The TEXAS TAKEDOWN

KATHRYN BROCATO

CRIMSON ROMANCE™

F+W Media, Inc.

Published by
Crimson Romance™
an imprint of F+W Media, Inc.
10151 Carver Road, Suite 200
Blue Ash, OH 45242. U.S.A.
www.crimsonromance.com

ISBN 10: 1-5072-0015-3
ISBN 13: 978-1-5072-0015-5
eISBN 10: 1-5072-0016-1
eISBN 13: 978-1-5072-0016-2

Cover art © Konrad Bak/123RF.

This book is dedicated to

Robin Alewine

Jeanette Alewine

Yvonne Berryton

Ann Caldwell

Celia Crittendon

Bonnie Klepac

Beverly Manne

Maria Martinez

and

All the other wonderful neighbors of Dolores Brocato

at the Georgian Apartments in Houston

CHAPTER 1

"You want me to *what?*"

Tyler Reid regarded the woman sitting on the other side of his desk with the expression he usually reserved for discrepancies in financial records. Perhaps the afternoon heat had affected his hearing. It was early June and already sweltering, but he'd thought he was well adapted to the Houston weather.

"You heard me," the woman repeated, enunciating clearly. Her knuckles were white from her grip on the arms of her chair. "I want you to help me find out who killed Daniel. It's been almost six months and the police still haven't arrested anyone. Somebody has got to do something."

She meant him. Tyler still couldn't understand it. He was an accountant, for Pete's sake, not a television private eye. He knew his way around a chart of accounts, but he lacked even a rudimentary knowledge of crime detection. Anyone else would have known and respected that fact, but apparently not Berry Challoner.

Her brother, Daniel Challoner, had been Tyler's college roommate and best friend. Though they'd been complete opposites in temperament, each felt he had found a brother. That was, up until six months ago, when Daniel had been found shot to death in the doorway of his apartment. Police investigators found no clues that would explain Daniel's untimely death. The official explanation was that the murder was probably a case of mistaken identity. Although Tyler understood and sympathized with Berry's distress at the lack of action from the Houston Police Department, he wasn't crazy enough to try and take the case out of their hands.

He regarded her in frowning silence. He recalled Berry at Daniel's college graduation ceremony. She'd worn a hot pink dress made of some floaty, gauzy material. He was surprised to realize how many conclusions he'd drawn about her because of that dress, considering he was usually such a logical and unimpressionable sort of man.

She looked different now. The wide, feathery brows still gave her face an exotic look, and her thick, shoulder-length, black hair called attention to a pair of large gray eyes that still managed to sparkle with life. But her smooth, golden skin looked sallow against the stark white blouse and navy skirt she wore.

The outfit was one Daniel would have approved of, but Tyler wished Berry had stuck with hot pink. It would have suited the passion and enthusiasm she projected much better than the clothes Daniel had always advocated for women in the business world. Daniel had believed strongly that women in business should avoid bright colors and feminine fashions because they distracted people from doing their jobs.

Berry's gray eyes blazed with fiery determination. She was not noticeably daunted by his lack of reaction. "There's something evil going on at that company where Daniel worked," she said. "I intend to find out what it is."

She sat on the edge of one of his leather office chairs, digging short, unpolished nails into the upholstery of the chair arms, and fairly glowed with determination and zest in spite of the drab clothes and the grief that still shadowed her expression.

Tyler had never seen anyone like her. No matter which of her emotions won out in the end, he had a bad feeling about whatever her "plan" entailed.

"I'm glad to hear somebody's going to do something," Tyler said diplomatically. "Would you mind telling me one thing?"

She studied him suspiciously. Tyler could think of no reason why she should be suspicious of him. He was a man made to be walked on by women, and they usually figured that out within five minutes of meeting him.

"What is it?" she asked.

"Did you dress like that because you thought it would help me agree to your proposition?" He indicated her skirt.

Her soft mouth with its upturned corners tightened, then relaxed. "I have no idea what you mean."

But she did. She swept him with a glance that held as much self-castigation as it held irritation.

Tyler abruptly realized he was failing to play the part of the stuffy accountant. He wondered what on earth she wanted him to say then decided to go with the truth.

"I liked you better in that shocking-pink floating stuff," he said.

Berry abandoned her pretense of ignorance and looked both surprised and pleased. "I was hoping to present you with an image you could understand. I mean, every time I met you, you didn't seem to approve of my appearance, and I haven't noticed any improvement during the last few years."

Tyler kept his mouth from falling open with an effort. He supposed he'd been wearing his usual frown every time he saw Daniel's little sister. That scowl was the only protective device he had, and he usually put it on the moment a woman who wasn't a flashy blonde walked into his view. Flashy blondes who liked having money spent on them were far safer in the long run. A man knew where he stood with them.

"I like pink," he said.

"Well, I didn't know that. You were Daniel's good friend, and I—" Berry broke off and looked down at her skirt as if thankful to direct her attention to another subject for a moment. "If I'd realized you didn't have Daniel's hang-up about dark skirts and white blouses for businesswomen, I'd have saved myself a few dollars. My green sundress would have been much more suited to this weather."

Tyler bit back a smile, careful to maintain his expression of stern disapproval. "Actually, if you'd worn the sundress, I would have been impressed with your good sense. As it is ... "

"Sorry. It isn't convenient for me to change and come back. You're going to have to imagine the green sundress." She smiled at him. "I never understood why Daniel was such a pain about business clothes. I'm glad you're not like him."

So much for intimidating her with his act of scowling disapproval. Berry had immediately detected his soft inner core and went straight for it.

"Daniel was way too attractive to the women he worked with," Tyler said. "He got fired from his first job because his secretary put out the tale that they were lovers. She was such a looker everyone believed it, but the truth was that she wanted his job. Ever since then, he wouldn't have a secretary who wasn't male or a really plain woman."

"Daniel hated being fired," Berry agreed. "He was used to winning, and he intended to keep winning until he became the chief executive of a major company." She paused and added, "Thanks for telling me that. Daniel just said he had changed jobs to 'further his career.' I knew there was something he was hiding."

"He wasn't hiding it precisely. It really bothered him that he could get fired from a good job when he hadn't done anything wrong."

Berry grimaced. "I can believe that, but it's still no reason for him to lecture me about not applying for a job until I changed my style. I'm just glad you're not like him."

Tyler relaxed. He might as well. She'd figured him out, just as every other woman in his life had. He had no doubt he was about to ruin the next few days of his life making a fool of himself by trying to play detective.

Berry sat on the edge of her chair. Her dark hair tumbled forward as she leaned toward him. The aura of feminine energy radiating from her slender body hinted at lithe strength, intelligence, and passion for life.

Tyler thought suddenly he'd give anything for a vacation and a chance to experience life with the same passion as Berry Challoner.

He was only thirty years old, and already tired of his job and the good life he was living.

"Although I spent six years in school studying a little of almost everything," Berry said, lifting her pointed chin with dignity, "business is one of the few areas I know next to nothing about."

"That's hard to believe," Tyler said.

He forced himself to think back. As a college student, Berry had provoked Daniel to awed annoyance by her apparent determination to take at least one course in almost every scientific discipline offered at the University of Texas at Austin. She had been so interested in everything, Daniel had been afraid she'd never declare a major.

But she had graduated at last, apparently in order to come to Houston and investigate Daniel's murder. He wasn't so sure that was an improvement.

"I'll need some help if I'm going to find out what happened to Daniel," she said. "So I thought, why not ask you? You were Daniel's best friend. You ought to be as interested as I am in what really happened to him."

"Be reasonable, Berry," he said. "How can I help you find out who killed Daniel? Unless, of course, he was shot by a runaway spreadsheet."

His ill-timed levity bounced off the wall of determination that surrounded her.

"It isn't funny." She frowned at him, hands clenched in her lap. "You can interpret any facts I discover, for starters. I figure money is somewhere at the back of all this. It always is, isn't it?"

"Money?" He regarded her in wonderment. "Daniel was still young, and he'd just bought a new car. He didn't have enough money to make him worth killing."

But despite the flaws in her reasoning, Tyler was conscious of an amazed gratitude that his name had occurred to her when she decided she needed help. He was fed up with both quarterly reports and the government branches that required them.

Solving a mystery would be a heck of a change. Solving the mystery of Daniel's death would be even more satisfying.

He pictured himself accepting police accolades for his brilliant detective work and had to smother derisive laughter. He was always the last person to solve literary or television mysteries. When it came to murder, he was about as brainy as a blade of grass.

"What facts are you intending to discover?" he asked. "If you don't know anything about business, how are you going to find out facts that require interpretation?"

She stiffened, and her wide brows drew together over her nose. "You needn't knock yourself out trying not to laugh. I know I'm explaining this badly."

"Sorry. I'm probably still in shock." Tyler wondered how she knew he was smothering laughter behind his unrelenting frown. "No one has ever requested my assistance in solving a murder before. This is something of a red-letter day for me."

"It's an honor, all right." She relaxed, regarding him in a confiding way. "You're the only man I know who's capable of helping me with this."

"Is that right?"

He had to hand it to her. No doubt she thought a little flattery would sucker him into participating in her scheme.

"I don't think the police even thought about looking into matters at Farley Brothers where Daniel worked," Berry said, turning her intense gray gaze on him. "It's high time someone did."

"So you think Farley Brothers, Inc. is up to something ... nefarious?" he asked.

"Well, of course it is," she burst out. "Think about it. Daniel Challoner, star college athlete, a man who graduated at the top of his class, murdered for no reason anyone can discover, within a few months of starting a new job. Look first at the people at that office. That's what I say."

He had to admit that catching Daniel's killer would give him great pleasure. The idea that Berry might succeed where the police hadn't, and with his help, held a certain charm.

Either that, or he had been a lot more bored lately than he'd suspected. "You have a point," he conceded. "But it could also be possible that Daniel formed an unsavory connection outside the office—"

Berry leaped up. Her eyes flashed gray fire, and her small fists clenched. "I thought you were Daniel's *friend*."

"Hey, take it easy." Tyler rose and came around his desk to her side. "I just want to be sure you've thought of all the possibilities."

Berry tossed back her dark hair and faced him. Her chin was tilted up in a challenging manner. "When Daniel first introduced you to me, I was thrilled he had a good friend like you. It certainly won't be the first time I've jumped to the wrong conclusion about a man."

Tyler bit his tongue. Berry was irresistible to male science majors. She'd been engaged at least twice that he knew of during her college career, engagements that had lasted two and three weeks before she claimed she'd made a mistake and gave back the ring.

Tyler knew only one thing at the moment—he couldn't let her just walk out of his office. Not when she'd infused the day with an excitement he hadn't felt in far too long a time.

He laid a hand on her arm. Touching Berry was like touching a live wire. He could feel her energy pouring into him.

"I've always believed in Daniel's integrity," he said, forcing his mind back to the problem at hand. "When the police turn up nothing in a murder investigation, you have one of two possibilities. Either Daniel was killed by random accident, or he was killed because of some reason no one knows about. Your theory is that Daniel was killed for an unknown reason, right?"

Berry faced him. "You'll help me prove it?"

"I'm as interested in finding out what happened to Daniel as you are," he hedged. "Let's talk about this a little more."

Berry allowed him to lead her back to her chair. He seated her with ceremony, chiefly so he could lean over her and breathe in her crisp, flowery fragrance. The blondes he favored usually smelled powerfully of expensive perfumes with names like Poison.

He wondered suddenly if time hadn't done its job in healing the hurt from his broken engagement to Alicia Cameron, who had used him to hide her intention of marrying a man her father disliked. The experience had shaken him badly enough that he had refused to date anyone who might have been marriage material.

Or had he been waiting all this time for Berry Challoner to walk into his office?

"I gather you already have a plan." He straightened reluctantly and reminded himself that Berry was likely to cause him a lot of trouble over the next few days.

"I do."

Tyler recognized that hopeful look. It was the same expression his younger sisters had used when they wanted him to aid and abet them in schemes they knew their parents would frown upon.

"I gather you're not ... engaged or anything right now?" He settled behind his desk.

"I quit getting engaged about two years ago. It got to be boring. Except for— Well, never mind that. Suffice it to say, I'm fed up with engagements. From now on, I'm avoiding entanglements with men."

Tyler believed this about as much as he believed Berry had a sensible plan for finding out who had killed Daniel.

He also recalled thinking Daniel should have taken more time to listen to Berry's plans and concerns and offer brotherly advice. But time was one thing Daniel had never had a lot of. If he managed to dash off a quick email to his sister once every few weeks, it was a minor miracle.

"That's good," Tyler said.

Why he thought Berry's avoidance of men was good, he didn't care to speculate. If he didn't know better by now, he obviously deserved whatever trouble she caused him.

"I abandoned the engagements so I could spend more time in chemistry lab," Berry said. "Things worked out better that way."

"I thought you kept getting engaged to guys you met in biology and geology labs." Tyler pretended to study papers on his desk.

Berry narrowed her eyes on him. "Who told you that? Daniel?"

Tyler said nothing about the weekly letters Daniel had tossed at him, saying, "Read it for me, will you, Ty, and tell me what kind of reply to send."

Berry had written reams of detail about her life to Daniel, but Daniel had been busy with his own life and hadn't paid much attention. He'd figured Tyler was more experienced at being a big brother than he was.

"Daniel thought you spent so much time in science labs, you were falling in love with your lab partners because of propinquity," he said.

Her gaze fell. Tyler noted she had long, dark lashes that covered an expression of deep loneliness—a loneliness he suspected had existed for a lot longer than the six months since Daniel had died. Daniel and Berry had never been close in spite of the efforts Tyler knew Berry had made.

"He was probably right," she admitted. "The guys in science labs were the only men besides Daniel I had a chance to get to know under real-life conditions."

"Real-life conditions? Science labs?" Tyler tried to remember the two college biology labs he'd suffered through. "Since when is dissecting a fetal pig a real-life condition?"

"You know what I mean. You're working together on a project, so you get to know each other as partners instead of just concentrating on the man-woman aspect. I figured if I liked a man in a biology lab, I'd probably like him in the kitchen and around the house. After all, marriage is a partnership, isn't it?"

"You have a point there," Tyler conceded. Her reasoning made a weird sort of sense. "Is that why you stayed in school so long?"

Daniel had feared she was destined to be a professional student. He hadn't listened when Tyler had suggested that perhaps Berry considered her professors and lab partners a surrogate family.

A faint hint of red tinged her smooth, golden skin. "Actually, I just felt … unprepared for life. So I'd decide to major in something else in hopes of feeling a little more prepared by the time I graduated."

"There's nothing that prepares you for life like getting a job. Are you leaving school at last?"

"I had all the requirements for a degree in earth science, so I went ahead and graduated." Berry's gray eyes darkened with emotion. "Now that school is off my mind, I can concentrate on Daniel."

"Daniel thought he was lucky to have a sister like you," he murmured.

Suspicion darkened her gaze. "He never said that, and you know it. Why do I keep getting the feeling that you're setting up something of your own here?"

"Okay, but he did notice how hard you worked at maintaining family ties."

That had to be true, he figured. It would have been hard not to notice, even for someone as basically egocentric as Daniel.

"Daniel and I were the proverbial oil and water," she said. "He liked sports and business, and I liked books and science." Her face clouded, and tears glistened in her gray eyes. "Still, he was my brother, my only family, and I loved him."

Tyler nodded sympathetically. Their mother had died when Berry was eight years old, and their father, a few months after Daniel's graduation from Rice University. That had left Berry and Daniel with no one but each other.

And now, Berry Challoner had no one.

"And what's worse is that he seemed to be changing just before he was killed," Berry added. "When he got the new job, he called me and told me he had named me as the beneficiary on his life insurance policy. He even said he loved me."

"And now you're wondering if he had some sort of premonition that he was going to die?" Tyler asked, surprised.

She frowned and shook her head. "No, because Daniel had that 'never give in' mentality. It's more like he was beginning to grow up and understand what was important in life, like friends and family."

"I see," Tyler said. He had noted the change in Daniel's thinking, also.

"I intend to set the record straight so Daniel can rest in peace." Berry's fingers tightened on the chair arms.

Tyler detected a strange quiver in her voice. "Do you have some reason to think he isn't resting in peace?"

"Well, how can he? Everyone thinks he was up to some nonsense like dope dealing or gun running." Her eyes flashed gray fire. "Do you know what really frosts me?"

He shook his head. If he died the way Daniel had, Tyler wondered suddenly, would his sisters personally go in search of his killer? He considered the question a moment and came up with a doubtful maybe.

"Everyone in Orange, where we grew up, thinks Daniel died a drug addict. All his old friends, his old teachers, even our neighbors." She swallowed hard, obviously furious. "You'd think they'd listen to the autopsy report that totally cleared him of drug use. But, no, that's not the way it is. Daniel is guilty until I can prove him innocent."

Tyler was silent, watching her. He kept his face dourly impassive. He strongly suspected Berry was burying her anger at Daniel for ignoring her most of her life beneath a passionate desire to bring his killer to justice. Although he couldn't blame her, he knew better than to think she—with or without his help—would find Daniel's murderer.

"Besides, Daniel sent me an email the day before he was killed," she added unwillingly. "I have no idea what it meant, but I intend to find out."

"What?" Tyler leaned forward. "Are you telling me you have a clue in your possession that you haven't given the police?"

"I did give it to them, for what that's worth." Berry scowled at him. "They don't think it means anything. But I think it does."

"So what did it say?" he asked, fascinated.

Berry pulled a folded sheet of paper from her purse and handed it to him. "He says not to be worried if I don't hear from him for a week or two because he'd be out of the office working on a special assignment for Mr. Walter Farley."

"And what does Mr. Farley say about this?"

"The police said he explained it was something private he wanted Daniel to look into for him, but since Daniel was killed before he began the assignment, they don't believe it had anything to do with his death."

Tyler studied the sheet in silence for a moment then handed it back to her. Berry refolded it carefully and stowed it away in her purse once more in equal silence.

"Well?" she demanded at last. "Are you going to be like the police detectives and tell me to run along and see a grief counselor?"

He couldn't repress a smile. "What would happen to me if I said that?"

She smiled back reluctantly. "Haven't you ever read a murder mystery where the accountant is found lying across his desk, strangled by the power cord of his own computer?"

"I can't say that I have. Would you mind answering another question for me?"

She regarded him curiously. "It depends."

"Daniel always called you Razz. What were your parents thinking when they named you Raspberry?"

She was like a berry, he decided, watching her face brighten into a sunrise of a smile. She was a luscious, spring dewberry; the type he used to treasure in his youth when he'd turn over some leaves and find a single, hidden berry, full of deep red juice and flavor.

Tyler studied her while ostensibly keeping his attention on the scribbles he was making with his pen. Yes, he could see why young men accustomed to staring at test tubes would fall for Berry Challoner. Gazing on her, even dressed in that drab secretary's outfit, restored his faith that one woman could hold all a man needed of excitement and pleasure.

"Did Daniel tell you my name was Raspberry?" she asked. "It's a family joke. I have this awful old great-aunt who claims to be rich, but the only thing she ever used her alleged money for was to threaten the family into doing what she wants. She wanted me named for her, but Daddy named me Beryl instead after my mother's mother. He told Aunt Mary my name was Raspberry." She chuckled faintly. "Daddy said he'd been wanting to give her the raspberry all his life. Daniel has always called me Razz for that reason."

"I had a grandfather like that," Tyler said. "When he died, the family held a celebration."

"Exactly," Berry said, nodding vigorously. "Aunt Mary managed to alienate every member of her family. By the time I was born, there were only two members of her family left alive for her to alienate—my father and my father's cousin. That's why she was so hot to have me named after her."

"Since your father officially gave her the raspberry, I presume you were struck out of her will."

Tyler scribbled some nonsense on his work pad. He'd better stop noticing how attractive Berry Challoner was. He never looked twice at a woman if she wasn't a blonde. Everyone knew that.

She smiled. "Assuming Aunt Mary actually had any money to leave. Daddy always doubted it because nobody had ever seen her show any signs of having money."

"What happened to her? Are you sure you're out of her will?"

"The last I heard, Aunt Mary was still living in Newton and being as mean as ever," Berry said positively. "Daniel and I never even met her. Considering how mad she was at Daddy over the naming rights to me, I'd be amazed to find out she left me five cents."

He figured he should return to the reason for her visit. "Berry, what if we find out Daniel was dealing drugs or doing something else that was illegal?"

"He wasn't."

Tyler knew absolute conviction when he heard it, and he heard it in Berry's voice. She echoed his own feelings about his best friend.

"Then why do you think he was killed?"

"It's obvious he knew something that was dangerous to somebody," she said, in the best television-detective-show tradition. Her pointed chin thrust forward, and her eyes glowed with enthusiasm. "I'll bet he stumbled on something at Farley Brothers, something he might not have even known was dangerous. I'm telling you, Tyler, there's something going on at that place, and I intend to find out what it is."

Tyler concentrated on maintaining his mistrustful expression. He had been in business as a Certified Public Accountant for enough years to have seen almost every type of tax-reporting evasion in the book. That sixth sense nagged him that Berry Challoner wasn't telling him everything.

The telephone on his desk buzzed. After regarding it balefully for a moment, Tyler picked it up. The caller was his sister, Debra, who had just gotten engaged and was calling him all the time with wedding planning ideas. Before the wedding took place, she was likely to drive Tyler crazy.

"You've got to help me, Tyler," Debra said.

"I'm busy with a client right now." He tried to inject more annoyance into his voice. "Get Martin to help you."

"That's why I'm calling you," Debra said. "Martin's boss is sending him to London tomorrow. I need an escort to the Pin Oaks Ball tomorrow night. Please, Tyler. There's no one else I can ask on such short notice."

Tyler frowned. He despised charity balls. He especially despised charity balls in the company of either of his sisters.

"Try Dad," he said.

"I did. He said you'd take me. Please, Tyler. I wouldn't ask if it wasn't important. I have to turn in a report for the paper, and I can't very well go without an escort."

"Why can't you? Other society reporters do."

He glanced at Berry. She was pretending not to listen to the conversation. He noted suddenly that she had Daniel's profile. The way she turned her head to the side accentuated the resemblance.

"Well, I can't," Debra said unequivocally. "I need someone to go with me. Please, Tyler. I need you."

Tyler melted inside, although he was careful to maintain his frowning demeanor. He was a sucker for women who needed him and he suspected Debra knew it.

"Oh, all right," he said. "What time?"

"Sevenish." Debra's voice went from cajoling back to its usual spunky tone. "Thanks, Tyler. You'll have a good time. I promise." She hung up.

"I'll bet," he muttered. He replaced the receiver and glared at the phone.

Berry said nothing. She turned her face toward him, and all resemblance to Daniel vanished.

Tyler watched her closely. She looked as though she longed to say something but was restraining herself.

"Where were we?" he asked.

"I was telling you Daniel probably stumbled on something at Farley Brothers he didn't know was dangerous. I'm going to find out what it is. With your help, I hope." She gazed at him pleadingly. "Actually, I can do this myself, but even if I get into their computers, I won't have the faintest idea what I'm looking at. I figure you will."

Again Tyler suspected Berry was hiding something from him. He studied her slender, exotic face and wondered what it could be. More to the point, how much trouble could he get into if he was discovered aiding and abetting someone who had broken into the Farley Brothers' computer files?

He decided he didn't care. Berry needed help. And to tell the truth, no amount of good sense kept him from wanting to do his bit to put Daniel's killer behind bars.

"In that case," he said, letting his gaze dwell pleasurably on her radiant, honey-gold complexion, "you'd better fill me in on your plan."

CHAPTER 2

Berry narrowed her eyes. Just when she thought she had a handle on Tyler Reid, some nuance of his voice told her she'd missed something vital. Perhaps Tyler knew the truth about why Daniel had been killed and didn't want to tell her.

She dismissed the thought immediately. From everything Daniel had said, Tyler was so honest he'd tell her straight out.

Daniel had always praised Tyler's financial abilities and intelligence to the highest, and Daniel had been the kind of man who rarely credited anyone but himself with intelligence. That meant Tyler had a lot on the ball in terms of business knowledge.

When she'd realized she needed an ally who understood business, his was the name that had leaped to mind. Now she wondered if she might not have made another of her famous mistakes.

Accountants were not supposed to be six feet tall, with broad shoulders and athletic builds. Somehow she hadn't noticed these things about Tyler the other times she'd met him. The way he'd frowned at her pink gauze dress at Daniel's graduation had kept her from wanting to know him better.

This was not a good time to notice he had thick, chestnut-colored hair and broad, slashing brows that set off startling turquoise eyes. His well-cut nose balanced a chin that erred on the side of aggressive. It was too bad he usually looked as though he'd eaten something that disagreed with him.

Why he was so gloomy, Berry didn't know. Daniel had told her Tyler had loving parents and two beautiful younger sisters, so she knew he hadn't been mistreated during his youth. Both his parents were in good health, and his sisters were doing well. He had gone to work for his father's accounting firm immediately after graduation and Daniel always said it suited Tyler better than anything else he could have chosen to do.

For an instant she let herself gaze at the magnificent specimen of elegant manhood facing her. He looked as though he had stepped out of an advertisement for expensive men's clothing. She must be crazy to let herself notice Tyler Reid, especially when she'd just finished with Grady Craig. After Grady, she had sworn off men and engagements forever.

Fortunately, Tyler wasn't likely to be interested in her. They were complete opposites, after all. Tyler was a steadfast, upright, correct businessman and she was a …

She wasn't sure what she was, except that she was a woman with a college degree at long last and three broken engagements.

The office door opened suddenly, and an older version of Tyler stalked in, clutching a manila folder. "Tyler, I've got to have the P and L statement for the Magician's Supply House by tonight. I'm not going to be able to get to it because—excuse my interruption, ma'am—your mother demands my attendance at that silly charity ball tomorrow tonight and I have to get my tux refitted."

Tyler regarded his father wryly. "Sorry, Dad. Debra is demanding my attendance at the same ball. It'll be all I can do to get Quinoa's quarterly reports done on time."

The older man ignored these words and proffered the manila folder. "See if you can get this statement done first. It's more important."

Tyler frowned heavily. "Dad, I—"

"Nice to meet you, ma'am," the older Reid said, bowing gracefully to Berry. "I have an appointment waiting. Excuse me, please." He exited as swiftly as he'd entered.

Berry pretended not to notice Tyler's look of weary resignation. She glared indignantly at the older man's back in spite of his graceful apology for interrupting. Daniel had said something about Tyler's relatives taking shameful advantage of his extreme good nature. Someone ought to do something about it.

"Sorry for the interruption," Tyler said. "My father thinks he has special privileges because he owns the company."

She forced a smile. "Daniel thought he had special privileges because he played football for Rice. I had to turn a plate of spaghetti over on top of his head in order to change his attitude."

Tyler set the folder aside. "Did it work?"

"What do you think?"

"It didn't work." He smiled, and his entire face was transformed. "I doubt if burying Dad beneath the entire contents of a file drawer would work." His face fell instantly back into the impressive frown. "Go ahead, please. You were going to fill me in on your plan for investigating Farley Brothers."

Berry remembered suddenly that Tyler had been engaged once himself. If he could smile like that, she wasn't surprised. But why wasn't he married?

Daniel had claimed Tyler was still single because he didn't have time to court a woman properly. Daniel had further said Tyler had given up girl-next-door types when his engagement ended and was now dating expensive blondes exclusively.

But that was the sort of male-chauvinist statement Daniel was always making. Berry dismissed it. Tyler had probably discovered he'd made a mistake, just as she had.

Watching him, she thought for a moment she'd caught a glimpse of something that rattled the very core of her femininity, something that said he could satisfy all her needs. Then she decided she'd been mistaken. Once more he looked like a mistrustful accountant who thought she was cheating on her tax returns.

She returned to her subject. "My plan is very simple. I intend to investigate that company from the inside."

His turquoise eyes widened. "What?"

"You heard me." She tossed her hair back. She had good reason to feel pleased with her efforts so far. "Monday morning I have an interview with Felix Farley himself. He needs a top-flight executive secretary."

"Oh, Lord." Tyler closed his eyes briefly, as if questioning his own sanity. "And here I thought you intended to hack into their computer system." He opened his eyes again. "I knew this would mean trouble."

"I'm using a fake name, of course." She smiled wryly. "Look at it this way, Tyler. At last I'm getting a job. Daniel would be proud. Believe me, by Monday morning, I'll look the part."

"The part of what?" he asked, looking baffled. "An executive secretary or a private investigator?"

"I'm going to look like an executive secretary who wouldn't mind being chased around the desk by the boss." Berry's enthusiasm revived as she reviewed her plan. "I've read some experts on the subject of sex and the office, and—"

"Sex and the office?" Tyler interrupted. His voice rose.

"Well?" Berry demanded. "What would you call it? Offices are happy hunting grounds to a lot of women, you know, not to mention men." His expression of outraged disapproval gave her a certain amount of enjoyment. "Also, I've listened to Daniel. If I dress the opposite of the way he thought a secretary ought to dress ..."

Tyler choked, and Berry wondered suddenly if he was trying to keep from laughing. It was hard to tell. His face remained set in its impressive scowl.

"Let me tell you something, Tyler. The Internet is full of good advice for women working in offices, and I have been studying it. Felix Farley is going to fall all over himself trying to hire me."

Tyler didn't like that, and she had no idea why not. After all, getting hired by Felix Farley was crucial to her investigation.

"And once you're hired?" he asked.

"Once I'm hired, I'll have access to the computer system and the file cabinets. Once we find clues, we can tell the police where to search for Daniel's killer."

"I see."

He didn't sound convinced, but Berry had expected that. She knew it took some time to convince people she had followed correct scientific procedure in developing her highly original plans of attack.

"You'll see," she said. "Mark my words. There's a drug ring or something worse operating inside Farley Brothers."

Tyler's broad, slashing brows raised. "As a matter of interest, what could be worse than a drug ring?"

"I don't know," Berry said darkly, "but we'll recognize it when we find it. Maybe it's a sex slavery ring, or something to do with arms smuggling."

Tyler stared at her a moment, then his sensual mouth twitched. "I hope you haven't convinced yourself I'll come crashing through the office door and beat up all the gun-toting bad guys if you get yourself into trouble."

"They'll never know anyone's on to them," she promised. "Besides, superhero abilities have nothing to do with a man's true worth in a crisis, and I ought to know."

"I suppose you should." Tyler sounded even more doubtful. "Daniel was a great all-around athlete, after all."

"How else do you think I learned men who chase balls around for fun tend to be deaf and blind when a woman needs help?" She looked at him hopefully. "What I want is a man who will use his skills and intelligence to help me when I ask. A man who'll do me the honor of assuming I have a certain amount of intelligence myself, and that I won't ask for help unless it's necessary."

Tyler didn't look at her. Thick, dark lashes veiled his eyes, and his mouth remained downturned. He toyed with a pencil. Berry decided she shouldn't have mentioned Daniel's athletic ability. Men were notoriously sensitive about things like that.

"You needn't worry," he said. "If you yell, I'll come running with ten freshly sharpened pencils to use as deadly weapons. So your theory is that Daniel saw something compromising?"

Relieved, Berry smiled brilliantly. She should have known Tyler wasn't stupid enough to compare himself to Daniel. He knew his own talents and valued them rightly.

"That's right." She nodded vigorously. "Or maybe he didn't see anything, but someone thought he did. Daniel wasn't murdered randomly like they say. I think whoever killed him meant to kill Daniel and no one else."

She paused for effect, but Tyler said nothing.

"I'm going to be doing a lot of snooping into things like accounts and inventories," she went on. "I'll need help in knowing what's important and what's not."

He nodded. Berry liked the confidence in his own abilities that nod indicated.

"Go on," he said.

"Also, I want the security of knowing there's someone who knows what I'm up to, someone who'll keep an eye on me." She took a deep breath. The way he avoided her gaze was beginning to grate on her nerves. "There's one other thing you can help me with, if you don't mind."

He looked up at that. "What is it?"

"Can you suggest a decent motel near Farley Brothers? I found several possibilities online, but—"

A most peculiar expression passed over Tyler's face. "If I'm supposed to keep an eye on you, then maybe you'd better plan on staying with me."

• • •

Berry dropped down on the drab bedspread of her motel room with a sigh of relief. After leaving Tyler's office, she had changed clothes and spent the rest of the afternoon finishing up the shopping for her upcoming role as an executive secretary who might not mind sleeping with the boss.

It had to be ninety degrees outside, and the humidity was roughly equivalent to the temperature. She was hot and tired and damp, and her green cotton sundress was badly wrinkled after being pulled on and off so many times.

"You'd better appreciate this, Daniel," she said aloud, kicking off her sandals. "Houston is the last place in Texas where I care to spend several weeks of my precious summer."

Near the window, the Venetian blind slats were open just enough to admit rays of the late afternoon sun. Dust motes danced in the sunbeams. Berry fancied she saw the specks dancing in answer and shut her eyes quickly.

"And if you don't appreciate it, that's tough. I don't take orders from you. Especially when you're no longer around to enforce them."

She opened one eye. The dust swirled. The hair on her scalp lifted gently and she snapped her eyelid down again. She was definitely going crazy. She'd spent weeks talking to the walls and imagining she heard answers. Now she was investing dust particles with Daniel's personality.

"Look. I've gone above and beyond the call of duty. I've even enlisted your best friend to help me." Her voice shifted from reasonableness to a distinctly aggrieved tone. "You never told me he was the type of man who invites women to move in with him the minute they ask for his help."

A cool breeze stirred the air. Berry rubbed her arms, where the fine hairs defied gravity. She told herself it was the cold temperature of the room after the heat outside that was giving her goose pimples.

At the same time she knew better than to tell Tyler that she felt almost as if Daniel was the driving force behind her sudden move from Austin to Houston. There was no way she could explain things like dust motes with personality and voices in her head.

"I've got the job interview and some outfits that'll knock old Felix's socks off. What more do you want?" She added swiftly, "Don't answer that. Whatever it is, you won't get it. I've done enough for you already."

Coolness touched her heated forehead as if someone had laid a hand on her brow. Berry's eyes flew open. She fell over backwards, heart pounding, and scrambled to the far side of the king-sized bed.

"Don't do that!" she yelled.

Someone pounded on the door. Berry reluctantly withdrew her attention from the beam of sunlight, where the dust motes danced about in agitated fashion. At that moment, she would have sworn Daniel stood beside the bed, offering what comfort he could.

Not that she could ever admit that. Tyler probably thought she was crazy enough already.

"Berry? Are you all right?" Tyler sounded ready to kick the door in. "Open the door."

Panting with residual fright, she edged off the bed and circled around it, keeping her distance from the patch of light. She was going nuts. Losing touch with reality. Totally freaking out.

The moment she slipped back the chain and pulled open the door, Tyler surged inside, ready for battle. He still wore his business suit, although he'd loosened his tie and discarded his jacket. His shoulders strained the white cotton of his shirt when he jerked open the closet door.

He glanced around swiftly then crossed the room to peek inside the bathroom. Once he was satisfied there was no one else in the room, he turned to Berry.

"Who were you yelling at?"

Berry kept her back to him and tried to pull herself together. "No one. I'm afraid I ... talk in my sleep."

"You were taking a nap?"

"You needn't sound so astonished. I do take naps occasionally."

It was stupid to sound so defensive, but she was still rattled from her own imaginings. Rubbing her arms vigorously, she shot a surreptitious glance at the beam of afternoon sunshine, now warmly golden, with only a few particles of dust floating lazily in the light. Her imagination had run away with her again. She had definitely lost it.

Tyler's voice became heavily reasonable. "I've been waiting for you the last half hour. Five minutes ago, you weren't here."

That figured. Men. They were conspiring against her, even those who, strictly speaking, were no longer alive to bug her.

"I guess I must be more tired than I thought."

He closed one hand lightly around her upper arm. Such was her state of mind, she started violently and tried to jerk free.

"Hey," Tyler said gently. "What's been going on in here?"

"Sorry. I was … having a bad dream when you knocked," Berry improvised. "It's getting to where I hate to doze off. I'm telling you, Tyler, if I don't find out something soon about Daniel, I'll probably be a candidate for the funny farm."

Since that was the absolute truth, sincerity rang in her voice. Tyler looked sharply at her. Without the frown she considered a part of him, he looked comforting and dependable.

"That bad?" He put a hand beneath her chin.

Berry refused to meet his uncomfortably searching turquoise gaze. She wasn't sure whether it was her own thoughts or his touch that kept her pulses pounding.

"Only when I first wake up," she said, and forced a smile. "What are you doing here?" They were supposed to meet for lunch at a deli in the Galleria tomorrow so he could give her a key to his apartment.

"I decided you'd better move in now while I'm available to help you. I'd forgotten that silly charity ball I have to attend tomorrow night."

He sounded thoroughly satisfied, a fact which made Berry suspicious. She stared at the floor, thoroughly confused.

Tyler tapped her chin with one finger until she looked up. "Berry, what's wrong?"

"Nothing. It's just that … a lot has happened lately."

Strong arms went around her. "It's been rough on you, losing Daniel." He hugged her hard. "I tried to call and check on you several times after the funeral, but you were always out."

That had been because of her late, great *whatever* with one Grady Craig, but the less said about that to Tyler, the better. She hated having anyone, especially Tyler, know how stupid she had been.

She didn't know what was more disturbing, Tyler's sympathy or the fact that he was holding her against his strong, hard body, resting his warm hands on her bare shoulders. Her nose pressed into his shirt. She cautiously absorbed the odors of starch, cologne that reminded her of a green forest, and a unique, masculine scent that she knew instinctively was Tyler's alone.

"Are you sure you're okay?" He moved his hands up to knead her shoulders. "Maybe you should invest in a good massage."

He could say that again. Most of her trouble was due to her own over-active imagination. Sighing with pleasure, she let herself enjoy his warm, soothing touch. She hadn't felt this degree of comfort since her father died and Daniel had spent a full five minutes hugging her after the funeral.

Berry rubbed her eyes. Behind Tyler, the dust particles thickened and swirled as if something had stirred them up.

"I see you put on the green sundress after all," Tyler said.

"Can you blame me?"

He chuckled, a deep rumble of his chest that sent shivers down her back. "I like a little color on a woman."

The dust particles settled slowly. Berry heaved a sigh of relief. She was imagining things again. If this kept up, she'd have to make an appointment with a good psychiatrist.

"I guess I'm just tired," she said, and forced herself to step back. "I wanted to finish up most of my shopping today."

He smiled and glanced curiously around the motel room at the myriad boxes stacked against the walls. "Why is a lot of shopping necessary for a few weeks as Felix Farley's secretary? You must have already spent a good portion of Daniel's life insurance policy."

"I'm getting ready for my real job at the same time," she invented. Anything to keep from telling him the new wardrobe was part of her disguise. Something told her Tyler wouldn't take kindly to the idea that she needed a disguise, especially the kind of disguise she had in mind. She'd spring that on him later.

"Oh? What's your real job going to be?"

"Well, actually, I don't know yet." Embarrassed, she turned away. "Right now I don't want anything distracting me from finding out what happened to Daniel."

His brilliant, blue-green gaze swept the room once more then came back to her. "Do you have a career track in mind?"

"I had thought about working in a chemistry lab at one of the refineries. And lots of companies are hiring science majors these days to keep track of their environmental impact." She thought fast. "Plus I can teach almost any high school science course. I took all the required education courses."

"That sounds fascinating," Tyler said, to her astonishment. "You must be qualified for at least a dozen positions. You can tell me more tonight."

She looked at him, uncertain how to reply.

"Let's get you moved," Tyler said. "After that you can have a hot shower and relax. I'll be working late at the office, so the apartment's all yours."

Berry shifted uncomfortably. "I've never lived with a man before. What's the etiquette for dealing with visitors?"

"You aren't living with me," Tyler said, laughing. "You're spending a couple of weeks in my spare bedroom while you take care of a little personal business. There's no etiquette involved."

"There isn't?" Berry cleared her throat, remembering her reaction the first time she'd called Daniel and a sleepy woman answered. "What happens when your mother discovers there's a woman sharing your apartment? Or your dad comes over and I answer the door in my robe and slippers?"

"It won't happen. They never bother me at home." He saw her suitcase sitting in the partially open closet and reached for it. "Besides, you'll probably be through with your investigation before they even know you're here."

Berry nodded, unconvinced. "Thanks for helping me. If I can get settled this weekend, Monday will go that much more smoothly."

He was silent a moment, opening the suitcase on the bed for her. In equal silence, Berry opened a drawer and scooped out her nightshirt and robe. She had no idea how to explain to Tyler the shock her presence in his apartment was likely to cause his relatives.

"Are you sure you want to go through with this investigation?" He moved back and shoved his hands into his pockets.

"Of course I'm sure. I wouldn't be here otherwise."

"I suppose not."

He lapsed into brooding silence and stared absently at the beam of light poking through the blinds. Berry lifted out her beautiful new underwear and wrapped it in a lacy slip while casting suspicious glances at the light beam. She headed toward the suitcase with the bundle of underwear, wondering if Tyler saw anything peculiar about the behavior of the dust motes.

He turned toward her suddenly. "I've been doing some preliminary investigating of my own this afternoon."

Startled by the abrupt movement, Berry dropped her bundle. The slip unrolled, and a shower of pastel panties fell to the dark green carpet, along with one lacy white bra.

"Here, I'll get that." Tyler stooped and reached for a pair of pink silk panties.

Berry ground her teeth and glared toward the light beam. Now Tyler was bound to think she'd dropped her underwear at his feet on purpose.

"What did you find out?" she managed.

Eyes narrowing, he glanced up. "Farley Brothers is a conservative automobile parts company that's been operating in the black for some time now." He smoothed the lacy cup of her bra with his thumb absently while he looked up at her. "Where other companies are going broke, Farley Brothers is making a tidy profit. That fact leads an accountant to assume the good people at Farley Brothers are tending to business rather than running drug rings on the side."

Berry watched his thumb out of the corner of her vision. Her face flamed, but she managed to keep her voice steady.

"Whatever Daniel saw might have been a side venture run by a couple of employees."

"That's possible."

Tyler didn't sound as though he thought it was possible. To her horror, he looked as though he suspected her of covering up something. His wide, sensual mouth tightened, but he didn't press her.

"Each of the three Farley Brothers presides over two of the six stores in the chain," Tyler added. "Felix's two stores are outperforming the other four stores two to one."

"Really? How interesting. What do you think it means?" Berry was unused to feeling totally ignorant about a subject, considering the wide range of her education, but this was why she'd come to Tyler.

"Without more data, I can't be sure." He glanced down, realized what he was doing with his thumb, and smiled. It was a purely male smile that affected Berry almost as much as if he'd directed it at her. "It could mean a lot of things." He gathered the scattered bits of pastel nylon and held the pile out to her. "It could simply mean Felix is a better manager than the other two brothers."

Berry swiftly tucked the underwear beneath her robe in the suitcase and ignored her own racing heart. "Daniel was technically working for Walter. Walter's the CEO."

"He's also the oldest, and the one who founded the company."

He rose smoothly and stood watching her with the mistrustful frown she'd come to recognize as a shuttered look. Wondering what lay behind the shutters was beginning to drive her crazy. She just hoped she was right in assuming he wasn't attracted to her. Otherwise, the complications of sharing his apartment could become horrendous.

She hastened back to the drawers, chiefly to have an excuse not to face him. "I told you I don't understand much about business. But Daniel told me when he first got the job that Felix was bucking for top dog. That might mean Felix is up to a lot of things that might be dishonest. That's why I picked him to investigate first. Also," she added, "my research shows he's the one most likely to hire a sexy new secretary."

Tyler nodded. "My informant also adds that Walter is long past official retirement age, and Felix is complaining aloud about his senility. Thurlow Farley retires next year. He's the middle brother."

"Do you think Walter Farley is going senile?" The drawers were mostly empty. Berry scrabbled through them again to look busy.

"Walter Farley is still the main force behind the company," Tyler said. "He and Thurlow founded it as young men, when Felix was in his early teens. Felix is lucky he was allowed in on the deal."

Berry turned toward the suitcase with a pair of jeans and two T-shirts in her arms. Behind Tyler, the dust motes danced in the sunbeam. Berry caught her breath and ignored them.

"Daniel said Felix was a complete jerk."

Tyler laughed and moved to adjust the blinds. The sunbeam glanced off his hair, turning it to golden-red fire.

"Felix was probably scared Daniel would outperform him and take his job." He turned toward her. "Daniel was brilliant."

"So I was told, by Daniel himself," Berry said. "It wouldn't surprise me to learn Felix Farley killed him in a moment of supreme annoyance with Daniel's natural arrogance."

Without his mistrustful frown, Tyler's face took on the look of a mischievous boy. He grinned at her. "Daniel believed in tooting his own horn, didn't he?"

She smiled and looked away, blinking back sudden tears. "I used to wonder how he kept any friends."

"Are you through packing?" He studied her. "Let's get you out of here. You could probably use a good nap."

She didn't argue, knowing he'd discerned her tears. Within five minutes, she had scooped her razor and toothbrush off the bathroom counter and had bundled everything willy-nilly into the suitcase. Tyler carried it outside for her and she popped the trunk of Daniel's car.

"Good Lord." Tyler peered into the trunk of Daniel's still new jade-green Mustang. "Did you buy the entire boutique?"

"Just about," Berry said. Tyler had to place her suitcase on the passenger side of the front seat because the back seat of the car was also stuffed full of new purchases. "Felix Farley is going to take one look at me and start panting."

"Is that right?" Tyler stared at the stack of plastic covered dresses lying full length across the trunk. Then he transferred his enigmatic, shuttered gaze to Berry's face. "Why do you need a new wardrobe to accomplish that?"

Berry refused to let herself ponder the meaning behind those words. Reading meaning into a man's words nearly always got a woman into trouble.

"Tomorrow, I'm having a complete makeover." She smiled with anticipation. "I'll be a raving beauty when I walk into his office Monday morning."

Tyler's gaze wandered over her meaningfully. "There are those who would say you're a raving beauty now."

Fortunately, she knew better than to believe that. "Felix Farley probably wouldn't be one of them, and he's the man I've got to impress. According to Daniel, Felix has a beautiful young wife and a beautiful young mistress."

"Daniel was right, except that the beautiful young mistress has recently dumped Felix for an unmarried man."

"I'm hoping Felix will take a fancy to me. If I can interest him for a couple of weeks, he'll probably give me access to anything I want in the office."

Tyler scowled at that but only said, "Actually, you may get your first chance to make old Felix eat his heart out even sooner. I just learned he's attending the Pin Oaks Ball tomorrow night. Would you like to come along and meet him?"

CHAPTER 3

Tyler came home the following afternoon filled with anticipation. Berry was getting what she called a "complete makeover." The prospect of watching her charm Felix Farley at the Pin Oaks Ball that night made him actually look forward to the event.

Debra had been resigned when he'd told her he was bringing a friend. Tyler grinned, wondering what Debra would think of a made-over Berry Challoner as opposed to his usual blonde.

He unlocked the door of his apartment, halfway expecting to find Berry watching television. Instead, the small living room was as usual, except for a fist-sized chunk of rock, four fashion magazines, and a book on how to format business letters on his coffee table. He regarded the coffee table with resignation and wondered why women felt clean, bare surfaces begged to be covered with knickknacks.

He looked around for further evidence of a feminine presence. Sure enough, a few branches off one of the oleander bushes lining the parking lot now graced his entertainment center. Every woman in his family loved to stick green stuff in a glass, plant it on a bare surface, and call it an "arrangement."

Somehow satisfied by these observations, Tyler went to his bedroom. The door to Berry's bedroom was closed, but Daniel's green Mustang had been parked in the slot beside his. The sporty jade car filled him with a peculiar sense of *déjà vu*. He half expected to find Daniel lounging on his sofa.

Tyler showered hastily and dressed in the evening clothes the ball required then returned to the living room, checking the time on his cell phone. He looked up, startled, when a woman in pink unfolded slowly from the dark leather sofa.

"Who—?" He broke off and stared.

36

Berry stared back. She seemed to find him as interesting as he found her, but he barely noted her fascinated gaze. He was too busy wondering what she'd done to her eyes. His mouth felt as if he'd eaten dust and his heart pounded in his ears.

He'd swear he had never seen this woman before in his life.

Her long, deep-pink gown was made of some material that almost begged him to touch it. The soft, prim lines emphasized her figure and her long elegant neck. Tyler wanted suddenly to stroke his fingers over the smooth golden skin of her exposed throat.

Her shoulder-length hair had been cut short and styled into clusters of Betty Boop curls that hugged her head. The new hairdo gave her an entirely different, highly sophisticated look. Added to the sophistication were overtones of another, more subtle quality—one that invited male interest. Tyler couldn't pinpoint the precise items creating the invitation, but his body recognized it and responded.

As for her eyes … He studied her face again, uncertain of what to think about her eyes, other than that they had radically changed color.

"Is that one of the outfits designed to enslave Felix Farley?" he managed to ask.

"How did you guess?" She turned for his inspection. "My research indicates bosses enjoy seeing a woman in slinky, fitted dresses. When you invited me to the ball, I thought I'd give the theory a serious field test."

He received this information in frowning silence and observed the way the dress hugged her derriere when she turned.

"My research also indicates that many men have fixations on high heels." Berry held out a slender foot shod in a fragile pink pump with a three-inch, stiletto heel. "The higher the heel, the more sexually available they think the woman wearing the shoe must be."

Tyler cleared his throat with difficulty. Berry's legs were a connoisseur's dream. The leg that peeked tantalizingly from a slit in the side of the pink dress looked long, golden, and perfectly tapered to a slender ankle.

"Well?" she asked.

"Well, what?"

She brimmed with effervescent enjoyment, Tyler realized, and practically overflowed with eagerness to get her investigation into gear. He felt relieved to rediscover the woman he'd met yesterday beneath the sophisticated facade.

Berry posed like a model. "As a typical professional man who employs a secretary and who works in an office, what do you think? Am I on target?"

He couldn't resist smiling. "Honey, I don't know what kind of research you're reading, but I do know I like long, slinky dresses and high-heeled shoes. If a secretary wore an outfit like that in my office, I wouldn't get a bit of work done."

Instantly, her air of enthusiastic enjoyment deepened. "Great. That's the idea. Would you mind telling me why you couldn't get any work done?"

Tyler decided to let her have the truth. As a scholarly researcher, she no doubt appreciated truth.

"Maybe it's because that dress is designed to emphasize a woman's differences from a man," he said. "It shows off every female curve you have and calls my attention to them. If a woman wore clothes like that in my office, I'd be thinking about having sex with her instead of working."

Berry's eyes widened. Tyler stared again. He still didn't know what to think, or say, about those eyes.

"That's brilliant, Tyler. None of the research I read said it that clearly. You've just summarized the idea behind every single item of clothing I bought for my investigation."

Tyler cleared his throat. She thought he was brilliant. No wonder she kept getting engaged. Most men spent their entire lives in search of such a discerning woman.

He reminded himself Daniel's little sister was notoriously mercurial. He'd be safer dating expensive blondes. He knew where he stood with them.

"This could be the beginning of a major study of female clothing in the office and its effect on male executives. I can see it now," Berry said enthusiastically. "Do you think the emphasis on bright colors is more of the same reasoning?"

"Do you mean designed to call a man's attention to the fact that he's looking at a woman instead of a man?" Tyler couldn't believe he stood there discussing the differences in male and female clothing with a woman who had no idea that he yearned to show her graphically what her dress made him think of. "Probably. Men's business wear is so drab we long to look at something feminine and colorful."

Berry grimaced. "Maybe it isn't your wardrobe that needs perking up. Maybe it's your attitude toward your work. I probably shouldn't say anything, but you look like you could use a vacation. If you want my opinion—"

"I don't have time for a vacation," Tyler interrupted, not eager to hear more along those lines. He remembered his frown. "Besides, I'm counting on you to refresh my outlook on my work. By this time next week, I want to be deep into the sinister accounting methods used at Farley Brothers."

She bobbed her head, pleased. Obviously, she fully expected that to be the case. "Before we're through, you'll be thanking me for letting you in on my investigation."

"Believe me, I already am." He sought a neutral subject. "Would you mind telling me what that rock is doing on my coffee table?"

"It's a special rock." She touched it lovingly. "It's a limestone conglomerate I found on a geology field trip."

"It looks like something you dug out of a driveway." He frowned at it. "It's shedding dirt on my coffee table."

"There's a story behind this rock," she said, with dignity. "Where I go, it goes."

"Don't tell me. I don't want to know. Are you ready? Debra is going to meet us in the hotel foyer."

Tyler tried not to stare at the vision on his arm as he walked her down the metal staircase toward the parking lot. Then she turned her face up to him. The flash of color from her formerly gray eyes distracted him so much, he stumbled.

Berry stumbled with him. "I'm not used to these heels," she confided, "but for a few weeks, I figure I can stand anything."

"I'm not sure I can. What have you done to your eyes?"

"My eyes? What's wrong with them?"

The innocent expression on her sparkling face didn't fool Tyler. "They're purple. That's what's wrong with them. If you're thinking that color looks natural, you'd better think again."

"They're violet," Berry corrected. "Just look at me, Tyler. Not even Daniel would recognize me now."

"Don't kid yourself." Tyler felt his frown came back in full force. Who but Berry Challoner would be crazy enough to think purple contact lenses constituted some sort of impenetrable disguise? "No one has purple eyes. If you want a new eye color, what's wrong with brown or blue?"

"I want to be eye-catchingly different," she said and gurgled with laughter at his expression.

He had to admit she was definitely different. What was more, she was right. Daniel probably wouldn't know her. For some reason, her deeply purple eyes added to the disguise. She looked like a young Elizabeth Taylor—someone who wouldn't mind tumbling into bed with a man on the first date.

Tyler handed her into his Porsche, staring down at the silky length of her legs as she drew them in. The slit in the pink dress showed the lace edge of a pale pink slip. No doubt the slip was another concession to a male boss's love of color.

"Lord help us." He sucked in his breath. "I'll be lucky to survive this investigation of yours."

"I won't be in your way," she assured him eagerly. "Everything depends on what information I'm able to find."

He let his breath out. Although he didn't expect much from her efforts, he did hope she had enough success to keep at it a couple of weeks. He needed the diversion.

He balanced his palms on the car roof and leaned in to watch Berry stroke her fingers appreciatively over the leather upholstery of his Porsche.

"When you bought this Porsche, Daniel didn't waste a minute," she said. "He ran right out and bought that Mustang."

Tyler's jaw dropped. "He what?"

"You heard me." She turned her head to study the dashboard, but Tyler suspected she was deliberately avoiding his gaze. "He couldn't stand it that you could afford a better car than he had, so he sunk every penny he'd saved into that Mustang."

Tyler found his tongue. "Daniel knew I bought this car because I inherited money from my grandfather that should have gone to my dad. When Dad wouldn't take the money, what could I do but use it on the car he's secretly wanted all his life but refuses to buy? Dad loves cars."

"Daniel didn't believe you." Berry touched the stick shift reverently. Her formerly short, sensible fingernails, now almost half an inch long, were painted bright pink.

"My dad drives this car more than I do," he protested, mentally reeling.

Her purple gaze met his. "Daniel couldn't outspend you, so he tried to out-*sport* you."

Hearing that Daniel Challoner of all people had been jealous of his Porsche gave Tyler the feeling that he'd been punched in the chin. He shook his head, dazed, and straightened to stare at Daniel's jade Mustang.

The fancy mag wheels caught his eye and he remembered twitting Daniel about buying a car with wheels that were almost certain to be stolen. Daniel had scowled and pointed out a nick in one of the wheels that he demanded the dealership replace. Daniel had died before the matter was settled.

"I see you kept the car, sporty wheels and all," he said, through stiff lips.

"I needed a car, and he'd already paid a lot down on it. Besides, that car reminds me of Daniel and what I've got to do."

Tyler changed the subject. "As a matter of interest, what sort of information are you searching for at Farley Brothers?"

"I won't know it until I see it." When she saw his expression, she added, "The truth is, I've been so worried about getting myself hired, I haven't had much time to lay out a methodical search plan."

Tyler came around and got in beside her. "Have you ever worked in an office before?"

He leaned on his steering wheel, the better to watch her expressive face. The pink dress made her skin resemble golden satin. He wanted to run his finger over her cheek.

"Not exactly," she said.

"What does that mean?"

She looked embarrassed. "It means that although I'm fair at typing letters and taking dictation, I've never actually worked as a secretary."

Tyler blinked. "Frankly, I'm surprised to know you can type and take dictation."

"Well, it's been a few years. In high school, I thought I'd be a secretary, so I studied office technology. Daniel said I'm better than most secretaries they hire these days."

"Daniel had reason to know," Tyler said. "He went through three secretaries inside of six months when he started at Farley Brothers."

"That was because Felix kept hiring secretaries with stunning physical attributes and no skills," Berry said, in austere tones. "I'm going to present him with the perfect combo—skills and a gorgeous exterior."

"Believe me, he'll hire you." If Felix didn't hire her, Tyler thought he might hire her. He'd never been so entertained in his life despite the way she kept him feeling as if he'd drunk too much champagne. "You have a history of regularly changing your mind about your career, don't you?"

Her purple eyes focused on him. "The problem is that there are so many interesting things out there." She indicated the world outside the Porsche. "Until I've sampled a few of them, how can I decide for sure what I want to do the rest of my life?"

Tyler started the car and backed out. He'd never considered anything other than earning his degrees and going to work for his father's accounting firm. Such indecisiveness was foreign to him. Or it would have been, if he hadn't been experiencing such a deadly boredom lately.

"What are you planning on doing first, assuming you get hired?" he asked, in order to stave off his thoughts.

"The first order of business will be to look for anything you tell me is sensitive data," Berry said with the boundless enthusiasm he'd come to expect from her.

Tyler wouldn't let himself smile. "Like what?"

"That's your job. You're supposed to tell me what's sensitive and what isn't. Mainly, I just hope to notice anomalies," Berry said, blithely unaware that her escort was fighting back incredulous laughter.

Somehow he managed to keep a straight face. It was exactly as he had suspected. Berry Challoner wouldn't know an office anomaly if it bit her on the ankle.

"Are you sure you want to go through with this? After all, it'll mean at least two or three weeks out of your life. Why can't you accept the fact that Daniel was probably the random victim of some drug dealer who hit the wrong apartment?"

"Because I know he wasn't," Berry said simply. "This is something I have to do, Tyler. What are a few weeks compared to my brother's life and reputation?"

He could not reply to that. He joined traffic on a main thoroughfare, reflecting that he had a week, maybe two, of entertainment ahead before the people at Farley Brothers checked out Berry's phony references and fired her.

Assuming they actually hired her.

"What did you say on your resume that got you an interview?" he asked.

"I listed two secretarial jobs with enormous responsibilities, of course—along with a glamorous physical description that describes me as a trophy secretary. If Felix is still hiring women who can't type or use a computer, he should be doubly eager to get hold of me."

Tyler said something about the admirable state of Farley Brothers' last balance sheet. Not that he expected her to pay any attention to such a boring thing as profitability.

"The key to Daniel's murder is lurking somewhere at Farley Brothers," Berry declared. "The police couldn't find it, but I will."

He glanced at her, noting the expression on her face as she studied the Houston skyline. Berry's ardent interest in everything around her was her most attractive characteristic.

"What name are you using?" he asked, reluctantly returning his gaze to the street ahead.

He still found it incredible she had actually managed to land a job interview at Farley Brothers, using a false name and false credentials. It was something he'd never have thought of doing.

He thought wryly that was probably what was wrong with him—nothing so daring would ever have occurred to him.

"My new name is as classy as my resume. I used my great-aunt's name," Berry said. The smile she turned on him encouraged him to laugh with her at the irony. "Her name was Mary MacGregor, and Daddy said she was pure Scotch all the way down to her toenails. Also, Mary is close enough to Berry so that I'll take notice when someone addresses me."

Tyler's head whirled as he contemplated becoming an auto parts marketing specialist at Farley Brothers under some name like Schyler Creed. His untried imagination couldn't get him past the secretary manning the front desk of the Farley Brothers executive suite.

"Is this the rich old aunt who got the raspberry from your dad?"

"Who else? She may as well be of use to her great-niece."

"You'll feel mighty silly if you find out Daniel was actually killed over your great-aunt's money," Tyler said, and smiled at her expression.

"I'll feel mighty silly if I find out she has any money, period," Berry responded. "Be serious, Tyler. There's something bad going on at Farley Brothers. You've got to help me find out what it is so we can take them down."

He was silent a moment. "Didn't Farley Brothers send a representative to Daniel's funeral?"

Berry nodded and raised her wide, feathery brows. "Walter Farley came himself."

"And you're counting on a new wardrobe and a phony name to keep him from recognizing you?"

Berry's smile grew. "No one paid much attention to me at Daniel's funeral, including you. You have to admit, a new hair style makes a big difference in a woman."

"It's only been six months since Daniel died. Don't you think you might jeopardize the police investigation if you go through with this?"

Her slender, exotic face took on an expression he could only describe as adamant. "What police investigation? If the police were going to find anything, they'd have found it by now. I'm not wasting another minute."

Tyler wisely shut up.

"Mary MacGregor even has a Facebook page and a LinkedIn profile, complete with a selfie of my new look. And I'll be carrying phony ID cards," Berry said. "If anyone at Farley Brothers snoops through my purse—"

"Snoops through your purse?" he interrupted. "You've been watching too many spy movies. Farley Brothers is an ordinary, above-board chain of auto parts stores."

"Well, naturally, that's what everyone thinks," Berry said. "If there was any hint of scandal connected with them, believe me, the police would have been onto them already."

A thirty-five-year-old corporation operating in the black and with no hint of a bad reputation or a scandal anywhere in its balance sheets simply could not be hiding a murderer.

Or, could it? Tyler glanced at Berry.

It was ridiculous. He didn't believe it for a minute. This wasn't a movie or a thriller. This was real life. In real life, what something looked like was usually what it was. As much as he'd like to bring Daniel's killer to justice, he and Berry were not likely to succeed where trained police investigators had failed.

He decided to play along anyway. If Berry wanted thrills and chills, let her have them. He'd enjoy himself watching her. Berry Challoner was just what the doctor ordered for a man who had been feeling bored and unsettled recently.

"I suppose it never occurred to you that, if what you suspect is true, you could be in serious danger?" he asked, tongue-in-cheek.

"Of course it has. That's one of the reasons why I came to you for help. If I disappear, I want you to raise holy hell until someone unearths my body."

Tyler's throat felt paralyzed for an instant. He choked, recollected himself, and felt paradoxically irritated. "Don't be ridiculous," he came back quickly. "You won't find a thing at Farley Brothers unless Felix Farley has an unsuspected drinking problem."

Berry smiled at him. Tyler's throat shut down a second time, and for an entirely different reason.

"If he has, I'm going to discover it," she said. "The problem is I get carried away when I have a pet theory."

No kidding, he thought. "Farley Brothers stores are selling auto parts all over Houston, and they're actually making money at it. That means they're paying a certain amount of attention to business."

Berry smiled wryly. "Thanks, Tyler. That's what I need to be told. If I'm not checked, I tend to get overly enthusiastic."

Berry's matter-of-fact acceptance of her own weakness told him he had stumbled across a rare treasure of womanhood. No wonder men fell all over themselves proposing to her. Tyler studied her covertly.

He thought of Berry's thick, dark hair against a pillow, and of entangling his fingers in it while he kissed her. His entire body reacted. He was in for a cold shower tonight. He could see it coming. He'd traded boredom for physical torture.

"While we're driving," Berry said, "can you give me a quick course in auditing procedures? I might need to do some fast field audits if I'm able to get into the company books."

She expected him to teach her advanced accounting procedures in one well-stated paragraph?

"I'll be happy to," he said. "Five minutes should—"

She burst into laughter. "You sound exactly the way I sounded when Daniel asked me to tell him, in one sentence or less, the geologic history of Big Bend National Park."

"I'm not surprised," Tyler said.

"I so glad I came to you," Berry said cheerfully. "We're going to work really well together."

"That, we are," Tyler agreed. "In fact, our partnership will probably work out better than any of your engagements."

"Daniel told me I was the only woman he knew who had been engaged twice before she was twenty," she said abruptly. "Do you think something is wrong with me?"

Tyler cleared his throat. "I've been engaged once, myself, but it turned out my intended was using me to keep her father from finding out about the guy she really loved. In my opinion, it's a lot better to break an engagement than to seek a divorce."

"That's what I thought. I'm such a sucker for a man who swears he needs me. But my last engagement cured me of that. From now on, I'm not getting engaged until I'm the one who needs the man."

Tyler agreed wholeheartedly with that. "So tell me more about your job prospects after you're finished with Farley Brothers."

"Actually, I don't have any job prospects," she confessed. "I know I ought to have, but since Daniel died, I haven't been able to think of the future beyond Farley Brothers."

"You might decide you like the auto parts business, but somehow I can't see you as Felix Farley's secretary for the rest of your life."

Berry looked down at herself with enjoyment. "I'm trying to look like a rich man's expensive mistress, but once I've found out who killed Daniel, I'll tone things down for a more professional appearance."

Tyler glanced at her. "Now that you mention it, everyone at the ball tonight will probably wonder how long I'll be able to afford a classy mistress like you."

At the hotel, he turned the keys over to the attendant and handed her out of his Porsche, holding his breath as she unfolded to her full, exquisite height. The silky, fitted pink dress looked high-necked until she bent forward.

He suddenly found himself peering straight down the neckline. The top edge of her brassiere was all pink lace and tiny satin ribbons. Above it, her smooth, golden skin inflamed his imagination into speculating about what the undergarment covered.

Tyler wasn't prepared for the all-encompassing desire that swept through him. He wanted to shove her back into the car and haul her home to his bed.

"Are you aware that a man can look down the front of that dress?" he ground out.

To his frustration, she looked delighted. "You can? Great. That's the effect I was hoping for." She fluttered long, mascara-coated lashes. Behind the lashes, her incredible, purple eyes twinkled at him. "My research says bosses like Felix love it when a dress that doesn't look low-cut gives him a glimpse of forbidden delights. Do you have any idea how long I had to shop before I found this little number?"

"About this so-called research of yours ..." he began.

Berry's soft laughter further inflamed his already reeling senses. "Don't ask."

Tyler guided her into the opulent hotel foyer with its famous crystal chandelier and thick carpet. Standing beside Berry in the extravagant gloom, he intercepted at least three interested male stares directed at her.

"You're a menace to the public," he said through his teeth.

"I've never been a menace before." She cast an interested glance at the glittering chandelier.

"Here comes my sister."

Berry clutched his arm. "What do you think she'll say when she meets me?"

"If she knows what's good for her, she'll say, 'How do you do, Miss MacGregor.'"

Debra burst in through the front entrance in her usual haphazard manner and barreled toward him. She was a tall, slender woman with Tyler's chestnut hair and turquoise eyes. She gave the flyaway impression of one who was always late and not quite dressed in spite of having every hair and article of clothing in place.

"There you are, Tyler. I've been tied up in traffic—" She broke off upon catching sight of Berry.

Tyler didn't need an interpreter to tell him what the expression on Debra's face meant. She might as well have shrieked, "Bimbo!" at the top of her voice.

"Debra, I'd like you to meet Mary MacGregor," he said. "She's an executive secretary in search of a job."

Debra made an obvious effort at pretending to believe this. "How do you do, Miss MacGregor? Have you been in Houston long?"

"I've just moved here from *Austin*," Berry said, darting a swift glance at Tyler's impassive face. "Tyler *very* kindly offered to bring me tonight in *hopes* of—in *hopes* of—"

"She has a job interview with Felix Farley at Farley Brothers Auto Parts Monday morning," he interjected, choking back laughter. "I thought she might like to meet him under more casual circumstances."

"Oh, yes, indeed." The falsely hearty agreement in Debra's voice nearly undid Tyler's gravity. "There's nothing like a little preview of the …" She looked Berry up and down, "Prospects. Tyler, can I speak to you a moment?"

"Later." He took Berry's arm in an unmistakably proprietary fashion. "I promised Mary a personal introduction to Farley. Let's go in. We're late as it is."

Inside the ballroom, he whispered in Berry's ear. "Let this be a lesson to you. Mastering ditz talk requires one heck of a lot of study."

"I keep on telling you," Berry said. "I have real *skills*."

Behind her long, thick lashes, a strange purple light began to glow. Tyler observed it with trepidation, but before he could warn her to behave herself, his father hailed him.

"Hi, Dad," Tyler said with a cool nonchalance he was further and further from feeling. "I'd like you to meet Miss Mary MacGregor."

He watched closely as his father shook Berry's hand and caught the fulminating glance Debra exchanged with his father. Not by a word or action did Mason Reid indicate he saw anything amiss with his son's date. To Tyler's further enjoyment, Mason obviously failed to recognize her as the plain woman he'd met the day before.

Later in the evening, when he was able to exchange a word with Tyler alone, Mason said, "Your new interest is quite a looker. I've never seen anyone with eyes that shade of purple before."

"They're violet," Tyler said, straight-faced. He followed Mason's gaze across the big room to where Berry stood in the center of a group of people.

"I think I'll have all your work audited," Mason continued, in those same meditative tones. "Just as a precaution, you understand."

"Of course, Dad. Can't say that I blame you." Tyler raised his brows and let his gaze caress Berry's derriere. "I suppose this means I'll have to resort to having you murdered so I can collect my inheritance and continue to afford her."

"Be reasonable, Tyler," Mason said gently. "Whatever you inherit from me still won't be enough to keep a woman like that in the style to which she's no doubt accustomed. Just what do you think you're up to?"

"Come on, Dad." Tyler smiled at Berry's backside, still marveling that his father obviously did not recognize her. "Look at her. Whatever she costs me, you've got to admit, she's worth every penny."

CHAPTER 4

"Actually, I'm very *skilled* at typing," Berry said to a man named Baxter, half-lowering her eyelids suggestively. "*And* in computer spreadsheet use."

She refused to glance at Tyler lest he detect a silent plea for rescue. He must have introduced her to half-a-dozen wealthy older men on the lookout for pretty young women. Without his reassuring presence at her side, the assessing male stares she attracted almost frightened her.

Tyler suddenly reentered the conversation. "She even transcribes dictation." He placed a large, warm hand at her back.

"Maybe you'd like to work for me," Baxter said, leering at her. "I've got a computer program that does transcription."

"Why, that *does* sound nice," Berry said, deliberately pitching her voice higher and widening her eyes. "I'd have ever so much more time for," she paused and glanced meaningfully at her perfect new nails, "*other* things."

Being a bimbo was a lot harder than she'd thought. It took all her wits and intelligence to pretend she was a dilettante with no particular plans beyond finding a rich protector who'd let her play at a job.

"If Farley falls through, she might give you a call, Baxter," Tyler said.

Berry tried not to look relieved that Tyler had taken her over again. She'd garnered three job offers, but Felix Farley had yet to appear. That made the evening a total loss as far she was concerned.

Debra's contemptuous stare met her gaze. Wincing inwardly, Berry elevated her nose and gazed winsomely at Tyler.

Celia Reid, Tyler's mother, approached. "Mr. Farley has just arrived. I'll be happy to introduce you, Miss MacGregor."

Berry met her assessing glance with one of wide-eyed insouciance and wished it weren't necessary to maintain her cover. She could have loved Tyler's willowy, blonde mother. But the fewer people who knew her identity, the better in this case.

"Thanks, Mom, but I'd better do it myself," Tyler said. "A man doesn't like to renege on a promise to a beautiful woman."

Berry restrained herself from thrusting her elbow into his ribs. Had she really thought Tyler Reid was the handsomest man in the room? Obviously, she had been viewing him through gratitude-tinted glasses.

"Maybe I'd better introduce her," Mason Reid said. "He'll probably be more likely to—er—see her as a competent secretary."

"Consider Mom's feelings, Dad." Tyler drew Berry against his side. "Should you be showing this much interest in beautiful young secretaries?"

Celia's face betrayed no sign of fear or antagonism. "Nonsense, Tyler. As if I'd mind Mason doing a simple kindness for Miss MacGregor."

Berry elbowed Tyler under the cover of his dinner jacket. He took her hand and laced his fingers through hers.

Debra pretended not to notice, but Berry saw the tightening of her every facial feature. Mason eyed their clasped hands and raised his brows. Celia looked frozen.

Tyler's wicked enjoyment of the situation was plain to Berry. She couldn't understand why his family didn't realize he was taking great pleasure in teasing them with his latest bimbo.

"Come on, B—Mary," Tyler said. "Let's meet your future employer."

Debra made a great and obvious effort. "Good luck, Miss MacGregor. It's really too bad the Houston job market started shrinking before you moved to town."

Berry smiled brightly. "I'll just have to rely on my *excellent* training. After all, it's my *major* asset."

Tyler choked back a laugh. "Mary has a truly spectacular resume."

"I'll just bet," Debra muttered.

"Felix will hire her," Tyler predicted, grinning. "Heck, even Dad's dying to hire her."

"Yeah," Debra said, aside to her mother. "He'd like to find out just how much you've spent on her so far."

Berry bit her lip. She put one hand on her hip and struck a pose then fixed a predatory stare on Felix Farley.

"It's a good thing I've lived such a quiet life so far," Tyler said. "I've got plenty saved, enough to give Mary quite a fling for the next few weeks. How about it, Mary?"

Berry couldn't resist tossing him an ostensibly adoring look that smoldered with promise.

Debra's eyes narrowed. "Since when have you traded in blondes for brunettes?"

"Since I met Mary, of course," Tyler said.

"Debra, kindly remember your manners." Celia Reid's blue gaze studied Berry from the top of her curly head to her ridiculously high-heeled pink sandals.

Mason regarded Berry with a gaze of fascinated horror.

"Oh, *look*, Tyler," Berry said. "Here comes Mr. Farley. *Do* hurry up and *introduce* me. I can't stand the suspense another *minute*."

"Your wish is my command, angel."

Tyler kept her tucked against his side as he led her across the big ballroom. Berry thought she felt the collective stares of the Reid family boring into the center of her back.

"Do you have to pretend I'm taking you for every cent you've saved since you left college?" she asked in low tones.

"Why not? It's what they expect, and God forbid that I not behave as they expect."

Berry noted the annoyance in his voice. "The only thing they *expect* is that your women be blonde instead of brunette."

"It's never too late to sample something different," Tyler returned. "Where'd you learn to talk like a bimbo?"

Berry was inordinately pleased. "I've worked on my diction, of course."

"I'd say you've succeeded," Tyler said grimly. "There must be six old gents who'd like to murder me and take you home with them."

"Then let's hope Felix falls for me, too." Berry realized he was getting immense pleasure out of teasing his family with a brunette bimbo instead of making an effort to meet one of the beautiful women present. "Do you know what's interesting? Since the time I met you, you've done nothing but frown—until you realized your family thinks you're being led down the primrose path."

Tyler grinned. Berry had to admit when he smiled, he was extraordinarily attractive.

"It's good for them," he said. "Look at it this way. You're paying me back for all the trouble I'm going through on your behalf."

"That's what I thought." Tensing, she directed a blindly brilliant smile in Felix Farley's general direction. "Okay. I'm ready. Let's see if my research was on target with regard to potential bosses."

Felix Farley turned politely when Tyler tapped his shoulder, looking bored. Berry's heart raced with the awareness that everything depended upon the next few minutes and her stomach jittered. Now she just needed to manage not to throw up on him, or faint, or anything else that might hint that she didn't find him totally desirable.

Felix Farley was a well-preserved man in his late fifties, with iron-gray hair, jaded hazel eyes, and a deep tan derived from expensive vacations in places like Acapulco. When his gaze fell upon Berry, his eyes widened then narrowed with speculation.

Berry fluttered and bent forward slightly as if bowing.

Felix gazed fixedly at the front of her dress. Blushing fierily in spite of herself, Berry straightened her shoulders and held out one exquisitely manicured hand. Her hands were cold with anxiety, but maybe Felix wouldn't notice that.

Felix took her hand, glancing at the useless, decorative nails approvingly. Wild triumph roared through her veins. Felix liked her already. She was going to get inside Farley Brothers, the first major step toward clearing Daniel's reputation.

Energized, she smiled sweetly at Felix and kept her mind focused on Tyler Reid. His thick, chestnut hair looked like burnished mahogany in the muted lighting. How could any woman look twice at Felix when Tyler was in the room?

In the middle of performing introductions, Tyler's voice almost choked off, but he managed to finish the sentence. When he resumed, he sounded like a man who was speaking through gritted teeth. Berry realized he must have noticed her effort to allow Felix a glance down the front of her dress.

"Miss MacGregor tells me she has a job interview with you first thing Monday morning," Tyler said. "She's been dying to meet you and Mrs. Farley."

He was wasting his time drawing Jennifer Farley into the conversation. Felix noticed no one but her. If that hadn't been precisely her objective, she'd have felt thoroughly ashamed of herself.

Jennifer Farley, a coldly precise, pale-blonde beauty, didn't seem to care what her husband did. Instead, she gazed speculatively at Tyler. Berry squelched an astonishing surge of jealousy and concentrated harder on Felix.

Felix held Berry's perfectly manicured hand in his for a moment longer than was necessary. "I'll look forward to Monday morning, Miss MacGregor. You may be just the person my office needs."

"Moving to Houston and searching for just the *right* position is so *exciting*." Berry glowed with ardent interest in Felix's office. "An executive assistant at my level looks for *challenge* as well as worthy surroundings, and most of all, a *gentleman* she can be *proud* of and look up to. A *successful* man who can teach her *new things* about the art of business. I want to devote all my *skills* and *heart* to that man."

Felix's tongue was all but hanging out. Berry hoped she'd hit on every sentiment dear to Felix's heart, based on the few things Daniel had said.

"I can see you're a true professional, Miss MacGregor." Felix's leering smile grew. "Something tells me you'll suit my office perfectly." Others claimed Felix's attention then, but he turned to her and said, "Until Monday morning."

Berry gratefully let Tyler lead her toward the dance floor at the far end of the enormous room. Dizzy with her own success, she contemplated snagging a glass of pure Kentucky bourbon from the nearest waiter's tray.

"If you dare let that old goat look down your dress again, I'll strangle you," Tyler said, almost snarling. "On Daniel's behalf."

Berry caught Felix's gaze on her as she pivoted gracefully. Probably watching her bottom, she thought, more satisfied than ever with the dress. She tilted her head back to smile up at Tyler, exposing her slender, vulnerable throat. Across the room, Felix Farley's eyes widened hungrily.

"Don't worry, Tyler." The research she had done with regard to sex and the office had paid off in spades. She felt herself glowing with triumph. "The idea is to make him think he's about to see something. There's nothing actually visible but the top edge of my bra."

"That's too damned much," Tyler snapped.

His broad brows were drawn together and he sounded almost jealous, but she knew that was unlikely. He probably had gone into big-brother mode, reacting the same way he would if one of his sisters had worn such a dress.

"My first priority is to get hired," she offered, in placating tones. "The idea is to create desire, and that's what the neckline is all about. On Monday—"

"Monday you're wearing a turtleneck and a skirt down to your ankles."

Tyler spoke through gritted teeth. Definitely, he had taken on the role of big brother to Daniel's little sister.

"Maybe you're right." She nodded seriously, and her dark curls brushed his arm. "We don't want to give him too much all at once. The important thing is to keep him guessing."

"Getting hired is the least of your worries," he said dryly. "Felix hasn't taken his eyes off you yet."

"I can't thank you enough, Tyler. You've made my investigation a lot easier."

She smiled warmly at him. Tyler had come through for her in an unbelievable way. When her investigation was done, she'd have to buy him a suitable gift that would adequately express her appreciation. Perhaps she'd give him a colorful painting for that sterile living room of his.

Tyler drew her into his arms on the tiny excuse for a dance floor. Berry's thoughts went on hold abruptly. Tyler arranged her body against his and guided her in a slow waltz. She stiffened automatically, unsure how she felt about being embraced like this by Tyler Reid.

"What are you doing?" she whispered. They could barely move in the crowded space.

"I'm giving old Felix a chance to admire your beautiful rear end, what else?"

Tyler sounded a bit sour. Berry relaxed into his hold, reflecting that Tyler made a much more satisfactory big brother than Daniel ever had.

"In that case," she said, "how about maneuvering us around so he can?"

"Are you kidding? The man's got X-ray vision where you're concerned." He guided them past a swaying couple. "Seriously, Berry, don't you think you're taking things a little too far? You'll be lucky if Felix doesn't chase you around his desk the minute you're officially employed. You've given him every reason to think you're amenable to what he obviously has in mind."

"I couldn't take the chance of not being hired," Berry said simply. "It's better to experience a little sexual harassment rather than risk not getting in."

Tyler drew in a quick breath. "Do you have any idea how big a risk you're taking?"

"Oh, I don't think the murderer is going to be interested in me." She smiled sunnily at him. "I'm going to put on an act of skilled secretarial stupidity, if you can imagine such a contradiction in terms."

"I'm not talking about whatever danger you're in from the murderer. Assuming there is a murderer at that company," he added, exasperated. "I'm talking about Felix Farley. Do you think for one minute he's going to let you lead him around by a ring in his nose? That man is accustomed to getting what he wants from women. And if you don't know what he wants from you, I'll be happy to explain it."

"Lighten up, Tyler. Of course I know what he wants from me. Any woman would. He's careful to make it very clear."

She smiled encouragingly. It was nice having a man around who cared enough to look out for her.

"Felix won't ever get caught on a sexual harassment charge," she went on. "One thing he's got is enough sense not to make passes at women who don't give him the proper encouragement."

"No one can say you didn't give him the proper encouragement," Tyler grumbled. "Did you learn those moves in one of your science labs?"

Berry chuckled appreciatively. "I read a lot. And I've been watching a lot of daytime television shows and paying special attention to the home wreckers."

"I'd have said you were channeling a professional mistress," Tyler said in acerbic tones. "I never thought a woman could actually walk like that in real life."

"It's these shoes," Berry said, choking with delighted laughter. "That's why I forced myself to buy them. You can't help but walk like a vamp in three-inch heels."

She glanced idly over Tyler's shoulder and caught a glimpse of a blond man who vanished instantly behind a dancing couple. Her breath left her body in one giant gasp of shock.

"Berry?" Tyler leaned back slightly so he could look into her face. "Are you all right? What is it?"

She jerked her attention back to Tyler and reached for her common sense. She'd been mistaken, of course. Why would Grady Craig be in Houston?

"I'm fine. I thought I saw someone I knew." She took several deep breaths in hopes of calming her pounding heart. "It was such a surprise, I reacted without thinking."

Tyler looked over his shoulder. "Who was it?"

"The person I saw looked like a man I dated a few months ago," she said. "His name was Grady Craig."

"Was? Is he dead?" Tyler frowned and scanned the glittering crowd behind him.

"He's still alive. At least, I suppose he is." She was definitely losing it. Of all the subjects she'd like to hide from Tyler, Grady Craig led the list. She still couldn't believe she had been credulous enough to fall for Grady's lies. The whole Grady Craig fiasco made her question her own good sense.

"One of your ex-fiancés, right?" Tyler frowned heavily. "Where is he?"

"I was mistaken," Berry said firmly. "I don't know why I reacted so strongly. It was a shock to see him here, that's all."

"Are you sure?" He turned them so he could scan the crowd suspiciously.

"Of course, I'm sure." Berry deliberately calmed herself and changed the subject. "It's a trick your mind plays on you … "

Her voice faded as she realized abruptly what construction Tyler was likely to place on this in regard to her relationship with Grady Craig.

Tyler relented. A small smile broke the frowning gravity of his face. "In that case, let's give this place the old raspberry. I don't want you to faint in here."

"You mean leave?"

"It's ten o'clock. We wasted two hours waiting for Felix to show. Now that he's seen you, how about letting absence make his heart grow fonder?"

"And his memory more explicit." Berry knew she ought to remain in case Felix wanted to dance with her, but she'd seen enough of Felix—and Houston's elite—for one night. "Let's go. What about your sister?"

"She's got Dad and Mom to look out for her." Tyler's face took on a mischievous look. "We might as well give their imaginations a little more fuel."

Berry considered that while Tyler guided her toward his parents. She could just imagine what they were going to think when she and Tyler disappeared just as the main event of the evening, a charity auction, was about to begin.

Tyler's parents were gracious, but Berry noted Debra's expression of surprise, then of worried suspicion.

"She's surprised to find you still with me," Tyler commented, handing Berry into his Porsche.

"Stop looking down the front of my dress, you pervert." She placed a hand protectively over her neckline. "I suppose she thought I'd pick up some rich old man and leave with him. What a mind your sister has."

Tyler chuckled warmly. "Keep it up, Challoner. You're doing wonders for my image."

"Careful, Tyler. Your dad's probably going to have your bank account attached on the grounds that you've obviously lost your mind."

For some reason, Tyler found that exquisitely funny. Berry eyed him curiously while he almost doubled over with laughter.

"I'm serious," she said. "If it looks as though I find you more fascinating than all those rich old guys we met tonight, there's got to be a reason, right? They probably think you've tricked me into believing you're rich."

Tyler straightened at last and came around to climb in beside her, still laughing. "I never knew I had it in me."

"Your horizons are expanding exponentially. Besides, I might see something more in you than your alleged money." She thought on it a moment. "I hope I run into your sister again during the next few weeks. I'll tell her I'm thinking about ditching the high life and marrying you because you have such a cute frown."

Tyler groaned. "Please. Don't do me any favors. Dad will audit all my clients' books for sure."

Berry chuckled, enchanted at the thought. "Did he say he was going to do that? How do you audit books, anyway?"

Tyler guided the Porsche expertly into traffic. "That's a question best answered over a good meal. What do you say?"

"Is this where I coax you into spending a huge sum on a genuine Maine lobster and a bottle of rare old wine?"

Tyler laughed. "You can try."

"Lucky for you, I'm allergic to seafood." She eased the pink sandals off her feet, sighing with pleasure. "If this is what a mistress has to put up with, she deserves every dollar spent on her."

"Next time, buy a pair of shoes an inch or two shorter in the heels," Tyler said with a remarkable lack of sympathy.

"Thanks so much for introducing me tonight. You've made my job easy Monday morning. Felix can't wait to hire me."

"That's for sure." Tyler lapsed into brooding silence and turned down a street lined with restaurants and neon signs.

"Don't worry about me, Tyler," she said gently. "Believe it or not, science labs are great training grounds. I've been chased around my Bunsen burner by several professors in my time."

Tyler said nothing. He turned into a restaurant entrance surrounded by wildly colored neon. "Here we are. Don't forget to ask for the wine list."

"Humph," Berry said, faking a scowl. "What's this supposed to be? I thought you were taking me to a posh restaurant where I could order lobster and practice my come-hither gazes."

"Sorry. If Palais-de-Burger isn't good enough for you … "

Berry's phony scowl morphed into happy laughter. "I guess it'll have to do since I'm starving. Thanks, Tyler. If I had to sit up straight in some fancy restaurant after what I've been through tonight, I'd have curled up and died."

Tyler smiled. "You were looking a little jaded. I thought a burger and fries might get you back to normal."

Tyler was a great man, Berry decided. It was almost as if he'd read her mind when the image of a hamburger had passed fleetingly through her thoughts a mile back.

"Thanks. It will." She studied the menu displayed on a lighted board with gratitude. "I was in danger of forgetting how real people live. It was awful, Tyler. Are there really women who'll put up with those old men just to have a lot of money and go to events like that one?"

"I thought you'd researched the matter thoroughly. You ought to know more about it than I do."

"After tonight, my heart no longer accepts what my mind tells me. I'll have the double cheeseburger and an order of fries, please. I've been so nervous, I've hardly eaten a thing since lunch."

Tyler dictated their order into the microphone. "Want to take a drive by one of the stores Felix manages? Maybe it'll give you some background."

Berry's enthusiasm revived magically. Tyler was unbelievable. Why hadn't she gotten to know him before?

"That would be great. Then I can impress Felix with my firsthand knowledge of his business."

"Only you could consider looking in a store window firsthand knowledge of Felix's business."

"Think about it." She gestured emphatically. "How many of Felix's previous mistresses have bothered to go look at one of his auto parts stores?"

"You do have a point." He rested his forehead on the steering wheel as if overwhelmed, but Berry saw his shoulders shaking with his silent laughter. "If he doesn't proposition you first thing Monday morning, something's wrong."

"Do you think he will?"

"Don't look so hopeful unless you intend to say yes."

Berry smiled. "If he propositions me right away, I'll more or less have him where I want him."

He lifted his head to stare at her. "You think so?"

"I'll explain about what an honorable woman I am, and how I have to break up with my current boyfriend before I move in with him. It'll take me at least two weeks—"

"Are you crazy?" He sounded completely floored. "Look, Challoner, let me explain a few of the facts of life to you. Felix Farley isn't used to waiting for what he wants. If you aren't careful, you'll find yourself in a situation you won't like at all."

Berry considered that seriously. Obviously, Tyler was editing his words heavily in deference to her maidenly ears. And although she, too, suspected keeping Felix on a string might prove far beyond her powers, she had no other ideas that would get her into the main office of Farley Brothers and keep her there for a few weeks.

"I've got it all planned, Tyler." She tried to project her usual optimism in hopes of covering the fact that she had no idea how to keep Felix dangling. "I know exactly what I'm going to say, and how I'm going to act."

Tyler's frown came back in full force. "Now where have I heard that one before? Oh, yes. That was what Debra said when I caught her climbing out her bedroom window one night to meet some creep at a bar. She was seventeen at the time."

"Did she really?" Berry tilted her head to the side. "What did you do?"

"Shut up, Challoner. You're trying to change the subject."

She was, but he wasn't supposed to know that. "I'll bet you followed her to the bar and walked in just as he made a heavy pass, right? She was so grateful to see you; she swore she'd never do it again, right? That's what I thought. Well, don't worry, Tyler. In this case, I'm not expecting you to gallop to the rescue like the cavalry. If worse comes to worst, I'll just have to quit the job, that's all."

She had no intention of quitting Farley Brothers until she either found out why Daniel was murdered, or she was fired and escorted off the premises. But Tyler didn't need to know that either. At least, not right away.

Tyler watched her. "What are you thinking now?"

"I'm considering ways to avoid quitting as Felix's secretary until I'm ready to leave."

"Why don't I believe you?"

"Heavens, Tyler, I don't know. Maybe you've gotten too suspicious in your old age."

She had to remember Tyler's experience in the matter of divining what was going on in the minds of his sisters. He might stalk into Felix's office one day.

They arrived at the service window, and Tyler reached for their order. "There's definitely something about looking out for little sisters that makes me feel old and suspicious."

"Is this where I remind you that I'm not your little sister?"

"You're Daniel's little sister, and that's almost the same thing," he grumbled. "Don't open that. We'll unpack it and eat at home."

The Farley Brothers Auto Parts store came into view down the road from the Palais-de-Burger. Not even the broad, picture window filled with mufflers and gleaming chrome wheels took her mind off the odor of freshly cooked hamburgers emanating from the bag containing their supper.

"Looks like a going concern." She peered at a display of glittering wheels made of hundreds of wire spokes. "They've got a big warehouse attached, I see." She slid her feet reluctantly back into her shoes. "I'd better get out and look the place over."

"This is Felix's major money-making store." Tyler got out and came around to help her out. "It's making more than any of the other Farley Brothers stores, presumably because of Felix's personal attention."

Berry tried to picture Felix behind the counter of an auto parts store and failed. "Do you think he's ever actually been in here?"

"According to my sources, he visits this store all the time. The manager seems to be a friend of his."

Berry put her nose to the picture window and peered at the rows of well-stocked shelves behind the counter. "When I describe that cute little pyramid of wire wheels in the window, he'll know I've actually been here," Berry said cheerfully. "Let's go home, Tyler. I'm starving."

"You're a truly gung-ho employee." Tyler obligingly headed the Porsche toward his apartment complex. When they arrived, he slowed before nearing his parking slot. "Uh-oh. Is that who I think it is?"

Berry ignored the yellow taxicab that waited, motor running, in the parking lot near the two parking spaces allotted to Tyler's apartment and focused on the peculiar way Daniel's Mustang rested on the pavement.

The taxi door swung open, and Debra burst out. She clutched her purse in one hand and pointed an accusing finger at Berry with the other.

"I knew it!" she cried. "You've brought that floozy home with you. How could you, Tyler Reid?"

"Tyler," Berry whispered, aghast. "Someone stole the wheels off my car."

CHAPTER 5

Tyler looked from the jade Mustang with its axles resting on the pavement to his sister's finger of doom. For a moment, he didn't know which disaster to tackle first.

Nothing could be done about the four stolen wheels except call the police, which meant the car could wait. If he didn't do something about Debra, every occupant of the apartment building would think he was running a house of ill repute out of his apartment.

"Debra probably remembers Daniel's car," he said aside to Berry, "so don't call her attention to it."

Berry stared at the Mustang in a blank, stunned way and appeared unaware that he had a family crisis on his hands.

"What am I going to do?" she asked slowly. "I've got to have a car by Monday morning."

"You're going to call a garage tomorrow and buy four new wheels. That's what you're going to do." The words must have penetrated because she turned her blank stare to him. "Now stay quiet while I get rid of my sister."

He got out of the Porsche with lazy grace, looking forward to the next few minutes. Or he did, until Berry got out of the car in her ridiculously high heels and sashayed over to stand beside him.

"What do you think you're doing?" he asked Debra. He'd never realized she had such a dramatic streak in her character. "It ought to be clear you're very much in the way around here."

"I can't believe this." Debra looked from him to Berry.

"You've already said that." Tyler kept a wary eye on Berry. She still stared at her Mustang, although she'd taken care to strike a sexy pose. "What's so difficult to understand about a man's desire for privacy when he brings a beautiful woman home with him?"

"Beautiful!" Debra threw up her hands in the best drama queen fashion. "The only thing she cares about is your bank account. Why are men so stupid?"

Tyler bit back an admiring grin. He wouldn't have guessed Debra had it in her. "Now, Deb, be reasonable. Mary told me just a few minutes ago that I have a cute frown. What more can a man ask for?"

"A cute frown!" Debra's despairing cry was worthy of a better audience than himself, Tyler decided. "You're a bigger fool than I thought, Tyler Reid. If this wasn't worrying Mom and Dad so much, I'd let you get what's coming to you. But—"

"What's coming to him is me," Berry said suddenly. "Tonight." Her voice was pitched low and sweet, and the look she turned in his direction was enough to ignite a man where he stood. "I'm the best thing that ever happened to him."

Tyler hoped he could keep any expression of his feelings from echoing on his face while Berry's arms wrapped around his waist, and her soft body pressed against his in blatant invitation. He dropped his arm casually about her shoulders, completely the man about town who knows himself irresistible to females, and gave her a squeeze.

"Let's go upstairs, beauty," he said, "so I can get what's coming to me."

"You're doomed," Debra said in hollow tones. "Well, no one can say I didn't try."

"I'll remember to tell Mom that you tried," Tyler said. "She'll be happy to know your good manners are intact."

"Shut up while you're ahead," Berry hissed in his ear, and pretended to nibble his earlobe.

"You should be ashamed," Debra said to Berry. Her tone of despair was definitely worthy of the stage. "It's perfectly clear you've gotten your hooks into him but good. Oh, why can't you go pick on somebody else's brother?"

"Every man is some woman's brother," Berry said. Only the quiver in her husky, sexy tones betrayed her. "If you wanted to keep him safe from women like me, you should have appreciated him more."

Berry reached up, grabbed Tyler by the back of his neck, and pulled his face down. Wrapping her arms around his neck hard enough to choke him, she crushed her warm mouth to his. His entire body reacted. He crushed her against him and hoped he hadn't hurt her.

"Oh!" Debra cried. "You—you *bimbo!*"

She flounced back into the cab and slammed the door. The cab driver, who had been a disinterested spectator, rolled his eyes and backed his cab up slowly.

Tyler didn't know whether Berry's grip on his neck was choking him, or whether it was his own physical response. Be that as it may, she didn't mean anything personal by the hot kiss she pressed on his lips.

As soon as the cab pulled out of the parking lot, she let him go but remained standing in his arms, resting her forehead against his shoulder. Tyler held her, well aware that Debra would draw the worst conclusion, and further aware that Berry was inches away from breaking down.

"Take it easy, honey," he said gently. "We'll call a tow truck tonight. By tomorrow afternoon, you'll have your car back. Hey, calm down. Kissing me wasn't that bad, was it?"

"It was wonderful." Her voice rang with passionate sincerity.

Tyler kept a grip on himself with difficulty.

Berry choked on a sob. "It's just that I was looking at that car as one of my last links to Daniel, and after all, I've still got the rest of the car." She locked her arms around Tyler and buried her face in the hollow of his shoulder. "I'm just being silly. But I'd really like to punch your sister's lights out. How dare she act like you don't have a right to live your own life?"

The leap of Tyler's heart told him he was in danger of losing his grip on reality. "I never knew she was so good at melodrama."

Berry burrowed deeper into his embrace. "She sounded like a perfect idiot. Sorry, Tyler, but your sister brought out the worst in me. I couldn't resist doing the siren act."

"It served her right," Tyler said, and laughed. "Lord, what a night. My reputation as a Don Juan just went up about ten notches."

"I didn't know you had a reputation as a Don Juan. Daniel said—" She stopped suddenly. "Daniel said he did his best to fix you up, but you weren't interested." She straightened slowly away from him as the cab's red taillights disappeared down the street. "Needless to say, Daniel thought that kind of decency was absolutely uncalled-for."

Tyler registered the withdrawal of her soft body with regret and self-castigation. She was only asking for a friendly hug. He'd better not start reading anything more into it, or he'd be in real trouble.

"That must have been after my one foray into the world of engagements," he said. "At the time, Daniel had about four girlfriends."

Berry hugged herself and suppressed a slight shiver, even though the night was too warm to require a jacket. "I used to wonder what they saw in him."

Tyler's face remained shadowed as he leaned into the car to get the sack of hamburgers. "You didn't see much of Daniel these past two years, did you? Believe it or not, he was finally beginning to grow up in the area of relationships. When he was killed, he'd been beginning to get serious about one of the women he was dating. He actually told me he was going to quit seeing the others so he could concentrate on the one he was starting to really care about."

"Thanks for telling me that," Berry said, on a deep sigh. "Daniel died just as he was beginning to get some sense, and that makes me twice as mad. I'm going to find whoever killed him, or at least give it a darned good shot."

Tyler balanced the fragrant package that contained their supper. "Daniel wasn't a saint by any means, but he was a good man. I hope you find out something that will help the police catch his killer."

Berry, apparently restored to normalcy, marched around to get her purse. "Don't worry. I will."

Tyler held her arm lightly as they climbed the stairs to his apartment and wondered if the man-woman aspect of having Berry Challoner in his apartment was getting out of hand. Reminding himself she was Daniel's little sister gave him no help. She didn't feel like a little sister when he held her, and she certainly didn't look like one.

He wondered briefly what Daniel would say if he knew his best friend was thinking lustful thoughts about his little sister.

I'd say, "Go to it, old buddy."

Tyler jerked his head around. "Did you say something?"

Berry gripped the balustrade upon his sudden movement. "No, and I didn't hear anyone else say anything, either. Why?"

"I thought I heard someone," Tyler said. "Here, be careful. I don't care to have you fall back down these stairs and break your neck."

"Don't get snappish. I keep on telling you, these shoes have a purpose." She regarded him curiously.

Tyler made a rude comment about the shoes' purpose and unlocked his apartment door. He ushered Berry inside, then stood in the door and took a long, careful look around the parking lot before he shut the door. The only thing he saw was a dark-colored sedan cruising slowly past on the street. He was hearing things. Perhaps he'd been overworking lately.

Berry stood in the center of the living room watching him. "Are you looking for your parents to arrive?"

"To save me from you?" he asked, grinning. "That would be one for the books."

"Your family loves you very much," Berry said austerely. "Naturally, they aren't thrilled to think of you falling into the clutches of a gold-digger like me."

"Some gold-digger. You've even bought groceries." He'd opened his refrigerator door earlier and found it stocked with steaks and vegetables.

"Maybe I should give you the bills. A woman has to protect her bad reputation." Her smile vanished. "Do you know a good tire service that's open on Sunday?"

"Don't worry, honey." Tyler carried the food to the bar that served as a table. "All you need is four new wheels. Get plain ones this time. I told Daniel when he bought that car that he was practically issuing invitations to car thieves. They love to steal fancy parts off sports cars and sell them back to the owners." He chuckled. "I wonder if they'll notice that nick on one of the spokes. Let's call the police and report the theft. If the police recover them, we can identify your wheels by that nick."

Berry cheered up. "Maybe this is a good thing, Tyler. Without those fancy mag wheels, that Mustang won't look so much like Daniel's car any longer."

Tyler agreed and pretended to concentrate on getting out his cell phone to call the police. In reality, he was enjoying the way Berry removed her shoes and worked her toes into the carpet.

Then she removed a contact lens case from her little clutch purse and came to stand at the bar while she removed the purple—violet—lenses. He studied her face while he spoke to the police and admitted himself impressed. He'd never have dreamed different-colored eyes could give her such a totally different expression.

"You look like yourself again," he said, clicking off his phone. "There's something weird about purple eyes."

"Don't tell me. Gray eyes give me a girl-next-door look, right? Well, plain and ordinary doesn't get it here, Tyler. I've got to look like the sort of woman who expects to receive lots of money and presents from men regularly."

She reached hungrily for her cheeseburger and bit into it with the enthusiasm usually reserved for plotting the downfall of Farley Brothers, Inc.

Tyler remembered another woman who had eaten hamburgers in his company with that same enthusiasm. He'd found that ability to enjoy ordinary things enchanting, and had thought it boded well for the future. Boy, had he been mistaken. Learning that she thought of him as a friend who would help deceive her father had come as a major shock.

Frowning, he removed his dinner jacket and hung it over a chair. That reminder got his thoughts about Berry Challoner back under control.

Berry tilted her head and considered him. "What's wrong? You're frowning again, just when I was beginning to get used to your smile."

He smiled reluctantly. "I thought you said I had a cute frown."

"You do, but that doesn't mean I like it better than I like your smile." She sipped her cola. "What are you thinking?"

He couldn't remember the last time a woman had asked him that. If one ever had. They were probably afraid he'd start in on some lethally dull accounting anecdote.

"I was thinking of a new method of analyzing the figures you're going to bring me Monday afternoon," he said.

Berry's gray eyes widened with renewed vigor. "Really? Do tell me about them. And while you're at it, tell me what figures you'll need. And how to find them in the computer files—"

"Hold it, hold it." He should have known. Accounting methods were very much on Berry's mind right now, in spite of the fact that she knew less than nothing about them. "I was just kidding. Actually, if you should happen to get hold of any balance sheets or company work sheets, I'll use time-honored, generally accepted accounting principles to analyze them."

"Oh? Well, how about telling me about those? How do you look at a balance sheet and tell whether a company is doing well or going broke? I've always wondered."

Berry's slender, golden face held an expression of such powerful interest; Tyler was surprised he didn't instantly launch into an explanation of generally accepted accounting principles.

"There are several things to look for," he said. "We'll take a look at the official Farley Brothers financial statements tomorrow if you're interested."

"Oh, I'm interested, all right," Berry said, looking ferocious. "I'm very interested. If you can tell me what to look for so I can prove they're lying about everything, we'll be in business."

Tyler bit his tongue and managed not to laugh. "We'll get on it tomorrow after we've had your car towed to the tire place."

"You don't know how much I appreciate your help." She fairly glowed with enthusiasm again. "Without you, I wouldn't have the faintest idea what to look for."

"I thought," Tyler said carefully, "you were going to be on the lookout for anomalies."

"I am. But it'll help if I know what's likely to be an anomaly."

Tyler, grinning, had to admit the truth of that.

•••

True to his word, Tyler had the Mustang towed to a tire shop first thing the following morning. By noon, Berry had her car back with four new tires. In one fell swoop, the Mustang had lost much of its super-sporty look.

Berry jumped out of it happily. "I like it a lot better. No one will recognize it as Daniel's car."

Tyler, who had followed her back, climbed out of his Porsche. He looked weary suddenly, and Berry didn't like it. She had seen him talking on his phone several minutes before and suspected the conversation had much to do with his resigned expression.

"Don't tell me," she said. "You've got to go to the office, right?"

He looked at her and his frown lightened somewhat. "As a matter of fact, yes. My father claims to have forgotten the spreadsheets for one of our clients are due out on Monday morning."

Berry didn't say, "Hah!" but she figured he could read her face. "Doesn't he know it's Sunday?"

"As Dad likes to say, when you own your own business, you throw away the key."

"Fine," Berry said. "He's an owner, too. Is he intending to help you with these spreadsheets?"

She figured the real reason Mason Reid was calling Tyler to the office was to feel him out about the bimbo he'd taken to his apartment the night before. Berry simmered with annoyance. The whole thing was her fault, but Tyler would be the one to suffer.

Tyler smiled, but Berry thought the smile looked forced. "He'll be there. He likes to work on Sunday afternoons when it's quiet."

She followed him up the stairs, flimsy high-heeled sandals clicking on the steps. She wore a new pair of white linen trousers and a purple halter-top that was tied beneath her breasts on the grounds that she might run into Felix or a member of Tyler's family.

"Daniel said you haven't taken a vacation in the entire eight years since you left school. Don't you think it's time you put your foot down?"

"The work has to get out on time." Tyler unlocked the door to his apartment and opened it so she could flounce inside. "What are you going to do while I'm gone?"

"I'm going to practice for my interview and hope that my so-called skills are the exact abilities needed in Felix Farley's office."

"According to Daniel, the only skill ever actually displayed by Felix's secretary was how to select a really nice nail polish from an online display."

"Really?" She regarded her laptop computer thoughtfully. "Maybe reviewing office procedures would be a waste of time. I'd better run out and pick up an elegant little manicure set. I'd never dream of actually filing one of these phony nails, but it won't do to disappoint Felix."

Tyler laughed. "When I get home, I'll help you practice taking dictation while sitting on a man's lap."

"I'll look forward to that," Berry promised. "In the meantime, maintain a stoic silence at the office. And if you can let your dad catch you gazing out the window and daydreaming ... "

"Please. If he ever catches me daydreaming, he'll have every piece of work I've ever done audited and probably have me committed."

"It would serve him right if you left him to do all that work by himself," Berry said indignantly.

But to her intense frustration, Tyler went wearily to his bedroom to shed his jeans in favor of dress slacks before heading to his office. She watched, gently boiling, as he went slowly down the stairs toward his car. It was ninety degrees out there. In her opinion, Tyler ought to be relaxing by the swimming pool with all the other apartment dwellers.

She was going to have to do something about the way Tyler's family took him for granted. She turned away from the window thoughtfully. If nothing else, she'd put a scare into them that would have them scrambling to pamper him and make him feel cherished.

Less than an hour after Tyler had left the apartment, his landline telephone rang. Tyler had said nothing about whether or not she should answer it, since he only kept it in case of hurricanes or other disasters. Berry let it ring three times, then picked it up and purred, "Hello?"

She heard a gasp that preceded a moment of shattered silence. The receiver crashed down in her ear.

Berry grinned and rushed to reinsert the purple contact lenses and buckle on the flimsy, high-heeled sandals. After a moment of thought, she clasped her new necklace around her neck. The center "diamond" occupied an interesting position at the very top of her cleavage.

Within fifteen minutes, the expected buzz sounded at the front door. Berry took a deep breath and minced daintily across the carpet to open it. Two stares, one of horrified turquoise and the other of interested green, met her.

"Why, Miss *Reid*," Berry simpered. "How absolutely *delightful* to see you again."

"What are you doing in my brother's apartment?" Debra demanded.

"Don't you think that's kind of obvious?" the other woman asked. "Cut the drama, Deb. Hi. I'm Kelley Reid, Tyler's sister. It's nice to meet you."

Berry allowed herself to look Kelley Reid over thoroughly before putting out one languid hand. Kelley had her mother's blond hair, and her eyes were green. Berry placed her age at about twenty and noted she shared Tyler's broad, slashing brows.

"How d'ye do?" she murmured, as if it was almost too much trouble to bother.

"We—uh—just stopped by to see Tyler for a minute." Kelley was obviously trying not to stare at Berry's eyes. "But since he isn't here, we'll just be on our way."

Berry rested her hand, with the long, pink nails on display, on the doorjamb and smiled a secret smile. "I'll tell him to call you *tomorrow*, if you like. He's going to be *busy* tonight."

Debra sucked in her breath.

Kelley elbowed her sister sharply. "It's not important. Please don't bother telling him we came by." She gave up all pretense of not staring. "Man, those eyes are to die for. Do you mind if I ask where you got them?"

Just what she needed, Berry thought irritably. A sister so likeable, she was going to have a hard time keeping up her bitchy act.

"Why, of *course* not," she gushed. "I was *born* with them. Bye."

She shut the door with a sharp click and remained with her ear pressed against it. Outside, she could hear Kelley adjuring Debra to get a life and butt out of Tyler's.

"He's thirty years old," Kelley argued. "Who do you think you are? His mama?"

"She's nothing but a low-down gold-digger!" Debra wailed. "Just look at her. I'll bet Tyler's the one who bought her that awful necklace. Somebody has got to do something."

"Well, it isn't going to be me," Kelley declared. "If Tyler doesn't know his way around by now, he's sure not likely to learn anything from us."

Berry watched the two women head for their car and fingered the maligned phony diamond necklace. It had been well worth the money, she decided, grinning.

She spent an otherwise boring afternoon Googling Farley Brothers for the six hundredth time, updating Mary MacGregor's Facebook page with several selfies and some breathless posts about the excitement of being in Houston and alternating between near-hysteria and calm determination when she thought about Felix Farley. Perhaps she could giggle and refuse to play footsies with Felix until after five o'clock. Then, at precisely four-fifty-nine, she could race for the elevator.

She set the computer aside. It was almost six, and Tyler still wasn't home. She went to her bedroom, removed the purple contact lenses, and changed into a pair of her own jeans, a soft, knit shirt, and a pair of flat slippers. She'd had enough discomfort for one day.

In the kitchen, she got out two steaks and prepared them to go into the broiler the minute Tyler got home. If he'd spent this long slaving over spreadsheets, he was bound to be hungry and tired.

Also, she thought craftily, if she presented him with a delicious hot meal, he might be less likely to jump on her for having some fun with his sisters.

•••

Tyler walked into his apartment at seven, dead tired and wishing he'd stopped to pick up hamburgers or a pizza. But Berry was waiting, and he probably ought to take her out to eat. It would also make for a better atmosphere when he lectured her about answering the telephone and the door when he'd specifically told her not to.

He shut the door behind him and sniffed the air in astonishment. He hadn't smelled that odor in his apartment ever. When he got home, he was usually either too tired to cook or rushing to get to the gym for a workout. He dropped his briefcase on the sofa, scowling at Berry's open computer, and peered into the kitchen.

She stirred something on the stove and looked like herself again, with her own gray eyes smiling at him and her cheeks red from bending over the broiler. She waved a potholder at him.

"Go put on something comfortable," she said. "I'm exhausted after tippy-toeing around in high-heels all day. We need to relax."

She was going to feed him a home-cooked meal, Tyler thought in astonishment. It would be the first time he'd ever eaten anything other than a frozen dinner or takeout in his own apartment.

He changed into a pair of khaki trousers and a blue knit shirt and joined Berry in the kitchen. Now that he thought about it, the lecture he planned to give her would go down better in privacy.

"Go ahead and sit down." She reached into the refrigerator. "The steaks will be done in a minute."

She set a bowl full of tossed salad before him and set out two bottles of dressing. He regarded the dressing in a dazed way. He hadn't been aware that he harbored any salad dressing in his cabinets.

"I've got fresh broccoli coming up," Berry informed him. "I'll bet your diet is atrocious. All frozen dinners and takeout."

"Don't tell me. You majored in home economics for a while, didn't you?"

"Actually, I just took two courses, one in basic nutrition and one in basic cooking techniques. I figured if I didn't, I'd never learn anything about how to eat. Daddy and Daniel both thought opening cans was the height of the art of cooking."

"I thought it was peeling back the foil on a frozen dinner."

He stared in a dazed way at the pot on the stove. Fresh broccoli. She was steaming fresh broccoli and broiling steaks. The next few weeks took on an added interest.

"So tell me about your spreadsheets." Berry checked the broiler. "Was it work that really needed to be done, or was it a ploy of your father's to get you out of my clutches?"

If Tyler hadn't been so tired, he'd have laughed. "It was a little of both, I think. He never said a word about you, but he did give me a lecture about allowing my focus to be shaken."

"That's always been my ultimate desire—to shake a man's focus. Do you think I'll succeed in shaking Felix's focus?"

"If you don't, it'll be because he's drunk."

"That's the nicest thing any man has ever said to me." She lifted the lid on the pot and peered inside. "Seriously, Tyler, what should we go after first? I might have only one chance to get into the company books. I've got to make it count."

"Just bring me whatever you can manage to get your hands on." Tyler shook himself mentally. He was too tired to think. Or maybe he was drowning in unaccustomed comfort. "If you do find anything, it'll probably be something unexpected. You can be sure they've already doctored the books to make most of the data conform to the figures they're publishing."

He rubbed his face and reflected that he had gone as off-the-wall as Berry Challoner, not to mention aiding and abetting in some sort of criminal behavior. Farley Brothers was not involved in anything illegal. Any data Berry managed to filch and bring to him for analysis probably wouldn't tell him a thing.

"That sounds almost like a scientific theory," Berry said enthusiastically. "You get up your theory, and if you can find one instance where the available data doesn't fit the theory, that theory is no longer valid. Accounting sounds a lot more scientific than the business stuff Daniel was always studying."

Tyler thought on this for a moment, blaming his slowed thought processes on a day spent clicking his computer mouse and peering at tiny numbers on-screen. "I suppose that's about what it amounts to. An auditor's job is to make sure all the available data matches what's listed in the books."

"And anything that doesn't match means somebody's cooking the books, right?"

Tyler grinned. "Possibly. What it definitely means is that somebody has some explaining to do. Which reminds me."

She sat down across the table from him and reached for the bottle of Thousand Island dressing. "Yes?"

"You have some explaining to do, young lady." He put on his best frown. "What the devil do you mean by opening the door to my sisters this afternoon?"

Her clear, gray eyes met his without a sign of embarrassment. "Do you call your sisters 'young lady' when you go to scold them?"

"Just answer the question." He had already lost control of the conversation, just as he always did when it came to feminine misbehavior.

"It ought to be perfectly obvious what I'm doing." She regarded him with amusement. "I'm setting you up for the vacation of your life."

CHAPTER 6

She was scheming to get his father to give him time off for a vacation. Tyler couldn't get over it. He even went to bed thinking about a travel-brochure vacation where he went snorkeling in clear blue water over white sand off some exotic Caribbean beach then spent the night dancing beneath swaying palm trees. The woman with him had dark, curly hair and violet eyes.

How he had gotten there, he wasn't even sure.

After a night spent with dreams of tropical paradises interspersed with fits of wakefulness, Tyler snapped awake to the odor of frying bacon. He showered swiftly and threw on his clothes. By the time he got to the kitchen, the odor of toasting bread had entwined itself with the bacon.

"Are you seeking alternate ways of paying your share of the rent?" he asked, sniffing hungrily.

Usually, he bought a doughnut and a cup of coffee on the way to his office. A real breakfast was a rare treat these days, available only in his mother's kitchen.

"I'm trying to be a good houseguest," Berry said, smiling at him. "Besides, doing normal things like cooking a meal is very calming to the nerves."

He noted suddenly she was wearing a pair of shorts and a pink T-shirt, although her hair and makeup looked perfect, and she was already wearing the purple contact lenses. "Why aren't you getting dressed?"

"My appointment isn't until nine, and it won't take me but twenty minutes to get dressed. Besides, I don't want to get bacon grease on my fancy new suit. Wait till you see what I'm going to wear, Tyler." She flipped the bacon. "You'll love it."

"That probably means I'll forbid you to leave this apartment."

Tyler got down a couple of plates from the meager supply of dishes his mother had given him when he got his first apartment. They had been used so seldom, he had to take them to the sink and wash dust off them.

Berry gurgled with laughter that held a nervous edge. "You might, but think what a waste it would be, with no one besides you to appreciate me."

Tyler watched her fry eggs and reflected that keeping her to himself wasn't such a bad idea. In fact, the thought of Felix gazing down or up her dress made him want to fight. He was definitely heading for trouble.

When Berry pranced out of her bedroom to give him a preview of her interview outfit a little later, his throat went so dry he couldn't speak.

"Well?" She twirled before him. "What do you think?"

She wore a pink linen suit with an oversized jacket and a very short, fitted skirt along with dark pink high, high heels, a masterpiece of sexy fashion that made vague pretensions at being business wear. She wore no blouse with it, and in the deep neckline, the fake two-carat phony diamond radiated splashes of colored light against her golden skin.

Any man looking at her would know exactly what to think of her secretarial skills. Tyler sighed and rubbed his forehead. He'd give almost anything to be there when Berry presented herself at the Farley Brothers main office.

So he could drag her out if Felix Farley so much as laid a hand on her, he admitted to himself.

Berry pursed her lips at him. She had painted on lipstick in a way that made her mouth look full and pouting for a man's kiss.

"I wish you were going with me," she said. "I'm so scared, I can hardly breathe. Everything depends on my getting this job. Everything."

Tyler suddenly realized he had a splitting headache and no wish to show up at his office. But he had quarterly reports awaiting him, and he'd definitely be an intruder if he behaved like some sort of glowering bodyguard at Berry's side when she entered Felix Farley's domain.

"Tell you what," he said. "I'll call Felix's office later this morning. Maybe we can meet for lunch. In the meantime, send me a few texts if you can. I want to know how it turns out."

Berry brightened. "I will. Lunch would be wonderful. Maybe I can give you my preliminary report."

"Your what?" The thought of meeting Berry for lunch improved his headache considerably.

"You'll be able to help me most if I keep you informed of everything I learn from the very beginning. By noon, I should have some idea of who the main players are, don't you think? You can guide me toward what I need to access next."

"I'd be amazed if you do," Tyler said drily. "Give yourself a few days at least, Berry. Starting a new job is hard enough."

"I don't have a few days." Berry clenched her fists as well as she could around the long, pink nails. "There's no telling when they might check the facts on my resume and find out Mary MacGregor doesn't exist. Or worse, that she does and she's nearly ninety years old."

"I thought you said your college roommate is giving you a glowing reference."

He stared at her feet. It should have been impossible to walk in heels that high, but Berry managed it.

"She is, but Farley Brothers might have an overzealous personnel manager."

Tyler still couldn't quite believe Berry intended to follow through with her investigation. But when he stood beside his car and watched her drive off in Daniel's Mustang, he realized abruptly that she was really going to do it. In the few short days he'd known her, he'd received a whole new outlook on feminine courage and imagination.

He sighed and rubbed his forehead again. He was late for work, and he didn't care. Worse, he had become so interested in Berry's assault on Farley Brothers he wanted to join her.

He looked up, eyes narrowing, as a dark sedan with tinted windows that had been parked on the street nearby suddenly took off in the same direction Berry had taken.

He told himself he was imagining things, but the car looked a lot like the same car he'd seen cruising past last night.

He firmly dismissed the thought. The direction Berry had taken was a widely traveled one leading directly toward the downtown area. Most of the cars driving past were headed there at this hour of the morning.

Tyler climbed in his car, thinking hard. There had to be something he could do to further Berry's cause. He certainly didn't want her quitting her investigation anytime soon. Not when just being in her presence restored his energy and his interest in life.

• • •

Berry drove herself to the office building that housed Farley Brothers, Inc. and parked in a nearby parking garage. By keeping her mind blank, she maintained her poise until she reached the eighth floor of the building and approached the glass door marking the entrance to the Farley Brothers suite.

Her control was only shaken once, when a businessman on the elevator stared admiringly at her and asked how much she charged.

"More than you've got," she asserted, lifting her chin.

Her heart pounded so loudly, he was sure to hear it. Clutching her small leather purse in both hands, Berry ignored his comeback and hurried toward the door. She resolutely pushed it open and walked inside, head up and chest leading.

"May I help you?" a woman asked. She didn't sound interested in helping, but Berry had expected that reaction from any female employee.

Repressing a gasp, Berry tried to look nonchalant. "I'm— Ber—Mary MacGregor. I have an interview with Mr. Felix Farley at nine."

She had almost ruined everything by giving her real name. If she didn't get her control back, she'd blow her own cover. She took several deep breaths while the woman tapped some keys and studied her computer screen.

The receptionist looked like an executive. To Berry's surprise, the woman's cool, brown eyes were filled with something resembling bleak dislike when they rested upon her. She squelched a strong desire to text Tyler for encouragement.

"Mr. Farley will see you now, Miss MacGregor," the woman said, curling her lip. "Please come this way."

Berry, hyperventilating, followed the darkly beautiful woman down the corridor to an office at the very end. The woman held open the door, announced, "Miss MacGregor," in ultra-refined accents then closed the door behind Berry.

She had no time to wonder what lay behind the receptionist's hostility. Berry gulped and stood blinking for a moment in the center of the dark, oak-paneled office. She forced herself to walk toward the man at the huge, mahogany desk that dominated the room, an office her research called a "power office."

"Good morning, Mr. Farley." She tried for borderline flirtatiousness. "*Thank* you so *much* for taking the time out of your *busy* schedule to see me. And for your wonderful *kindness* Saturday night in welcoming a new arrival to Houston."

Felix Farley contemplated her in silence. Berry's heart pounded with a strange mixture of horror at her own ditzy speech and fright at facing Felix Farley alone. Now was a really poor time to discover she hated her own speech.

As her eyes adjusted to the gloom, she realized Felix's gaze assessed her with lewd frankness. She felt a twinge of a new kind of nervousness when his bold stare rested on her chest. What had given her the idea that she could go through with this?

"I'm sure you'll suit me just fine, Miss MacGregor," he said. "Just fine. You seem ... very competent. Your resume is quite impressive."

His drawl gave his words a second meaning, and Berry shivered inside when he gestured toward the straight chair beside his desk. She swayed toward it, feeling like a beauty contestant on parade, and sank onto it with relief—until she noticed that his gaze focused hopefully on her upper legs.

Felix's gaze rose reluctantly when Berry kept her knees pressed modestly together. She managed somehow to keep from tugging her short pink skirt down.

"Well, Miss MacGregor," he said. "With the high recommendations of your previous employers, I have no questions at all about your ability."

Berry smiled prettily while she forcefully kept herself from collapsing with relief. "*Thank* you, sir. That means *everything* coming from you."

For a moment, Berry thought he was going to lean forward and place his hand on her knee. Instead, Felix leaned back when the door opened upon a knock and the receptionist entered.

Berry suppressed her smile of gratitude and studied the woman, noting her air of competence, from her dark pageboy to her dress-for-success tan suit to her plain brown pumps. Although the woman was strikingly beautiful, Felix Farley accorded her a frowning glance of total disinterest.

"I'm terribly sorry for interrupting, Mr. Farley," the woman said, "but Mr. Corrigan insists on seeing you about the inventory figures for the Westheimer number two store. He's on his way over."

Her voice was so full of meaning, Berry paid attention in spite of the many impressions crowding her mind.

Felix scowled. "Tell him he'll have to come back tomorrow. I'm late as it is. Will you have Miss MacGregor fill out the necessary papers? I'm sure she's going to suit me perfectly."

Felix turned away as he spoke, and Berry noted an incredible expression on the receptionist's lovely face, one composed of cynicism and—of all things—unrequited love.

Berry suppressed a gasp. She must have stumbled into a veritable hotbed of human passions, and all within her first five minutes on the job. Motives for murder suddenly beckoned from everywhere.

Berry's morning was a hectic jumble of new faces, papers to be filled out with her carefully planned and memorized falsehoods, and strange instructions her most thorough research hadn't prepared her to follow. Although she tried to stay alert for overtones and nuances, it was all she could do to keep the players straight as she sat behind the big desk just outside Felix Farley's office and tried to look as if she knew what she was doing.

A chunk of blue-quartz granite, cut and polished to show off the quartz inclusions, held a place of honor on her desk. It was literally the only thing about Farley Brothers that she felt she understood.

She herself had given it to Daniel after a geology field trip to the Llano uplift near Llano, Texas. Somehow it had missed being included in the box of Daniel's belongings that Farley Brothers had sent her after Daniel's death. Berry considered finding it on her desk an omen of her ultimate success.

She sent Tyler a surreptitious text message as soon as she was able and told him she had gotten the job.

A moment later, the telephone on her desk buzzed discreetly, and Berry searched for the instrument. It didn't even look like a telephone. "Mr. *Farley's* office. Miss MacGregor speaking."

"Ah, Miss MacGregor. I see you're already manning a desk."

Berry quivered with irrational joy at hearing Tyler's deep voice. "I *am*, thank you," she said. "Remind me to tell you *all* about it." After the morning she'd put in—all thirty minutes of it—she wanted nothing more than to get away from Farley Brothers for a while.

"I'll pick you up at noon," he said. "Be waiting at the curb in front of the building."

Tyler hung up, and Berry went back to her current task of searching the computer's address book program. No wonder people talked about stress in the workplace. She hadn't been here an hour, and already her blood pressure had likely skyrocketed.

The morning grew more surreal by the minute. The job of locating Bernard Warren's telephone number soon proved impossible and she had to ask the beautiful woman, whose name was Concetta Tomayo, how to find it.

"Try looking under Westheimer number two," Concetta said, with crisp contempt. "Mr. Warren is the manager." *Which any idiot ought to know*, her tone said.

"Oh, *thank you*." Berry simpered and went back to the computer.

Sure enough, she found the correct phone number under the "Westheimer #2" heading, but before she could call the number, another interruption occurred.

"I demand to see Felix Farley," a short, redheaded man snapped as he skidded to a halt before her desk. "If I have to wait all day, I will."

"Mr. Farley left the office a little earlier, sir," Berry said apologetically. "But I was instructed to call Mr. Bernard Warren—"

"Warren!" the little man said, breathing fire. "It looks to me as if Bernard Warren is most of the problem. If Mr. Farley doesn't care to talk to me, then I'll have to take my concerns to—"

"Mr. Corrigan," Concetta Tomayo said, approaching from Berry's other side. "Mr. Warren is on his way here. Isn't he, Miss

MacGregor? Mr. Farley said Mr. Warren would be happy to answer all your questions on his behalf."

"Bernard Warren is, at most, an unreliable source of information," Mr. Corrigan said in precise tones. "Furthermore, I'm beginning to believe Mr. Farley is just as unreliable." He glared at Concetta. "As are you, Miss Tomayo."

Berry succeeded in entering Bernard Warren's phone number, but when he finally answered, she literally could not hear him, nor could he hear her when she requested his instant presence in Mr. Felix Farley's office.

Over her head, Mr. Corrigan shouted accusations and Concetta Tomayo countered them with accusations of her own. Berry ignored Bernard Warren's repeated demands for her to speak up in favor of memorizing the insults that flew back and forth. She didn't understand much, but she hoped Tyler would be able to decipher the mess.

In the meanwhile, the only thing she understood was that she had stumbled into a hornet's nest of some kind of skullduggery. She just wished she knew what it all meant.

"Nepotism!" Corrigan shouted. "Nepotism of the most suggestive kind!"

"I'll have you know that I was hired because of my training and ability," Concetta yelled back. "How dare you say otherwise!"

"Never mind," Bernard Warren said, into Berry's left ear. "I think I see the problem. I'll be there shortly."

Berry started. She had forgotten about Bernard Warren on the other end of the phone line. "*Thank you*, Mr. Warren," she said, with heartfelt gratitude. "That would be most appreciated."

And how, she reiterated inwardly. She pretended she was totally deaf and got on with typing a batch of letters Felix had given her. At the same time, she thought on ways she could listen in on the conversation between Bernard Warren and Mr. Corrigan. Perhaps she could suggest she take notes on the proceedings.

But Bernard Warren never showed up, and Concetta Tomayo soon stormed back into her own office and slammed the door.

Mr. Corrigan planted himself on a chair beside Berry's desk. "You seem to be the only person in this office not connected with this farce," he observed. "Do you think you can locate Mr. Felix Farley? Tell him that he can talk to me now, or he can talk to me later, but if he talks to me later, I can guarantee he will not like what I have to say."

"Certainly, Mr. Corrigan," Berry said respectfully. "I'll do my best."

"That's all I ask," Mr. Corrigan said, and leaned back in the manner of one willing to wait an eon or two. "He's been dodging me for two days now. If he doesn't meet with me today, I'll have no choice but to turn in a report he won't like at all."

Berry quivered with eagerness. She pulled up the company contact list once more and plowed through it with determination.

"We can't have that," she said brightly. "Don't worry, Mr. Corrigan. I'm sure I can make him understand the *importance* of your visit." She hoped.

Well, Daniel, she said inwardly and touched the rock gently, *I hope you weren't planning on making Farley Brothers your life's work. I don't know what's going on here yet, but I'll bet it's both illegal and underhanded.*

By the time she blanked her computer screen and left the tiny anteroom that protected Felix's office to go to lunch, Berry had confirmed her opinion of Farley Brothers as a bastion of illegitimate activity. She just hoped she could remember the morning's events accurately enough to relate them to Tyler in an orderly fashion.

He awaited her at the curb in front of the building as he had promised. Berry slid swiftly in beside him, conscious of an overwhelming urge to fling her arms around him and kiss him.

"So how'd it go?" He glanced at the diamond in her cleavage, then her legs. "Have you hidden a sheaf of confidential documents in your undies already?"

"I've never seen so much sticky human passion in my life," she said, heaving an exaggerated sigh. "Believe me, Tyler, there's enough going on in that place to motivate a dozen murders. You won't believe what I'm about to lay on you."

Tyler smiled at her enthusiasm. "I can't wait to hear it. But first, I've just checked out Farley Brothers' most recent financial statements. I've got a friend who holds stock in the company. He emailed them to me this morning."

"Wow. The people accountants know." She shook her head. "It just goes to show. Not even a police detective could help me as much as you have, and in just three days. We're a team, Tyler, and together we're going to find out who killed Daniel."

"No doubt I've now gone completely whacko, because I really, really want to believe you, Challoner." He frowned at the busy street ahead. "However, the company appears to be doing better than ever. Just thought I'd mention it."

"Tell me about it," Berry said, with considerable feeling. "I spent the morning typing gloating letters. Felix is getting back at every single person who ever told him he'd never amount to anything."

"That must have been half of Houston. Felix appears to have been the brother most likely to wind up in jail. He partied through college and was involved in a fraternity hazing incident where someone died. What's more, rumor has it he got married on Walter's orders, so he could present a good image to the stockholders."

Tyler turned into the parking lot of the first café they passed. Berry regarded the picture windows with approval. The sooner they got settled in a nice, private booth, the sooner she could spill her information.

"I believe it, because he seems to be a vindictive sort who never forgets a grudge, and boy, has he got a list of grudges." She buried her face in her hands a moment. "I'll be busy on them the rest of the afternoon."

"Do you think he'll develop a grudge against me for taking his sexy new secretary right out from under him?" Tyler parked his Porsche in a slot as near the entrance as he could find.

Berry laughed. "Only if he finds out. But there's a gorgeous woman already working there, and she's in love with him. Oh, the atmosphere in that office!"

"In love with him? Are you sure? The guy has the morals of a tomcat."

"Bonkers over him." Berry nodded enthusiastically. "Unrequited love is practically choking out all the air in the place. Her name is Concetta Tomayo, and she's Walter Farley's assistant. She's acting as receptionist right now because: one, she has nothing better to do while Walter is on vacation, and two, the receptionist just up and quit last Friday, and three, someone has to ride herd on a wild and out-of-control accountant."

"You've lost me," Tyler complained. "Let's get out of this heat before you say another word."

He hustled her inside the cold café, where they chose an empty booth that looked as private as the little eatery could offer.

Berry settled into the booth and gulped ice water. "I'll be lucky if I don't need medicine for high blood pressure after a few more days like today."

"All right, what wild and out-of-control accountant is on the rampage at Farley Brothers?"

Berry leaned forward and lowered her voice. "His name is Nathaniel Corrigan. He's a short, redheaded guy, and he's putting down roots beside my desk even as we speak. He won't even leave to grab a sandwich or a cup of coffee." She glanced around. "In fact, I think I'll take him a sandwich and a cup of coffee and lay some heavy sympathy on him."

He regarded her askance. "I'll bet he loves violet-eyed women."

"Please, Tyler. You'll put me off my food. After this morning, I deserve a really good lunch." She studied the menu appreciatively. "I'll have the BLT with all the trimmings, and another wrapped up to go with a large cup of coffee."

"You can never go wrong with a good bribe." He placed their orders and turned back to her. "Why is this out-of-control accountant putting down roots beside your desk? Is he aiming to make Felix jealous?"

Berry shook her head and gave him a portentous wink. "Farley Brothers is undergoing an outside audit, and Mr. Corrigan is the accountant sent to do the dirty work."

Tyler gave her a look of stark astonishment. "What? An outside audit? Are you sure?"

Pleased with this response, Berry proceeded to enhance the effect. "It seems Mr. Corrigan has a few questions about something he calls 'internal controls.' According to him, the Westheimer number two store's manager, Bernard Warren, is responsible for both inventory and general ledger entries."

"I can't believe this." Tyler drew in a deep breath and stared at her in disbelief. "Well, Miss Mary MacGregor, much as I hate to admit it, you may have stumbled onto something."

Berry experienced a surge of gratified triumph. "I knew that company was hiding something. But I haven't got the faintest idea what he's talking about." She regarded Tyler hopefully. "What *was* he talking about?"

Tyler leaned back. "Tell me everything you learned. A lack of internal controls simply means that the opportunity exists for some creative bookkeeping to take place."

Berry mulled that over and grew more cheerful by the minute. "First, Concetta Tomayo came rushing in and told Felix that Mr. Corrigan was on his way over. The way she said it was so full of meaning, I knew something was up."

"I'll just bet." Tyler stared at her in fascination. "Go on."

"Felix was on his way to the golf course. When he heard that, he got into an even bigger hurry and said Bernard Warren should handle it. So I was designated to call in Mr. Warren while Felix made a wild dash for the door."

Tyler asked slowly, "That was a problem?"

"I'll say it was. I went through the address book program about five times before I finally gave up and asked Concetta who he was." She sipped more ice water gratefully. "I was trying to give an impression of total competence, but can you imagine how dumb I felt when I couldn't even locate a lousy phone number?"

"Concetta rubbed it in?"

"Without saying a word," Berry confirmed. "It turns out that Bernard Warren is the manager of the Westheimer number two store, which is under Felix's jurisdiction *and* is the most profitable store in the chain. It was one of those little facts that's so well known, no one bothers to enter it into their contacts list. Anyway, Mr. Corrigan arrived while I was punching in Bernard Warren's number, and he was breathing fire."

"I'd never have dreamed a boring auto parts business like Farley Brothers could harbor this much drama. Get on with it, Challoner. What did he say?"

"He demanded to speak to Felix at once and declared that he'd sit right there for the next two days if he had to. Concetta couldn't do a thing with him. In fact, the very sight of her seemed to set him off." She paused for dramatic effect. "Guess what, Tyler. Bernard Warren is Concetta's half-brother."

Tyler's eyes widened in a way that gratified Berry enormously. "Nepotism?"

"And how!" Berry felt her cup of happiness was now full. "Mr. Corrigan spent ten minutes shouting about how that kind of nepotism within a company 'invites—yes, *invites!*—ambiguities.' Which is the most accountantly thing I've ever heard, even if I don't know what it means."

Tyler dropped his forehead into his hand. "This is unbelievable. And you didn't even have to hack into the company books to find all this out. What happened next?"

"Well, Mr. Corrigan then huffed out that as an accountant, it is his duty to insure that the internal controls of the company are sufficient to guarantee accurate data, but in this case, he fears he cannot do that."

"Oh, God. Berry, you've hit the jackpot. What happened next?"

"Then he shouted that all the internal controls devolve upon Bernard Warren, and Bernard Warren is Felix's sandbox buddy."

"What?" Tyler looked as if he might choke.

"Felix and Bernard grew up together, went to school together from first grade on, dated girls together ... In short, they're such close friends, there's no doubt in Mr. Corrigan's mind that the two of them have cooked up a scheme to defraud the company."

"*He said that?*"

"Yes, he did, but that was because Concetta insisted on conducting a shouting match with him over my head while I called Felix's cell phone. When he didn't answer, I tried to find the phone number of his golf course. And do you know, I found it? It was in the contacts list under 'G' for 'golf course.'"

Tyler sat as if frozen in place and stared at her in stunned silence.

"Can you believe that? They didn't bother listing Bernard Warren, but they had five golf courses listed. I called two before I got the right one. Not that it did any good. If Felix wasn't answering his cell, why would he answer a page at the golf course?"

"Berry ... " His mouth opened then closed.

Their waiter arrived with sandwiches and iced tea. Berry kindly allowed Tyler some recovery time before she sprang more of her morning's discoveries on him. After the waiter departed, she squeezed lemon into her iced tea and added a spoon of sugar and refreshed herself with a sip.

"Anyway, Felix will be given the message as soon as someone can locate him on the golf course," she said. "How much do you want to bet that Felix doesn't show back up today? Or tomorrow?"

"From the sound of things, Felix is the sort who thinks bad news undelivered is somehow not bad news," he said at last. "I have to hand it to you, Challoner. It looks as though you were right. Something nefarious is going on at Farley Brothers. The big question now is: was it the cause of Daniel's murder?"

"I'll bet it was," Berry declared. "We know there was a reason Daniel was killed, and if he somehow discovered what Felix was up to, well ... Who knows what a man like Felix will do? What if he's a sociopath or something?"

"Accounting fraud doesn't mean Felix is a sociopath. It just means he's greedy." Tyler studied the tabletop, frowning, obviously deep in thought.

"What kind of fraud do you think could be going on?" Berry asked. "Oh, and Mr. Corrigan also said Bernard Warren was responsible for the inventory figures and for the general ledger entries. What does that mean?"

He looked up, gaze sharpening. "I can't know without having some figures. The possibilities are, quite literally, endless."

Berry thrust out her chin. "Then I'll get some figures. After all, Mr. Corrigan is going to be with me for a while—until Felix decides he can't dodge the man forever. So give me some questions to ask him. I'll bet I can narrow things down by early this afternoon."

Tyler nodded slowly. "I'll write a few questions down for you. In the meantime, you said Felix is getting his old grudges off his chest. What else did you find out in regard to that?"

"Apparently Walter is considered the brains of the organization, although the rumor is that he may be losing it." She laid down her sandwich and thought through the progression of her morning.

"He took off suddenly for New York last week, which thrilled Felix down to his toenails."

"It's another chance for Felix to prove his managerial worth, I'll bet."

"You're probably right. Felix is claiming Walter is senile, and that he, Felix, is now the driving intelligence behind the company's current profitability. Take that, all you old fossils who thought Felix would never amount to anything."

"How long have you been employed there? Three whole hours?"

"Three really, really *long* hours." Berry grinned back at him. "Obviously, you've been used to working alone in that passionless two-man office of yours, whereas corporate offices are veritable seething caldrons of mystery and emotions."

"I'll suggest to Dad that we hire a secretary." He reached over and covered her hand with his. "You can come stir Dad and I up when your investigation at Farley Brothers is complete." He added, "If it isn't already."

Berry smiled back at him. "You know, Tyler, I expected to think a lot of sad stuff about Daniel and his last days there. But within ten minutes of sitting down at my desk, I was too busy trying to keep from laughing out loud to grieve. Felix doesn't seem to think a secretary exists when he starts talking about all his dirty little secrets." She added gleefully, "I'll bet Daniel never knew any of this stuff, even after two years there."

"I have to admit, I'm impressed. In barely three hours on the job, you've done better than a professional detective," Tyler agreed. "I wonder if Felix is always this forthcoming in his letters."

"Let's hope so," Berry said devoutly. "I've never had such a good time typing letters in all my life."

"So Corrigan says internal controls are nonexistent," he said thoughtfully. "Did he apply that to the entire company, or just to one particular store?"

"He kept talking about the Westheimer number two store, which Bernard Warren manages. What does a lack of internal controls mean?"

"It usually means that the same person is responsible for several accounting operations. In this case, it sounds as if Bernard Warren is responsible both for the inventory figures and for recording payments in the general ledger. That means he could take items out of stock for his own use. Or he can charge personal expenses to the company accounts. It could mean a lot of things, and the fact that Corrigan brought it up probably means he's found some highly suggestive discrepancies in the store's accounts."

Berry practically quivered with excitement. "I get the picture. Accountants prefer a system with a different person responsible for each operation, right? So they can tattle on each other?"

Tyler gave a crack of laughter. "That's right. Otherwise, the opportunity exists for unlimited embezzlement."

"So, Mr. Warren could be driving a car built entirely out of parts the company paid for," Berry realized, thinking it over. She laughed suddenly. "Lord, Tyler, no wonder so many companies are going broke. These days, a company has to choose between paying lots of people to obtain proper internal controls, or paying a few people and letting them steal a little."

"Please, Challoner." He put his forehead on his hand again, obviously stifling laughter. "I'm going to have to remember that one for the next meeting of the CPA society. Did Corrigan give any indication that he thought someone was embezzling?"

Berry leaned toward him enthusiastically. "According to Mr. Corrigan, the inventory figures appear to be largely fictitious. He wants to know why, and he demands that Mr. Warren allow him to complete an inventory to prove it. Mr. Warren says he can go straight to hell and take his lying insinuations with him."

Tyler whistled. "Thousands of dollars may have been embezzled."

Berry regarded him with admiration. Now, more than ever, she realized how right she had been to ask for Tyler's help.

"How would Mr. Corrigan know the inventory figures are fictitious?" she asked.

"I'd guess he counted a few items on his own. That's standard procedure, just to verify that the inventory figures are likely to be accurate. But if he found some big discrepancies in a few items, he has good reason to assume the rest of the figures are phony."

Berry had never known accounting could be so fascinating. "That's amazing. When I find discrepancies in my bank balance, I just subtract until I get whatever the bank says is in my account."

"An outside auditor's job is to verify the company's figures," Tyler said. "If he can't, he tries to find out why he can't."

Berry cocked her head and thought on that. "And if he still can't, someone at the company is in trouble?"

"Big trouble. And not just with his or her employer. There's usually the little matter of unpaid taxes on the gains, not to mention the criminal aspect."

Berry drew in a deep breath and let it out slowly. "Well, Tyler, it looks like I signed on at Farley Brothers just in time for the kill."

CHAPTER 7

Tyler returned to his office reluctantly. Now that he had decided to cast aside a lifetime of conservative, boring behavior, he was ready to get on with it. He hadn't told Berry about the idea that had taken possession of his thoughts while they discussed her morning at Farley Brothers in case he changed his mind. The more he considered the idea, however, the more determined he became to carry it out. But common decency bade him inform his father of his upcoming absence.

He bypassed his own office and went straight to his father's. "Hi, Dad. I'm taking off for a few days. There's something I've got to take care of."

Tyler had never seen anything quite like the expression that passed across his father's face as he slowly lifted his gaze from the papers on his desk.

"You're *what*?" Mason said, in disbelief.

"I'm taking a few days off." Tyler regarded his father, frowning. "Is there something wrong with that?"

Mason's mouth opened slowly then closed. He stared at Tyler in a way that indicated total astonishment and something else Tyler couldn't put a name to.

"I haven't taken a vacation in the past few years," Tyler continued ruthlessly, "and in view of that fact, I think I'm entitled to a few days when I need them, no questions asked."

Mason sat unmoving, like a statue.

"I knew you'd agree." Tyler smiled and stepped back out the door with a farewell wave. "See you in a week or so, Dad."

He concentrated so hard on the plan that he'd hatched during his lunch with Berry, he didn't even waste time feeling guilty about the half-finished quarterly reports on his desk. The quarterly reports could wait. Fraud at Farley Brothers couldn't, not with Berry uncovering scandal right and left.

He drove directly to the nearest Wal-Mart. When he left the store, he wore a pair of dark slacks, a short-sleeved white shirt, a clip-on tie, and a pair of horn-rimmed glasses with plain glass lenses. Standing before the fitting room mirror, he slicked his hair straight back. He thought it went well with the glasses.

Then he drove down Westheimer until he reached the Farley Brothers Auto Parts store known in financial statements as the Westheimer number two store. After driving past it twice, he parked his Porsche about a block away, well out of sight of the store employees, and walked back.

He paused and peered in. Clerks who looked like mechanics manned the long front counter. In spite of his efforts, Tyler couldn't kid himself that he looked like one of them. He looked more like a computer nerd.

Tyler studied his own image in the plate glass window with sudden doubt. But what did he have to lose? he asked himself. He could always watch the men at the counter and reappear tomorrow in a different guise. He shoved open the door and joined the crowd at the long counter.

He took up a position to one side and watched a transaction closely. The clerk handled an intricate-looking piece of metal with hands that showed calluses and deeply ingrained grease stains. Tyler shoved his hands into his pockets. Perhaps he should have opened the hood of his car and checked the oil before coming in.

"Help you, sir?" a clerk asked.

Tyler started. "I'd like to see Mr. Warren. I'm here to apply for a job."

"We aren't hiring." The clerk eyed Tyler curiously.

This wasn't in the script Tyler had planned, but he improvised successfully. "I know, but Felix Farley thought Mr. Warren could find a place for me. I'm actually a bookkeeper, but I'm also a car buff and Mr. Farley thought I'd be helpful in the warehouse until a bookkeeping position opens up."

The clerk shrugged. "Bernard's office is over there. Go on in if you're sure he's expecting you."

"Thanks." His guess had been on target. Felix regularly sent people who approached him for jobs to Bernard Warren.

Tyler came behind the counter and raised his hand to knock. Then he heard shouting through the thin plywood door and paused with his fist in mid-air.

"We *can't* move it out tonight," a man shouted in exasperation. "For one thing, I've got a business to run. For another, I don't have that kind of manpower. Besides, he can't prove anything."

From the moment of silence that followed, Tyler gathered Bernard Warren must be on the telephone.

"Look," Warren continued. Tyler had to strain to hear. "It can't be done. How the hell could you have let this have happen? We've never had trouble out of the accountants before. What tipped him off?"

Tyler couldn't believe it. He hadn't even gotten the job yet, and already he was getting an earful. What the devil was going on behind the scenes at Farley Brothers?

"He must be on the phone," the helpful clerk said from behind him. "Here. You'll have to knock louder."

Tyler reluctantly stepped aside. He'd hoped to hear a bit more before making Bernard Warren aware of his presence.

"This man says Mr. Farley sent him over." The clerk poked his head fearlessly into Warren's office. "He's supposed to help in the warehouse until a bookkeeping position opens up."

Bernard Warren scowled at Tyler and slammed down the receiver. "Who did you say you were?"

Warren was a burly man about Felix's age, but he lacked the sophisticated polish Felix Farley displayed. He looked like a mechanic who had made good, and his clothes were a more expensive version of Tyler's current outfit.

"I'm Schy—Tyler Reid," Tyler said. He had no reason to give a phony name, he decided abruptly. "Mr. Farley sent me over to help out in the warehouse."

Warren put on a friendly smile after running a beefy hand over his face. "Sure thing, Reid. We're short of counter help today. Do you think you can act as sort of a gopher for the other guys until you learn our system?"

Just like that. "I'll be glad to help out in any capacity," he said gruffly.

He obligingly filled out a simple application without bothering to resort to lies. His only falsehood was a failure to list his education beyond his high school diploma.

Tyler spent the afternoon feeling lost and idiotic, running back and forth from the counter to the long aisles of automobile parts in search of computer-numbered parts. It wasn't nearly as easy as he'd thought, considering he was used to working with his brain rather than his legs and arms.

The store stayed open until nine that evening, and Tyler soon realized he was expected to stay until that time. He took a brief break and called his apartment.

"It's Tyler," he said hurriedly. "I'll be home at nine-thirty."

"Nine-thirty!" Berry exclaimed. "You worked all day yesterday. When do you get some time off?"

"I'll explain when I get there," he said, and clicked off his phone before someone saw or heard him.

Berry's attitude was a complication he hadn't expected. He'd be lucky if she didn't tackle his father about making him work long hours. Grinning, Tyler raced down one of the long aisles after a set of points for a 1970 Chevrolet Impala. He'd never had a woman jealous of his time off before. It was rather endearing.

• • •

Berry clicked off her phone, fuming, and glared at the chocolate pie she had just removed from the oven. Tyler wouldn't get home in time to appreciate the rich chocolate odor filling the air.

But the pie would be chilled and ready to eat by then, she thought, cheering slightly. No wonder housewives got angry when their husbands worked late.

Tyler's landline phone rang. She answered in Mary MacGregor's husky, purring tones.

"Who is this?" a man demanded.

Berry instantly recognized Mason Reid's voice. "Why, *hello* there, Mr. Reid. This is Mary MacGregor. How *lovely* to *hear* from you this evening. What can I do for you?"

"I want to speak to my son, if you please."

The formal, cool tone told Berry everything she wanted to know. "Why, he isn't *available* just now. May I have him call you the *moment* he gets in?"

"Do that, please. I'm at the office," Mason said drily.

Berry hung up the receiver and glanced at the time on her own cell phone with mild surprise. Tyler obviously wasn't working late at his own office.

Maybe he had a date.

She put her hands on her hips and considered the thought. She had no business feeling so jealous if he did. Her best bet was to pretend total disinterest in the state of Tyler's love life, considering the way she'd crashed in on him.

By the time Tyler was due home, Berry had a full meal prepared. He was not going to regret letting her stay in his apartment. He was saving her a lot of money, and providing her with a feeling of security besides. She owed him a few good meals, and no questions asked about where he'd been.

Someone knocked at the door. Startled, she swung toward it.

The pounding resumed, louder and more annoyed this time. Berry raced for her bedroom, where she swiftly inserted the purple contact lenses and shucked off her sensible jeans and T-shirt. The best she could do on such short notice was to fling on a fluffy, pink chenille robe and stuff her feet into a pair of pink high-heeled sandals and freshen her lipstick.

"Coming," she sang out.

She rushed down the hall to another round of pounding. But before she could reach the door, she tripped over an obstacle strung across her path. She fell heavily, sprawling full-length on the hall carpet.

Breathless, she lay still a moment. The knocking stopped and didn't resume.

Berry concentrated on getting her breath back until she heard a new sound. Gasping, she pushed herself up and stared toward the door, which was now swinging open of its own accord.

It was Tyler, and he looked both annoyed and curious.

"Who the hell was that at the door?" he demanded. "He ran off when he saw me coming."

Berry fought to catch her breath and speak. Something looked strange about Tyler, but she couldn't immediately put her finger on what.

"What did you do to your hair?" she wheezed.

"What are you doing on the floor?" He crossed the living room to her side and helped her sit up. "Are you all right? Say, you have one gray eye and one purple eye. Did you lose a contact? What the heck is going on?"

"Oh, no!" Berry wailed. "We've got to find it, Tyler. This is the only pair I've got."

"Oh, Lord." He switched on the overhead light to join her in combing every inch of the carpet. "Do you know who that was at the door when I came up?"

"I have no idea," Berry said irritably. "I was on my way to answer it when I tripped over something and fell. Maybe it's a hit man hired by your family to bump me off."

"Unfunny, Challoner." He sat back on his heels. "Were you going to answer the door in that outfit?"

"As a matter of fact, I was," Berry said defiantly. "I was in jeans, and that just won't get it. And by the way, your father wants you to call him. He said to tell you he was at the office."

"Did you tell him I was working late?" Tyler asked, grinning.

Berry looked up from her search. "No wonder your dad sounded so strange."

"If you answered the phone, I'll bet he did sound strange. For some reason, knowing I've got a woman in my apartment seems to be doing my family a lot of good. This afternoon, I told him I was taking a few days off, and he probably thinks you and I are about to take off for Tahiti." On his hands and knees, he scoured the thick green carpet closely. "What did you trip over? Or is that a fair question, considering the height of the heels on those shoes?"

"I have no idea." Berry sat back and studied the path she had taken from her bedroom to the door. "Nothing's there." She shrugged. "If something had been there, I'd have seen it earlier."

"It's those shoes."

"It wasn't the shoes," she said irritably and stuck out her right leg for him to view. "It hit me right above the ankle, whatever it was. See the mark?"

He examined the fading red mark above her ankle. "Are you sure this didn't happen in the fall?"

"I keep on telling you. Whatever gave me that mark is what tripped me and caused me to fall." Exasperated, she rose to her knees again. "Let's find my contact, or I'm in serious trouble."

Tyler resumed his search, grinning in a way that made her long to plant one of her stiletto heels in his ribs. "You can always wear dark glasses and claim a black eye."

Someone knocked at the door again, and Berry said, "He's back."

"Challoner, you look really weird with one purple eye and one gray eye." Tyler looked her over critically. "Better hide in your bedroom while I get rid of him. Careful. There's a contact on this carpet somewhere."

Berry gave him a regal glare, gathered her robe, and swept into her bedroom. For two cents, or maybe even less, she'd stretch a rope across the hall and trip Tyler up as he hurried to the door, or the phone, or—

Puzzled, she looked down at the ankle that had contacted the invisible obstacle. Now that she thought about it, it had felt remarkably like a rope that had been strung across her path. The fine hairs on her arms tickled as they lifted gently from her skin.

Somehow she managed to keep from running to open the bedroom door and look again at the area where she had been tripped. Things were getting too, too weird.

But one thing she did know. Tyler would call her totally whacko if she mentioned a ghostly rope across her path, so she added the incident to the growing list of weird events she'd experienced ever since Daniel had died.

The sooner she found out who killed Daniel, the better for everyone.

• • •

Tyler rose carefully to his feet, scanning the carpet as he did so, and went to the door with equal care. On the way, he noted once more the picturesque chunk of rock sitting on his coffee table. He had to hand it to Berry. Rather than flowers or interesting cushions, she decorated with rocks.

He checked the peephole then ripped off his tie and tossed it aside before opening the door.

"Hello, Dad," he said calmly. "What are you doing here at this hour?"

Mason made no move to come in. He stood on the landing and eyed Tyler with a grim expression Tyler hadn't seen since he was ten and had been caught red-handed in some boyish deviltry. "Have you lost your mind?" Mason demanded.

"Probably." Tyler assumed a wonderfully nonchalant pose. "You might as well come in. Mary—"

"No, thank you." Mason sniffed the air. "So. She's even got you cooking for her. I thought you had too much sense to let a woman wrap you around her little finger, but it's obvious I was badly mistaken."

"Come on, Dad," Tyler said. "You've cooked many a meal for Mom, and you know it."

"That's different." Mason raised his brows, but Tyler could see that beneath his pose of indifference, Mason was badly shaken. "Your mother and I are married."

Tyler gave a lazy shrug and used his fingers to fork his hair back into its usual style. "Why don't you come in and sample my chicken?" He hoped the delicious odor he smelled was chicken. "You can tell Mom what a great cook I've turned out to be."

Mason took another step back. "If we're lucky, your mother won't find out about this little aberration of yours."

"In the meantime, you might try having a little faith in whatever good sense you taught me."

"What good sense?" Mason demanded. "It's obvious enough you're not going to listen to a thing I say, so I'll be going. All I ask is that you not worry your mother with this—this woman you've picked up."

"Are you saying you don't want me introducing B—Mary to the family as my significant other?" Tyler suddenly wanted to drag Berry home to meet his mother under her own identity. As Daniel's sister, she would automatically be welcomed.

"Be reasonable, Tyler," Mason said gently. "Your mother is a broad-minded woman, but no woman is that broad-minded."

He went hastily down the stairs, leaving Tyler standing in the doorway.

Tyler shut the door and leaned against it. Was it only three days ago he'd been so bored, he welcomed any distraction? His life had suddenly become full of complications.

The major complication poked her curly dark head out of her bedroom. "Is the coast clear?"

"Temporarily." He straightened. "You'd better check on whatever it is you're cooking that smells so good while I have a look around for that contact lens of yours."

"My chicken!"

Berry burst out of her room, now wearing her own jeans and a pink knit blouse, with a pair of house slippers. Before rushing to the kitchen, she looked carefully up and down the short hall as if in search of obstacles. A moment later, he heard the sounds of the oven door closing and the rattle of a utensil against a china serving platter.

"Thanks, Tyler. Our dinner is saved." She appeared beside him, stepping carefully and scanning the carpet. "What did your dad want? Other than to get rid of me, I mean."

"He wants to know why I've suddenly lost my mind. It seems to him my insanity is connected to the fact that a beautiful woman has taken up residence in my apartment." He bent to inspect a bit of color on the green carpet. "Here's your contact. That must have been some fall you took."

He held out the purple lens on the tip of his index finger. Berry received it tenderly and hurried to bestow it in a small, plastic case after dousing it with lens fluid.

"Thanks, Tyler." She joined him in the small kitchen, where the table had been set invitingly for two. "What are you doing with that tie? It isn't your usual sort, is it?"

Tyler had long known women had unerring vision when it came to men's clothing. "It's a cheap clip-on. I thought it was appropriate to my new station in life."

"Your what?"

"Didn't I tell you? I'm now a counter clerk at Farley Brothers number two on Westheimer. If you can pry a few figures out of Corrigan, I'll be able to check them against the actual warehouse stock—"

"Oh, Tyler, you didn't!" Berry shrieked. She forgot about the dinner and flung herself on him, wrapping her arms around his neck. "Oh, thank you, thank you! We're this close to finding out who killed Daniel. *This close.*" She separated her thumb and her forefinger by about two inches and held them in front of his face and pressed her lips against his. "You're wonderful. No one but you could have done it."

Tyler's arms went around her body automatically. He pulled her against him and all exhaustion evaporated. Fresh energy suffused his body, energy tempered with fire that threatened to burn out of control.

"You inspired me," he said roughly and kissed her.

To his surprise, Berry kissed him back with such enthusiasm, he promptly forgot all his good resolutions about not making love to Daniel's little sister. He held her against him so that she felt the extent of his desire for her, but she didn't pull away.

Nor did she object when he pulled her shirt from her jeans so he could glide his hands over that smooth golden skin he had been dying to touch ever since he had first seen her. He couldn't get enough of touching her, of absorbing her passion into himself.

It couldn't be happening this fast, he thought dimly. But he could only count his blessings as he stroked his hands up and down her slim back, savoring her heat and her lithe softness.

He'd never felt this degree of desire for any of his expensive blondes. Now that he thought about it, he'd never felt anything like it for Alicia Cameron, his former fiancée, either.

Berry's long nails were in his hair, raking lightly against his scalp. He'd never realized the scalp was an erogenous zone before. Furthermore, she held him as if she'd never let him go, and that was the ultimate aphrodisiac as far as Tyler was concerned.

He lifted her in his arms and carried her to his bedroom.

...

Berry rode on waves of heat that carried her along like an ocean wave carried a canoe. Moments later, she felt cool air against her heated skin as Tyler set her feet on the floor and lifted her shirt off over her head so he could skim his hands over her body. Goosebumps covered her arms, and Berry shivered with delight. She felt weightless, boneless, and drowning in heat. She'd never felt anything like this before. She hoped it would go on and on.

He kissed her as if he'd been thinking of nothing but her all day. Nothing could have been more seductive. She locked her arms around him and kissed him back. She might never have this chance again.

He slipped his fingers into the clasp of her lace brassiere and unhooked it, then cupped her breasts. She fit perfectly into his hands, as if she had been built for him. He touched the tips with his thumbs and almost whimpered with the pleasure.

He drew back to stare at her and she looked back at him in wonder. Why had she waited this long to find a man who made all these exciting things happen inside her? She had believed no one could ever make her feel this way.

Well, she had been wrong, that was all. And now that she had discovered him and he wanted her, she wasn't about to lose the chance. She might never feel these things again.

She leaned into him and fumbled with the buttons on the cheap shirt he wore. That reminded her of the extremes Tyler was going to in order to help her investigation, and her desire increased tenfold.

He must have gone out and bought a pair of cheap slacks also, she thought, as her fingers fumbled at his waistband. No one had ever given her the help and consideration Tyler had. No wonder she had fallen in love with him.

That thought, rather than jolt her, gave her such a sense of rightness she almost gave everything away by telling him she loved him. Some innate caution deep inside, born of a lifetime of males who may or may not have loved her but who definitely would take anything she chose to give, kept her silent.

Besides, she thought through the haze of desire clouding her mind, if she said anything at all she might destroy the mood and cause Tyler to change his mind about making love to her.

He dropped his trousers on the floor and tossed his shirt aside, then he tackled the snap on her jeans and peeled them down her legs.

"You have the prettiest legs," he said thickly. "Those silly shoes of yours really show them off, but I'm afraid you're going to break an ankle wearing them."

"Don't worry. When the investigation is over, I'm going back to my flats and sneakers."

She felt his laughter against her neck as he lifted her and laid her on the bed. Incredibly happy, Berry wrapped herself around him, even though she thought she might die if he didn't make love to her instantly.

Tyler didn't disappoint her. He pinned her wrists to the pillow and held her there while he kissed her neck and teased her lips until she thought she would go wild with desire. When he finally entered her, the relief sent her spinning rapidly into a climax that shattered what was left of her composure into thousands of pieces.

When it was over, he tucked her against his side and lay on his back, eyes closed. She studied him in the semidarkness. Light coming in the open bedroom door highlighted the planes of his face. He looked so relaxed, Berry almost hated to question him, but she was dying to know.

"I can't believe you got a job at Felix's store. That's the nicest thing anyone has ever done for me." She kissed his shoulder. "I can't wait to see Mr. Corrigan tomorrow. I'll bet I can get him to give me all kinds of figures."

Tyler smiled and kept his eyes closed. "If you can get his figures on just a couple of items, I'll be able to get some idea of what they're doing. Although when I'm going to get a chance to do a count or two, I don't know. All I had time for today was trying to figure out how to tell one car part from another." He opened his eyes and turned toward her. "How was your afternoon? Did you find out anything new?"

Berry smiled back. "Mostly, I just picked up a few more hints and suggestions and spread huge amounts of sympathy over Mr. Corrigan. He really appreciated the sandwich and coffee and said this was the best he'd ever been treated in a situation like this."

"I'll bet it was. Outside auditors tend to be universally hated by the employees, especially the ones who are involved in embezzlement."

He threaded his fingers into her curls and massaged her scalp gently. She sighed with pleasure and wondered why such a simple action seemed to her so erotic.

"When I left the office at five, I met a woman from the office next door who claims she knew Daniel. She wants me to meet her for a drink after work tomorrow."

"Who is she?"

"Her name is Cammy Osborne, and she's a secretary at Wilburn and White, the law firm down the hall. She says she'll call me tomorrow to confirm."

"For a newly hired employee, you sure get around." Tyler shifted and came up on his elbow to lean over her. "How'd you meet her?"

"When I left the office after work, she was just coming down the hall and admired my outfit. We left the building together. She seems nice enough, but kind of spacey. Sort of like the druggies I knew in college, if you want to know."

He frowned and concentrated on curling a lock of her hair around one finger. "I don't like this, Berry. It sounds to me as if she planned to meet you." Pushing her hair back from her face, he added, "Tell her something came up and you won't be able to meet her, okay? Let's get this Farley Brothers connection solved first. Then you can expand the investigation into other areas."

Berry agreed readily and said nothing about her plans to stay after hours at her desk in hopes of discovering something in the computer system. "Earlier this afternoon, I pegged Concetta Tomayo as Daniel's killer. They passed over promoting her to hire Daniel."

Tyler chuckled. "Now that's a prime motive for murder if I ever heard one."

"That's what I thought." Berry poked him in the ribs. "Men have no idea how infuriating that can be to a working woman. She's still pretty steamed about it. I gained a lot of Brownie points by sympathizing heavily over the crass nature of men."

"Daniel told me himself that Walter Farley hired him because of his football record at Rice," Tyler said.

"If that isn't crass, what is?" Berry regarded the ceiling thoughtfully. "Seriously, Tyler, motives for murder seem to be lying all over the place in that office. I hardly know which person to investigate first."

"What other motives for murder have you uncovered today?" He resumed his gentle massage of her scalp.

"Well, Concetta hated my guts the minute she saw me because she's in love with Felix. But when I found out she's Bernard Warren's half-sister, I realized she must have known Felix all her life."

"So?"

"So that's why she's in love with him. She probably knew him when he was young and personable."

Tyler laughed and leaned over her again. "He's no longer young, but I didn't realize you thought he wasn't personable."

"He reminds me of a satyr or some other lusty old creep." She made a face. "I was thrilled when he ran off to hide at the golf course. I hope Mr. Corrigan sits by my desk for the next couple of weeks."

Tyler laughed. "Why is Concetta's love for Felix a motive for murder?"

"Obviously, she's been in love with Felix a long time, and maybe he even had an affair with her. What if she came on to Daniel in hopes of making Felix jealous?" Berry rolled her eyes. "You know how attractive Daniel was to women. What if Felix had Daniel killed because he considers Concetta his? Or Concetta killed him because he wouldn't cooperate with her plan to make Felix jealous?"

"Be reasonable, Berry." He stroked her hair back and kissed her eyebrow. "It's a lot more likely that you'll be the one Concetta murders if she's in love with Felix."

"You're probably right." Berry thought that over. "Concetta is beginning to like me a little since I'm such a sympathetic sort. We're agreed that Daniel Challoner had a silver spoon in his mouth, and that football-playing ability is a very poor predictor of success in the business world."

"Actually, success in team sports like football is supposed to be a good indicator of team-player ability in an office setting." Tyler stroked one finger around the edge of her lips. "I used to hate depending on other people. That's why I went into accounting, I suppose."

She smiled and lifted one hand to touch his face. "Because as an accountant, you get to be suspicious of everyone else's math?"

"We're told that most errors on tax returns are simple math errors."

Berry turned toward him. "So tell me about your first day in an auto parts store. Was it fun?"

"I have a few other words to describe it, but fun is not one of them." He paused as if gathering his thoughts. "But I did overhear a phone conversation between Bernard Warren and someone who wanted him to move something out of the store tonight. Warren refused and wanted to know what the caller had done to make the accountant suspicious, considering they'd never had any trouble out of the accountants before."

Berry's eyes went wide. "Wow! Maybe we should break in the place tonight and search it. I'll bet they're storing cocaine or diamonds in some of those parts. Or maybe even guns and gun parts. What do you think?"

She knew that two days ago, Tyler would have denied this possibility categorically. His education had progressed so well, he now gave the suggestion serious consideration.

"Warren flatly refused to move whatever it was. Therefore, it'll still be there when I get to work at seven in the morning," he said.

"Seven? Mercy, Tyler. Why so early?"

"That's when the store opens," Tyler said. "But I'll be off by four. I don't care for these late evenings."

"Good," Berry said emphatically. "Because that's exactly what I intend to tell your dad."

Tyler laughed and rolled her to her back. "That's what I like. A woman who's determined to spend some quality time with her lover."

"Is that what this is?" she teased. "Quality time?"

"Whatever else it is," he said, skimming his lips over her chin, "it's definitely quality."

CHAPTER 8

"Sorry about the chicken," Berry said much later that night as she set a plate before him. "It would have been really good if we'd eaten it right out of the oven the way I'd planned."

"I'm not complaining."

Tyler wouldn't have changed a thing about the night. As far as he was concerned, Berry's broiled chicken dinner was even better cold, especially after he had mind-bending sex with the chef.

"But the chocolate pie will make up for everything," she went on. "It's my specialty, and it ought to be good and cold by now."

"The food is perfect," Tyler said. "What are you planning to investigate tomorrow?"

"I'll know it when I see it," she said, ever optimistic. "If I'm lucky, Felix will be hiding out on another golf course all day, and Mr. Corrigan will be free to visit with me."

"Tell you what," he said, smiling at her enthusiasm, "I'll pick you up outside the building at five. We'll go have a nice dinner someplace and tell each other what we've learned."

"Sounds great. If things change, send me a text, and I'll do the same. Especially if I find some information you need to check out right away."

She perched on the edge of her chair, wearing nothing but his robe and nibbling on chicken, and he thought he had never seen anything so beautiful. She fairly glowed with happiness and passion, and he resolved to see that she kept that joyful enthusiasm no matter what.

The moment that thought crossed his mind, an image of the rock chunk on his coffee table arose in his mind. Somehow, he knew that rock was important.

"By the way," he said, "what's with that chunk of rock on my coffee table?"

To his amusement, she flushed and looked self-conscious, but she answered readily enough. "If strange people are going to keep knocking at your door, I thought I'd better have a good weapon readily available."

"That's a weapon?"

"Believe it or not," she said, now fiery red, "I've used it before, and it works."

He regarded her with fascination. "Maybe you'd better tell me all about it, Challoner. So I'll learn what not to say to you if I don't want that rock banged off my head."

She kept her gaze on her plate and forked up a bite of asparagus. "Believe me, Tyler, you don't ever have to worry about being on the receiving end of my rock."

"Come on, honey. Tell me what happened," he coaxed, suddenly positive the incident was important somehow.

"It's a sad but simple tale," she said reluctantly. "I met this engineer named Grady Craig several months ago. He gave me the grand rush, said the magic words, and next thing you knew, we were engaged."

"The magic words?" Tyler leaned forward. "What are the magic words?"

"Never mind that. Suffice it to say, he said them. But I knew I'd made another mistake within a week. For some reason, he meant to make me to fall for him, but I never could figure out why."

Tyler nodded. He looked at Berry's face and thought he knew darned well why. "You say he was an engineer. Where did he work?"

Berry shrugged. "He said he was a construction engineer, but he was lying. That's one of the reasons I broke off the engagement."

"You must have been emotionally vulnerable at the time. What else was going on in your life?"

"Come on, Tyler. Grady wasn't some creep off the street. He was a good-looking, professional type. Like you, in fact."

Tyler frowned across the table. "Thanks a lot."

"Well, he was. After years spent looking at guys in lab coats and jeans, it wasn't surprising I developed a weakness for business suits."

"You don't know how happy I am to hear that." Tyler wondered if she was telling the truth. "So what else was going on in your life at the time?"

"The usual," she said, and her face looked sad suddenly. "Daniel had called to yell at me about changing my major yet again. I had begun to realize I didn't really want to major in geology after all, and I didn't know what to do because none of the credit hours I'd racked up seemed to have anything to do with life as people lived it off-campus. So I guess you could say I was at loose ends. Then Daniel got killed and everything fell apart. I didn't care about my major anymore. I just graduated fast as I could with whatever degree I could get."

Tyler blinked a little at this summary, but he had to admit it fit the Berry Challoner he'd come to know from her letters to Daniel. "Did Daniel approve of your engagement to this Craig fellow?"

"Daniel was killed right before I met Grady."

Tyler frowned. Something inside him fairly screamed that this was important, but he couldn't see how. "Daniel hoped you'd marry the guy whose daddy owned a bank, but that fell through within three weeks. What is it with you, Challoner?"

"It's some sort of genetic weakness." She scowled back at him. "When a man starts telling me he needs me, I automatically stick out my left hand to receive the diamond."

Tyler leaned back against his chair, the picture of masculine arrogance. "Well, let me tell you what I need."

"Right." Berry folded her arms across her chest. "Careful what you say, or you may find yourself wearing my chocolate pie instead of eating it."

Tyler shook his head and grinned. "Since I seem to have forgotten to arm myself with a diamond, I'd better shut up."

Keep after her, the voice inside his head instructed. He glanced behind him suspiciously. Perhaps he was going schizophrenic.

"So Craig presented you with a diamond and you found yourself engaged," he said. "What happened when you decided you'd made a mistake?"

Tyler watched her, conscious of a possessiveness he'd never felt before in regard to a woman. If he presented her with a diamond and she decided it was another mistake, he didn't know what he'd do.

Berry kept her eyes fixed on the spicy chicken on her fork. "Usually, I manage to part friends with them." She cast one glance at him then returned her attention to her plate.

Tyler sat in surprised silence a moment, trying to hear what she wasn't saying. "But this time Grady didn't take it well. What did he do?"

Berry gulped. "Oh, well he …"

"Yes?"

"He got … pretty mad."

"Now that's an evasion if I ever heard one," Tyler managed to say gently, though the red mist surrounding him. "Did he hit you? Try to rape you?"

She cast him a fleeting glance. "How did you know?"

"If you had to use your rock, it stands to reason. Go on."

"He … said he was going to show me once and for all who I belonged to." She shrugged again. "He was already mad at me because I wouldn't go to bed with him. That was the main reason I broke the engagement. I just wasn't interested in him sexually. Probably because some things he said just didn't add up."

But she was interested in him, Tyler thought, on a surge of gladness. "Go on."

It was almost impossible to keep his voice neutral. He wanted to go in search of Grady Craig and teach him a few things.

"He slapped me and knocked me back against the window sill in my apartment. Luckily, that's where I kept my rock. When he tried to grab me, I bashed him in the head with the rock and ran next door. Grady was gone by the time the police arrived." She looked up and smiled. "I have to admit, that was my most dramatically ended engagement."

Tyler wanted to say many things. Nothing he could think of was appropriate.

"Forget everything I said about that rock," he said at last. "So the rock on my coffee table is the one that saved you from this creep?"

"That's the heroic rock. It's a piece of limestone, an edgewise conglomerate that I found on the petrology field trip in the Austin area."

Tyler laughed and shook his head. "You've lost me there. But since it saved you, it deserves a medal of some sort. Maybe we can have a bit of felt put on the bottom and polish it up so you can display it properly."

"Maybe you're right. The sharp edges drew blood," she said thoughtfully.

"Served him right. Did he call you to apologize?"

She grimaced. "He called and called. I blocked his number."

"Did you file charges?"

"You bet I did. As soon as he realized that, the phone calls ended." She looked up and he saw that her eyes glowed with residual fury. "And do you know what was weird about the whole episode? The police couldn't find him. Everything he'd told me about himself was a lie. No engineering school in the United States had ever heard of him, and no construction company in the state of Texas employed, or had ever employed, an engineer by the name of Grady Craig."

"He was lying about everything? Why?"

Tyler sat back, puzzled and disturbed. Con men usually went after women with assets like money or property. Berry Challoner had little of either. At least, that's what he'd assumed. Daniel certainly hadn't had anything beyond what he earned and had never said anything about Berry possessing an independent income. At least, not then.

"Are you really rich, by any chance?" he asked.

"Believe me, Tyler, if I were rich, I'd know." She gave him an exasperated look. "If it hadn't been for several well-timed checks from Daniel, I'd have been eating on five dollars a week more than once during my college career."

"I remember. You'd spent too much on new clothes." He smiled at her, recalling how he'd harassed Daniel into doing his brotherly duty. "He thought maybe he ought to let you starve so you'd quit school and get a job." He thought a moment, trying to remember everything Daniel had said when their father had died. "Berry, is there something you aren't telling me? Something you've forgotten about?"

She wrinkled her forehead. "What do you mean?"

"Do you own any annuities, or an old building somewhere, or maybe some land or old jewelry from your mom?"

"Tyler, what you see is all there is." She pushed a stray black curl off her honey-colored forehead. "I have Daniel's life insurance money, and that's it. When it's gone, my investigation is over. Can we talk about something else now? Grady Craig is not my favorite subject."

"There has to be some reason why this jerk came on to you so hard," he said. "I'd like to know what it is."

"If there's something about me that attracts men like him, I'd rather remain forever ignorant."

"Craig was interested in you for a reason," Tyler repeated doggedly, more certain of it than ever. "We ought to find out what it was."

She flung back her head. "I don't want to know, thank you. If I could erase the entire thing from my memory, believe me, I would."

"The guy was a con artist," Tyler said, with enormous patience. "You said so yourself. That means you had something he wanted. What about your great-aunt Mary? Are you sure you don't stand to inherit something from her?"

"Like what?" Berry resumed her dinner. "Even if she really had any money, Great-aunt Mary wouldn't leave two cents to me. She hated us because Daddy told her she was a dried-up old witch with twisted priorities. She told him he could forget having himself or his children mentioned in any will of hers."

Tyler shut up. It was obvious that Berry had no idea what Craig had wanted from her. His only consolation at the moment was the knowledge that Grady Craig, whoever he really was, had ruined himself forever with Berry Challoner.

But Craig had wanted her for a reason. Tyler thought suddenly of the dark car he kept seeing and frowned. Was it possible Berry was being followed? And if so, why? Next time he saw that car, he was getting the license plate number.

The whole thing was ridiculous, he suddenly thought. He had no imagination and he definitely wasn't given to speculation. He was an accountant, and a darned good one. He dealt in facts that could be substantiated by figures, whether electronic or penciled.

Perhaps the adventure of working as an auto parts counter salesman had oiled his rusty imagination into taking off like this on the subject of Grady Craig.

He thrust the thought aside and concentrated on his dinner. One thing his imagination could handle, and handle well, was how that chocolate pie he had seen in his refrigerator was going to taste.

Another thing he could handle was Berry Challoner in his bed. He could hardly wait to finish the pie so he could taste Berry again.

• • •

Berry parked her green Mustang in the slot beside Tyler's Porsche. Tired as she was, she had the joyous conviction that she was home at last. Coming home to Tyler felt so natural, it was hardly surprising that she already considered his apartment home.

She sat still a moment and analyzed what she felt. Of course, considering last night, and definitely after the day she'd had, deep gratitude and joy were hardly surprising.

She got out of the car slowly, sighing with weariness, and headed toward the stairs. Then she glanced up and saw Tyler on the landing waiting for her. He wore a pair of khaki trousers and a plaid shirt. The afternoon sun turned his brown hair into a halo of deep-red flame.

Oddly enough, he appeared to be staring at something beyond her. She turned but saw nothing other than a dark car gliding slowly past on the street behind her.

He leaned over the railing. "Have you ever seen that car before? It's almost as if it's following you."

Berry stood at the foot of the staircase and looked up at him. "I haven't noticed it before, but maybe I've picked up a stalker. After the day I've had, that would be the crowning glory."

"Wait till I tell you about mine," he said. "We can talk over a good dinner somewhere. You look too tired to cook, and I don't even want to think about it."

"Thanks, Tyler." Berry climbed the stairs slowly, pausing on each step. "My feet are killing me. Do you think we can go someplace where I won't have to wear high heels?"

"You can wear tennis shoes," he promised, holding out his hand to help her make the last two steps. "What happened? Did old Felix chase you around his desk?"

"Something like that," she admitted. "It's been a long, dreary day." She shook herself like a wet puppy. "But no one said this investigation was going to be easy."

"Better get out of those clothes, honey." Tyler studied her slim figure appreciatively. "Otherwise, I might forget myself and attack the bimbo in the yellow dress."

"You can't attack a dead person. It wouldn't be fair."

She wore a brief, sun-yellow suit with a bolero jacket trimmed in deep purple. Rather than button the jacket, she showed off a very sheer lilac blouse that revealed the lace of her bra. Worn with deep purple high heels and bright red lipstick, the outfit projected playful, sophisticated sexiness.

"In that case, we'd better see what can be done to revive you." Tyler watched her limp down the hall to her bedroom. "I've never been into necrophilia."

* * *

When Berry reappeared, dressed in a pair of dark trousers and a red silk shirt tied beneath her breasts, Tyler stood before his coffee table staring down at the chunk of rock.

"It's a stealth-rock," she said. "It's a deadly weapon disguised as a decoration."

"Why don't you get a gun? At least it wouldn't shed dirt all over the place."

He glanced at her feet. She'd exchanged the high heels for a pair of flimsy, flat sandals. Otherwise, she was still Mary MacGregor, violet eyes and all.

"Relax," he said. "We're going to a Chinese place nearby. You won't see anyone from Farley Brothers there."

"How do you know? I can't afford to let my guard down for one minute, considering everything I've gone through to get in at Farley Brothers."

"I'm beginning to hate that name," Tyler grumbled.

Berry laughed. "You aren't the only one. They'll never sell me an auto part, even if I live to be a hundred."

The Chinese restaurant sat like an island in the middle of a huge parking lot that was half-full. He looked at the broad, tiered blocks of concrete steps they'd have to climb and rejoiced that she had left her heels at home. He'd probably have had to carry her up.

The restaurant was crowded, but they didn't wait long for a booth. Tyler advised her about sesame chicken and egg rolls and ordered coffee to be brought immediately.

After placing their orders, he leaned back. "All right. Tell me what happened today."

"You name it, and it happened." She received her coffee with a look of profound gratitude. "I didn't find out a single useful thing today, except that Mr. Corrigan is coming tomorrow with demands for a one-on-one interview with Felix."

"That should be interesting, especially if you can manage to overhear the conversation." Tyler saw renewed vigor animate her weary face at this challenge and felt inordinately pleased.

"Don't worry. I'll find a way," she said fiercely.

"I spent the morning being ordered up and down those mile-long warehouse aisles without a minute to stop and count anything. Now they're trying to teach me how to look up parts on their computer. Frankly, it's a losing proposition."

"Come on, Tyler," Berry said, chuckling at his expression. "If they can do it, you can do it."

"The problem is, I don't want to do it," he grumbled. "Plus, in order to look up a part, I have to know what it is. Frankly, the only thing good about that job is that I'm learning to appreciate my own quiet office."

He was pleased to see the sparkle return to Berry's face. "See? I knew you needed a vacation."

"Some vacation. Tell me what happened with Felix today."

She sat staring at her coffee cup for a moment as if gathering courage. "You were right about Felix. Mr. Corrigan was gone, so I had no excuse not to go into his office when he called me." She shivered. "What a creep."

Tyler leaned forward, suddenly and irrationally furious. "Did he make a pass at you?"

Berry nodded and wouldn't look at him. "I mean, I expected him to—to try and kiss me and—and things, but I thought I could handle that."

Tyler was silent while he mastered the all-encompassing rage that swept through him. He should never have let her hire on at Farley Brothers dressed like an expensive mistress.

"And don't bother saying, 'I told you so,' because I'm perfectly willing to admit you were right." She smiled shakily. "I had no idea how to handle him. He had an answer for everything I said. He kept coming on and coming on until he had me bent back over his desk. Tyler, he actually wanted to make love to me on his *desk*. I was so grossed out, I couldn't think of a single viable excuse."

Berry sounded so outraged, Tyler almost laughed in spite of the fury that pounded through his veins. "How did you escape?"

"Concetta walked in on us. Can you believe that? He didn't lock the door." She took a healthy swallow of coffee and added, "I could have kissed her."

Tyler opened his mouth then closed it again. When he'd mastered himself, he said, "Maybe he planned the show to let Concetta know she had no hold over him."

"You may be right," she said. "That was the conclusion I came to later. Anyway, there I was on his desk, with my skirt up and his hands all over me. I was so embarrassed I could have died. But she saved me, Tyler. If she hadn't come in, I'd have had to do something desperate."

"Like what?" He glared, still furious at Felix, and at Berry for being so naïve as to think she could fend off an experienced libertine like Felix with mere words. "If he had you on his desk with your skirt up, it was already too late."

"No, it wasn't. There was a crystal paperweight on his desk. I already had my hand on it when Concetta walked in." She flushed. "These days, I always make sure there's a rock or a paperweight around whenever there's a man nearby."

Tyler's scowl deepened. "Are you telling me that rock on my coffee table was put there in case what happened last night in the kitchen happened in the living room?"

Her purple gaze met his and flashed away. "In case you failed to notice, I encouraged what happened last night. So why would I use the rock on you?"

"I've been afraid to ask." He noted her flushed cheeks and decided he'd better cease his line of questioning. "I hope this warns you to be better prepared next time you go into Felix's office alone. In fact, I'd suggest you stay out of his office at all costs."

He hoped she had received a sufficient fright to come to that conclusion on her own, but he had learned the hard way not to trust a female to arrive at the same conclusions a male would. Still, according to Daniel, Berry had quite a temper when sufficiently provoked.

"Did you really dump a bowl of spaghetti over Daniel's head?" he asked.

Berry gave him a demure smile. "Don't worry, Tyler. I promise not to dump a bowl of anything over your head. No way would you ever manage to deserve it the way Daniel usually did."

He considered himself warned and shut up.

"Tell me about your sisters," Berry said, after a moment of silence. "They seem so different from each other, I was fascinated. It was too bad I had to stay in character, or I'd have enjoyed meeting them."

He launched into a description of Debra's aspirations in the field of society journalism and her engagement to a man he hoped could corral her dramatic leanings.

"Kelley wants to be a vet, of all things. She's majoring in biology. It has Dad so baffled, he wonders if she's really a member of our family."

Berry chuckled. "I know what you mean. I was the only person interested in science in my family. They could never figure out why."

By the time Berry's sesame chicken arrived, her enthusiasm and energy had returned. She walked out of the restaurant on Tyler's arm, talking happily about her plan for listening in on Felix Farley's heart-to-heart talk with the auditor Nathaniel Corrigan—assuming it actually took place.

"Maybe I'll be able to find out some figures for you to check out," she said, purple eyes glowing. "If I do, I'll text you to do a count on the spot."

Tyler agreed. He forbore commenting on the fact that the figures several months back would be different from today's count. She would probably consider facts no excuse for failing to convict Felix Farley of fraud and murder.

They began the long descent down the wide tiers of concrete steps, and Tyler glanced at the cars coming and going on the long, circular drive that led to the restaurant. The area was so well lit, they might have been standing outside in broad daylight, even though it was eight o'clock and the sun was nearing the horizon.

A dark sedan with tinted windows cruised slowly out of the parking lot and crawled at a snail's speed up the drive. The hair on the back of Tyler's neck stirred gently. Some atavistic sense told him danger approached, even as his conscious mind ridiculed the idea. But the car looked a lot like—

Someone shoved him hard from behind. Tyler fell headfirst down the tall stairs, dragging Berry with him. She slowed his fall enough for him to twist and get his arms around her. Somehow, he managed to protect her from the worst. They rolled to the bottom of the stairs in a flurry of legs and elbows.

As they fell, four distinct, rapid gunshots rang out in the abrupt stillness. Bullets slapped into the stairs above them with solid thunks. They shot down the remainder of the stairs headfirst and rolled to a halt on the concrete below.

Screams rang out and men yelled. People nearby dove to the ground. Someone behind them yelled in pain. The world became a kaleidoscope of sound and flashes of light and color. Tyler hugged Berry beneath him in a world gone suddenly mad and felt her fingernails digging into the back of his neck.

Tyler heard the sound of a gunning engine, then screeching tires, then silence. Not more than a few seconds had elapsed since he'd begun his fall down the stairs. He raised his head cautiously.

Above them on the steps, a well-dressed man lay clutching his blood-splattered thigh. Everything remained strangely still and silent for a moment, then movement and sound began once more in surreal slow-motion.

"He's gone!" A teenage boy crawled out from beneath a car, gasping with excitement. "It was a black Corolla with a man inside."

"Better save it for the police," Tyler grated, profoundly shaken. Adrenaline raged through his body, but there was no one for him to fight. "Get some help for that man." He helped Berry sit up. "Berry? Are you all right?"

"I think so." She panted and trembled but remained game. "If you hadn't protected me, I'd probably have broken every bone I have." Clutching his arm, she shuddered with shock and residual fright. Her red silk blouse would never be the same, but she was alive. "What about you? That was some fall."

He knelt beside her on the concrete, staring at the long gouges in the concrete above them while he hugged her tightly and measured where he'd been standing when he began to fall.

According to his calculations, Berry had narrowly escaped death. One-tenth of a second later, and the first bullet would have struck her head. The second one, the one that had seared a long gouge in one of the steps, would have pierced her body.

"Who were they shooting at?" Berry asked, clenching her teeth against the tremors that shook her.

Tyler swallowed. "I don't know."

She could have died before he had a chance to marry her. Tyler forced himself to rise to his feet, in spite of a desire to continue shielding Berry with his own body. He measured the area visually with a calm that was at odds with the state of his insides.

What he saw did not comfort him. The bullet meant for Berry's head had traveled on and hit the man who had been a couple of steps above them on the wide, wooden stairs.

"They must have been aiming at that poor man behind us," she said. She added, in tones of censure, "I thought assassins always took care to check the gun sights before they did a job."

Even at a distance, Tyler could see the wounded man's Rolex watch and diamond ring. Hope rose within him. Maybe he was wrong about thinking the bullets had been intended for Berry. "Who do you think he is?"

"Maybe he's a Mafia don or something, poor thing."

Tyler grimaced. The man had expensively styled blond hair and cold, blue eyes of Anglo-Saxon extraction. At the moment, Tyler would have given anything if he could think the gunman was settling a score with a Mafia don.

"He looks more like an executive," he compromised. "I'd hate to think we're starting to see disgruntled stockholders and customers putting out contracts on top management."

Berry smiled. It was a faint, wavering smile, but it warmed Tyler's chilled heart. He sat back down beside her and hugged her close. "Are you sure you aren't hurt?"

"Me? What about you?" She clutched him. "Thanks for saving me, Tyler. If you hadn't pulled me down, I might have been shot. How'd you know they were about to start shooting?"

Tyler blinked. His brain seemed to have shifted into slow gear. He thought suddenly of the powerful shove against his back. But he hadn't noticed anyone close enough to them on the stairs to put that kind of power into a push.

The thought made the hair on his neck lift gently.

He looked again at the steps and measured the distance. The man who'd taken the bullet that would have struck Berry had been two steps up—too far away to have planted a hand in the center of Tyler's back and pushed, and that was what Tyler thought he'd felt.

"I … uh … saw a gleam of light reflected off what looked like a gun barrel," he said.

He just hoped the lie was believable. Something told him the truth would be regarded as highly suspicious.

CHAPTER 9

Tyler figured the only redeeming feature of the next few hours was Berry's company. She clung to his arm, shivering in the cold interrogation room at the police headquarters. Fortunately, she was still so dazed; she had no idea why they were being questioned with such thoroughness.

After two hours of hearing her repeat her story, Tyler grew exasperated with the official attitude. It was a relief when official attention focused on him for a change.

"Now, Mr. Reid," the detective said, looking at Tyler's written statement for the third time. "You say that you were warned of the danger by catching a glimpse of a gun barrel a fraction of a second before the shooting began. Yet witnesses say that the car windows were tinted so you couldn't see inside."

He had realized the police would pick up on that. "The car was cruising so slowly, I began to watch it. Someone rolled down the car window, and I saw light gleaming off what looked like a gun barrel."

It sounded logical. He just hoped it proved possible.

"You saw a gun? What kind of gun? What made you think you and Miss Challoner might be a target of gunfire?"

Fury raced along his nerve endings. He tightened his muscles and maintained his cool demeanor.

"I didn't think we were the targets," he said dryly. "I did, however, think we might turn out to be among those statistics known as 'innocent bystanders.' And I know nothing about guns."

The detective was silent a moment, eyeing him steadily.

Tyler stared back. In his heart, fury fought with the chilling conviction that Berry had indeed been the target. Something within him kept insisting that was the case in spite of his every attempt to squelch it.

"How well could you see?"

"Very well indeed," Tyler replied. "The sun was still up."

"What kind of car was it?"

"I didn't notice, except that it was a dark car. The parking lot attendant said it was a black Corolla with one man inside."

"You state that in spite of good light, you didn't notice the color or the make of the car?"

"Cars were never a hobby of mine."

"Your own vehicle is a late-model Porsche?"

"That's right." Tyler allowed himself to look amused at the implied rebuke. "I followed the recommendation of my father. He's been a car buff since his teens, but he would never allow himself to buy a Porsche. So I bought it for him."

After a moment of silence, the detective let the car pass and went on to a new topic. "Now, Mr. Reid, were you aware of the identity of the man standing somewhat behind you who was shot in the upper right thigh?"

"Of course I wasn't," Tyler said irritably. "Should I be?"

"What about you, Miss Challoner?"

Berry drew herself up. "No. I'm new to Houston."

Tyler congratulated himself on telling her to give the police her real name. He just hoped her name and picture didn't appear in any newspapers.

The detective scribbled something on a note pad. "When did you arrive in Houston?"

"About five days ago," she replied. "I told you, I graduated from the University of Texas two weeks ago."

Tyler shifted impatiently. "Well, who is the man who got shot? I've lived in Houston all my life, and I don't know the guy."

The detective looked at him steadily. "His name is Jackson Jacobs, a reputed drug dealer. His major clients are supposedly among the rich and famous."

Tyler let out his breath on a sigh of profound relief. Everything inside him sagged.

The insistent voice inside him called Jackson Jacobs's presence a coincidence.

Shut up! Tyler told the voice vehemently.

Berry hadn't been the target after all. The bullets belonged to this Jacobs fellow. Now that he knew that, he couldn't maintain his anger at the apparent police suspicion that he'd known about the hit ahead of time.

He ignored the dark—very similar—car he'd seen cruising around his apartment building. It was probably a coincidence.

"Since I'm neither," he said, "that explains my ignorance. Is there anything else you want to ask us, officer? I need to get Miss Challoner home."

"Just another few questions, Mr. Reid."

Tyler was so mellow from realizing Berry hadn't been the intended victim, he couldn't even work up a good snarl.

After taking them through the events of the shooting two more times, the police let them leave.

"Have you ever heard of Jackson Jacobs?" Berry asked as they exited via a side door.

"No." Tyler smiled grimly. "However, I'll make sure he isn't dining at the same place I am in the future."

He carefully helped Berry into his Porsche. In the hours since the shooting, he'd been growing steadily more stiff and sore, and he knew Berry was, too.

It was over. Berry was safe. The whole affair was a case of being in the wrong place at the wrong time. He gunned his engine and backed out swiftly.

"Are you sure you're all right?" he asked quietly.

"Do you mean other than my three cracked ribs, my bruised knees, and battered elbows? Yes, thank you." She chuckled faintly.

"I'm glad you happened to see that gun. Otherwise, we'd probably both have been killed by accident."

Tyler agreed, although he had noticed what the police had noticed—that Berry Challoner was the only bystander who'd have been struck by the bullets meant for Jackson Jacobs.

They were meant for her! The words skittered across his mind like a black spider.

Tyler stiffened and let himself consider the idea. What if Jackson Jacobs had been the innocent bystander? Berry would have looked like the innocent victim of another senseless shooting, and no one would have delved any further into reasons.

Tyler shoved the thought aside. He had seen no evidence to suggest such a thing, and if Jackson Jacobs was known to the police as a drug dealer, then of course the bullets were meant for him. Berry had simply been standing in the wrong place when the delivery of lead arrived.

• • •

Berry limped into Tyler's living room. Every muscle in her body protested. Tyler had protected her well, but she'd still bumped and scraped a great many areas. That meant Tyler had to be twice as sore and bruised as she was.

"I hope I don't have any huge bruises on my legs," she grumbled, looking at her elbows and forearms. "It won't do for Felix to notice any damage to the merchandise."

"Shut up, Challoner. I'm not in a very good mood at the moment." Tyler scowled at her. "At the moment, I wouldn't mind ruining Felix's dental work if he so much as looks at you."

He did sound very much on edge. Berry edged away cautiously.

"In that case, I'll just vanish into the bathroom and soak my soreness away in a hot tub of water," she said.

"You owe me, Miss MacGregor. Come here and pay up."

She glanced over her shoulder. His voice had dropped to almost a whisper, and he was frowning in the way Daniel used to frown when he was about to flatten someone.

Well, she wasn't exactly in any sort of good mood herself after rolling down a long flight of concrete steps like a snowball, losing a bit of skin at every bounce.

"You'd better watch yourself, Tyler Reid, or I'll—"

He crossed the floor in two easy strides. Berry tried to flee, but was hampered by her sore muscles. At least that's what she told herself. When Tyler's hands closed around her waist, she pretended to struggle.

"Why, Mr. *Reid*," she said, in Mary MacGregor's fluting voice. "I do believe you're jealous of Mr. Farley. *Shame* on you."

"Felix gets to look at you in those sexy getups all day, while I'm stuck with running at top speed up and down warehouse aisles stacked with automobile parts I never even knew existed. Something is definitely unfair about this arrangement."

She smiled at him as he lifted her in his arms and carried her toward the bathroom. "In that case, I'll see what I can do to even things up. We can't have any *unfairness* around here."

"That's more like it," he said, and set her feet on the floor beside the bathtub to take her gently in his arms and kiss her. "You taste like that police station coffee."

"So do you. Strong stuff, but it definitely restores your vigor."

She waited while he turned the faucets of the bathtub on and adjusted the temperature of the water, then stood in unresisting silence as he undressed her slowly, taking note of every scratch on her hands and the bruises on her elbows.

"I'll have to wear long sleeves for a week," she said. "Anything is better than trying to tell Felix what happened."

"True." He held her away from him and took his time just looking at her. "But I'll bet you can blame a lot of things on those high heels of yours. If you didn't look so delectable in them, I think I'd banish them to the dumpster out back." He pulled her into his arms. "Thank God you're not hurt. I don't know what I'd do if you'd broken an arm or something."

"I'm fine, Tyler. You broke my fall and kept me from banging my head all the way down. Considering that, I'm glad *you're* okay."

She slid her hands down his back. He felt so warm and solid, so dependable, definitely someone she could turn to, someone who would protect her from danger with his own body. Someone who had gone out of his way to help her. Someone she found irresistible.

Someone she loved.

She loved Tyler. Berry examined the idea with one part of her brain while the other part concentrated on the incredible pleasure kissing Tyler gave her.

She had never loved any of her three former fiancés. She could see that easily now that she understood the real power of love. She had been infatuated with the idea of having someone who cared about her, someone to call her own. But she had never loved any man. She'd gotten engaged as a cure for loneliness.

She shivered and kissed Tyler greedily. This was love, this longing to become one with a man. She couldn't get close enough to him. His clothes were in the way of that need. She struggled to get her hands beneath his knit shirt so she could feel his hot, bare skin beneath her palms.

"You're going to burn me alive," Tyler said, stringing kisses along her jaw. "But you know that already, don't you?"

"You're doing the same thing to me." She gasped and arched her neck when his lips found the sensitive skin behind her ear. "I've never felt like this before."

"You haven't?" Tyler nipped the soft, fragrant skin on her neck. "Then let's see if we can get the fire started."

He groaned softly as her questing hands brushed across his bare chest. Berry thrilled to the sound, sought to make him groan again, but he framed her face in both his hands and pressed his lips to hers in a kiss that sought a deeper response from her.

She gave herself up to his touch and felt him lift her and set her gently in the tub. To her joy, he stepped in behind her and pulled her back to lie partly on him as they soaked in the warm, soothing water.

"This feels like heaven," she said on a sigh.

• • •

Much later in the night, Tyler awakened and turned onto his back. He drifted in that pleasant state between waking and sleeping.

Time shifted. He was back in his dormitory room at Rice University. He knew that because Daniel Challoner's distinctive cologne scented the air. He registered the thought that his roommate must have just finished his morning shower.

Tyler sighed deeply and prepared to go back to sleep. The scent of cologne meant he had another hour in bed. Daniel always got up early. A man with four girlfriends, football practice, and a full course load had to get up early.

"I thought I'd try another way of getting through to you," Daniel said. "See if you can keep your mind in that dreamy state. Manifesting the image you expect is impossible if you're fully awake."

Tyler muttered in sleepy annoyance when Daniel touched his shoulder. Daniel knew how much he hated being bothered in the early hours of the morning.

The bed dipped slightly as Daniel sat down on the edge. Tyler half-opened his eyes. Daniel, his dark hair freshly combed, and smelling freshly showered, smiled reassuringly. His blue eyes crinkled at the corners in the way that kept four girlfriends enthralled, and his polo shirt matched his eyes.

Tyler was not a girlfriend and the crinkles at the corners of Daniel Challoner's blue eyes left him cold. "Get lost, you Neanderthal. I'm trying to sleep."

"Don't talk," Daniel said. "Just listen. Berry is in serious danger. This Grady Craig—"

"Grady Craig?" Tyler interrupted sleepily. "What about ... ?"

His voice trailed off. Something was wrong somewhere.

He remembered suddenly. Daniel Challoner was dead.

No, that was impossible. How could Daniel be dead when Tyler could feel the weight of his body pressing down the edge of the bed?

Maybe the reports of Daniel's death had been a mistake.

"Don't wake up," Daniel commanded sharply.

Tyler came awake with a vengeance. His heart pounded as he sucked in his breath and shot up in bed. He had attended the funeral and had looked upon his friend's face for the last time. Daniel *was* dead.

Daniel faded. Tyler saw his lips moving but could no longer hear his voice. Within a second, Daniel's image had completely vanished, along with the dent in the bed.

"You can't come in here saying something like that and then just fade away," Tyler said aloud.

But Daniel had. Tyler glanced at the clock he kept at his beside. It was just after five and still dark outside. He stared suspiciously around the room, but there was no hint of Daniel's presence. Still breathing hard, his heart pounding madly, Tyler plumped up his pillow and leaned back. He hardly knew what to contemplate first, Daniel's appearance, or Grady Craig.

Beside him, Berry slept soundly. If anyone was going to have some kind of visitation from Daniel, by all rights it should be Berry. Look at all she had gone through on Daniel's behalf. He curled his body around hers and let her warmth and comfort seep into him. Berry's presence guaranteed him a deep and peaceful night's sleep as nothing else could.

Grady Craig. Tyler thought suddenly of the man he had surprised knocking at the door of his apartment several nights before. The man had worn dark clothing, and Tyler had never gotten a glimpse of his face. In fact, now that he thought about it, the man had tried to avoid being seen.

Moreover, he had carried something under his arm that had been wrapped in a dark windbreaker. Could it have been a gun?

He thought back to the few facts he'd been able to glean about Daniel's death. The bullet, they claimed, had been fired from a .223 carbine. He had no idea whether that was a pistol, a rifle, or a shotgun. At the time, he hadn't asked.

Could the man have been Grady Craig? Tyler had no idea. This whole thing was nothing but a bad dream, most likely because of the Chinese food he'd eaten the night before.

Besides, why would Grady Craig want to kill Berry Challoner? More to the point, why would Grady Craig kill Daniel Challoner?

Nothing added up. That meant it had been a dream.

Tyler tucked the covers closely around Berry. He had another hour before his alarm would sound. He breathed deeply and closed his eyes, noting absently that the room still smelled of Daniel's favorite cologne.

He lifted his head and sniffed carefully. The spicy, metallic scent couldn't be anything but the expensive cologne Daniel had favored.

Did that mean the experience hadn't been a dream?

Tyler didn't know, but he did know one thing. Something weird was going on, and he was going to get to the bottom of it.

On that thought, he drifted slowly back into sleep, pleasantly conscious of Berry in his arms and her dark curls tickling his nose.

Later in the morning, after a good breakfast with Berry across the table from him, he dressed in his cheap clothes for another day at the Westheimer number two store and frowned at his own image in the mirror. He had questioned Berry thoroughly about her great-aunt, but she knew little other than where the woman had lived when Berry and Daniel were children. Before leaving his apartment, he called a private detective, a former policeman who was a friend of his father. He gave the detective all the information Berry had given him and asked for a callback as soon as possible.

Hopefully, he told himself as he drove to the Westheimer number two store, Berry's great-aunt was still alive and hating all her relatives, and her alleged money was either non-existent as Berry insisted or had nothing whatsoever to do with that dark car and the shots fired last night. Things would be much simpler if this was all about Felix Farley and not about Berry Challoner.

Tyler drove to his usual parking spot about two blocks from the Farley Brothers store and walked the two blocks. When he got off, he'd meet Berry at her office. By then, he might have some news for her.

"That your car, Reid?"

Tyler experienced a sinking in his stomach upon seeing Bernard Warren approaching. "Actually, it belongs to a friend."

"Must be a good friend," Warren said, eyes narrowed on Tyler's Porsche half a block away. "Not many people would entrust that baby to just anyone."

Endless talk about cars bored Tyler, and he'd heard enough car talk the past two days to make him want to buy a bicycle. But he'd learned a few things, too, and he was prepared in case anyone noticed the Porsche.

"Actually, it's my sister's boyfriend's car," he said. "They've taken off to Acapulco, so I'm babysitting their car and their apartment."

Bernard Warren gave the car a last, suspicious stare then disappeared into his office. Tyler told himself he'd better do some counts today, busy or no. He punched the time clock and hurried out to the counter.

"Reid," Rich MacKenzie, the experienced counter man greeted him, phone in one hand. He pointed down the long aisles to the rear of the store. "We just got a shipment in. Go see if there are any sunroofs for a '95 Camaro. Move it, will you?"

Before Tyler could head to the back, a customer entered, one very familiar to him. Tyler wavered between annoyance and exasperation. He did not need this today.

"I need to speak to you," Mason Reid said, fixing a stern glance on his son.

"Sure," Tyler said. "Come this way, please. We can talk on the way. As you can see, I'm rather busy, and Rich needs that sunroof now."

Mason, to give him credit, gave nothing away, but he stared at the tall shelves loaded with automobile parts they passed through with disbelief.

"For a man who claims to dislike car engines, you sure seem to have landed on your feet in the middle of every car engine part there is. What's going on here, Tyler?"

"It's a long story, Dad. Keep your voice down. I'm doing a bit of private sleuthing for a friend."

"You're *what*?"

Mason's incredulity would have been comical if Tyler had caught a glimpse of his father's expression, but they arrived at the rear of the warehouse section of the store where a myriad of wooden boxes stuffed with a hodgepodge of parts sat by the wall. A selection of fancy wheels, including a fine set of expensive mag wheels, rested against the back wall. Tyler sucked in his breath and reached out to turn the wheels so he could examine both sides. Surely, he must be mistaken.

But he wasn't. He knelt and turned one of the wheels so that he could view the characteristic nick in the gleaming metal—the nick Daniel had been fighting with the Ford dealership about, up until the day he died.

"Tyler, what's going on here?" Mason demanded in low tones.

Tyler let out his breath on a long sigh and glanced to the side. "It's a long story, Dad, and I have a feeling it's just about at an end."

He rose to his feet when Bernard Warren, his expression hard and suspicious, approached.

"What the hell are you doing, Reid?" he snapped, directing a hard stare at Mason.

Tyler faced him, suddenly furious. "The reason Nathaniel Corrigan couldn't reconcile the inventory is because you're integrating stolen car parts into the regular inventory. How long has this been going on?"

Warren's face froze. "I don't know what you're talking about. You're fired, by the way. Farley says he never sent you here. Just what the hell kind of game are you playing?"

"I think you know exactly what the game is." Tyler took his father's arm. "I'm a Certified Public Accountant and a private investigator, and this is my colleague." That wasn't entirely a lie. "These parts are stolen parts. If I call the police, I'll bet there are theft reports on most of these items." He pointed to the four mag wheels. "Including the wheels off Daniel Challoner's Mustang. Is that why you had him killed? Because he stumbled on your little scheme? I can prove those wheels are off his car, you know, just as Nathaniel Corrigan can prove the inventory you keep is actually much larger than the inventory you report on paper."

He could almost hear Mason's silent whistle, but the older man otherwise gave no sign that this was news to him. He maintained the same stern expression he had turned on his son earlier.

Warren's face whitened slowly. He stared in a horrified way at Daniel's mag wheels and cursed beneath his breath.

"Well?" Tyler said through set teeth. "Is that why he was killed? Because he found out about your little fencing operation?"

"No. No. You've got it all wrong," Warren whispered. He looked gray. "Look. I don't know anything about Challoner's death. I hardly even knew the man."

"The hell you didn't!" Tyler bit out. He'd never felt such a cold rage before. The thought of Daniel's life being cut short to cover up this petty fraud enraged him so much, he never thought of any danger to his own life if Bernard Warren was really a murderer. "If you didn't kill him, then you know why he was killed."

"Look, keep your voice down," Warren said earnestly. "I can see you've got the game all figured out. Let's go to my office. I'll tell you whatever you want to know. But you've got to believe me. This little scheme of Felix's isn't worth doing murder over. Whoever killed Daniel Challoner had nothing to do with us."

"We'll be the judge of that," Tyler said harshly.

He found it hard to hide his relief. If Felix Farley was responsible for Daniel's death, there was no reason for anyone to kill Berry.

That would mean the dark car, the bullets, and the strange urges in his head, not to mention the weird dream of Daniel this morning, were all products of his fevered imagination.

Berry was right, he thought, as he and his father followed Warren to the office.

When this was over, he was taking a long vacation.

• • •

The vacation began taking form in his mind the whole time he and his father faced Bernard Warren. When Nathaniel Corrigan arrived upon Tyler's phone call, followed soon after by Felix Farley, he had decided upon a tropical paradise, one where he could gaze on Berry Challoner in a tiny bikini any time he wanted. Daydreams of swimming in the warm Gulf of Mexico waters with Berry, lying in bed with Berry and walking the twilight beaches with her at his side interspersed accounting discussions of inventories and enhanced profits.

Lawyers for Felix and Bernard Warren arrived, along with representatives of Walter Farley, still very much in command of the Farley Brothers empire. The discussion dragged on, with Tyler alternating between fury and disappointment. Try as he might, he could not quite reconcile the blustering, red-faced Felix Farley, who had dreamed up the current fraud, with the cold-blooded murderer of Daniel Challoner. No doubt Felix was covering up a couple of other frauds that might not be so straightforward.

Felix's plan was simple enough. He wanted to replace his older brother as head of Farley Brothers, and he figured the way to do that was to operate the most profitable stores in the chain. His scheme had worked brilliantly for several years, until Walter became curious and decided to launch a personal investigation into the matter, hence the outside audit performed by Nathaniel Corrigan.

Oddly, no one seemed to question Tyler's presence, and no one asked who had placed him in the store.

Except Mason Reid, who tackled his son the moment the two of them got outside the building some time after four o'clock in the afternoon.

"Well, that was quite an eye-opener on an unusual aspect of fraud," Mason said. "So would you mind telling me who talked you into taking on this little job?"

Tyler laughed. He was free of auto parts for a while, and Berry could leave Farley Brothers now with a good conscience. His spirits shot skyward. Berry would be safe away from Felix and his crooked schemes.

"Sure, Dad," he said. "That would be Daniel Challoner's little sister, Beryl. She's the 'bimbo' currently in residence at my apartment. I'm going to marry her, by the way."

"That's Daniel Challoner's sister?" To give him credit, Mason's voice remained reasonably level. "What's going on here, Tyler?"

"To make a long story short, Berry thinks Daniel was murdered, so she concocted a scheme to get herself hired as Felix Farley's secretary so she could snoop through the company books for the secret that got Daniel killed. But she knew nothing about books or accounting, so she came to me."

"At least she had that much sense," Mason said in acerbic tones. "And she uncovered this fraud?"

"On her first day, she uncovered several good motives for murder." Tyler drew in a deep breath of relief. "According to her, the place was a hotbed of motives, including unrequited love, probable accounting fraud and nepotism. And she hasn't even managed to access the company books yet."

Mason stared at him. "Tyler, are you sure about this?"

"Yes, Dad, I am." Tyler knew his father spoke of his intent to marry Berry. "Believe me, she's nothing like the woman she tried to convince everyone she was the night you met her."

"I see." Mason stared at the sidewalk ahead. "So you're now convinced that Felix Farley's little fraud includes the murder of Daniel Challoner?"

Hearing the problem stated so bluntly brought back all the doubts Tyler had managed to squelch. "That's what's bothering me. I can't see either Farley or Warren as a murderer. If Daniel had discovered what they were up to, they'd have been more likely to offer him a bribe than kill him." He stopped in the middle of the sidewalk and took out his cell phone. "That's why I asked Peterson to look into an elderly relative of the Challoners who claimed to have a lot of money."

He scrolled down the list of text messages. "Berry says Felix went racing out this morning after a call from Corrigan. That was because I called Corrigan." He scrolled again. "Well, I'll be. She got into the bookkeeping system and she's printing out everything she can." He laughed, delighted. "That should be some fun for you and me."

A moment later, he found the text he'd been awaiting. "Peterson found the great-aunt. She's still alive, and sure enough, she's changed her will. Come on, Dad. We've got to get to Farley Brothers' offices before Berry gets off."

Mason appeared to realize they were walking down the street away from Farley Brothers, where he had left his car. "Where are you going, son?"

"I've been parking far enough away so that no one saw the Porsche, for all the good it did. Warren saw me this morning, but my education has progressed so well, I was able to spin a good lie about my sister and her boyfriend taking off for the Caribbean and leaving me to babysit the car." He led the way toward his Porsche. "You'd better ride with me. I don't like the looks of this at all."

"What are you talking about?" Mason complained. "Is there a murderer loose at Farley Brothers or not?"

"There's a murderer loose, all right," Tyler said grimly, "but I'm growing more and more convinced that the murderer is more likely to be interested in Berry than in fraud at Farley Brothers."

"What?"

"I think Berry was right. Whoever killed Daniel meant to kill him."

"But ... *why*?" Mason was clearly at sea. "You're saying someone else, someone outside of Farley Brothers, killed Daniel? For what reason?"

"It's one of the oldest motives for murder there is." Tyler punched the keypad to unlock the car doors. "The possibility of a big inheritance. Let's go, Dad. I don't want Berry left alone for a minute."

Mason looked as though he had taken a punch to the jaw, but he gamely got in the car and buckled on his seatbelt. "I think I'm beginning to see the attraction of this new life you're suddenly living. All this fraud and danger." He watched as his son spun the wheel and accelerated out of the parking lot with the tires squealing a protest. "It's really quite exhilarating, isn't it?"

CHAPTER 10

Berry dressed in one of her most eye-catching outfits, a short-skirted, tightly fitted red linen suit with long sleeves that would cover the bruises on her arms. She applied makeup liberally to the bruises on her legs and topped it with a pair of opaque pantyhose before leaving the apartment in the midst of a misty rain. Hopefully, by the time she arrived she would regain her enthusiasm for sneaking into the Farley Brothers computer files.

She arrived at Farley Brothers offices and had to give herself a pep talk. After all, if Felix tried to come on to her again, she could always quit. In the meantime, the longer she held him off, the more she could snoop through the bookkeeping files and make a few printouts. She settled behind her desk with a sweet smile directed at Concetta and another of equally sweet respect for Felix.

"Good morning, Miss MacGregor." Felix's knowing smile made her toes curl with intense dislike. "Would you bring your pad in, please? I have some instructions for you."

Berry knew this was a ploy. Felix used a digital recorder for instructions as well as dictation. He also played golf in the mornings. Why did it have to rain today of all days?

She sought desperately for an excuse and decided to go for indignation. *Mr. Farley, I am not that kind of girl!* That might last her until eleven, when Nathaniel Corrigan had scheduled an appointment with Felix. She fully expected Felix to find urgent business elsewhere shortly before eleven.

The telephone buzzed discretely. Berry lifted the receiver, praying for succor. "Mr. *Farley's* office."

"Nathanial Corrigan here. Is this Miss MacGregor?" The accountant sounded both pleased and excited. "I've just gotten a call from a fellow—don't know who he is, but he says he's an accountant and knows you—at the Westheimer number two store. He says he's found the reason for the discrepancies in the inventory counts. I'm going out there right now to check it out."

Berry stared blindly at her calendar note of Nathaniel Corrigan's eleven o'clock appointment. "Yes, Mr. Corrigan. What time shall I tell Mr. Farley to expect you?"

Corrigan gave a sarcastic laugh. "Tell him I'll get back to him."

"Oh, *dear.*" Berry's heart beat rapidly with excitement. She hung up the receiver and put on a distressed look before going to the door of Felix's office. "That was Mr. Corrigan. *He* says—" She had to stop and swallow, her mouth had gone so dry. "He says someone called him from the Westheimer number two store *claiming* to know the reason why there were *discrepancies* in the inventory figures. Mr. Corrigan is going there now to check it out. He says he'll get *back* to you."

"What?" Felix's ruddy complexion turned a peculiar, pasty shade. "He can't do that."

Berry fluttered, her hand at her throat. "Oh, Mr. *Farley.* What do you think he could *mean?*"

Felix uttered several words that didn't fit the expensive office decor. "Get Warren on the phone. Now." He slammed both hands, palms down, on his desk.

Berry obediently scurried back to her desk, tapped in the number and asked for Mr. Warren. She hardly knew whether to faint with gratitude or quiver with excitement.

"I'm sorry," a nervous-sounding male voice said. "Mr. Warren isn't available at the moment."

Nothing Berry said got Bernard Warren to the telephone, either then or the six other times both she and Felix tried.

She could hardly contain her excitement. Clearly, something big was up, but there wasn't a thing she could do except flutter helplessly every time Felix spoke. Felix marched between her desk and his, alternately cursing and yelling for Concetta, who had apparently gone to a meeting of the sales staff. He and Berry both tried to raise someone at Westheimer number two, and so long as Felix hovered nearby, she couldn't even shoot a text message to Tyler.

Felix was red with either fear or fury—Berry couldn't decide which. "I'm going out there myself, Miss MacGregor. Cancel all my appointments."

The moment Felix exited, Berry sent Tyler a concise text message detailing what had happened on her end. In spite of checking her phone every few minutes, Tyler didn't text her back, but then, if he was involved in whatever was happening at Westheimer number two, she couldn't expect to hear from him until things settled down.

Time crept by. Berry typed busily on an unimportant report and tried to keep her fingers off the telephone buttons. At intervals, she tried accessing the bookkeeping files, but they had been password protected. She tried various names and passwords, but nothing worked. She thought on ways of getting Concetta to part with a password and considered ransacking Felix's desk on her lunch hour for clues.

Concetta returned just before noon, so Berry flicked off her computer terminal at precisely eleven-fifty-nine and sauntered toward the door. Concetta disappeared into one of the sales offices, leaving the front desk empty. Berry slipped out, hoping to avoid her notice.

"Oh!" a woman exclaimed, the moment she stepped out the door. "Mary! What luck. I was so hoping I'd run into you. How about lunch?"

Berry turned, startled. Cammy Osborne, the secretary from the legal office down the hall, approached. She was a rabbity-looking young woman with white-blond hair and pale blue eyes. Berry thought it unlikely Daniel would have given her the time of day, but who knew? She owed it to herself to find out as soon as possible what the woman knew.

"Hi, Cammy. I can't go to lunch today, but thank you." She intended to spend the entire hour hoping to hear from Tyler. "I'm meeting someone." She hoped her voice implied she was meeting a lover.

"Then let's have a drink together after work. What about it? I've got to tell you something really important as soon as possible." Cammy leaned forward, her pale face twitching and secretive. "I'm afraid someone's going to ask questions soon. I'd like to get your opinion about what I should do." She looked portentous. "After all, we're both outsiders."

"Of course." Berry glanced around swiftly and wondered why Cammy Osborne thought she was an outsider. "Where would you like me to meet you?"

"How about right here? Then we can walk there together. There's a bar only half a block away."

"Fine. See you here at five."

Berry dodged around a corner and left Cammy Osborne behind with a gasp of relief. Something about the woman's fixed rabbit-like stare and nervous twitching made her uncomfortable.

She ate a bowl of soup and a few crackers at the first floor delicatessen and tried phoning Tyler. He remained unavailable.

Big things were up, and Tyler was in on them. She could hardly wait to get off work to find out what he'd discovered. In the meantime, she really, really needed to access those bookkeeping files.

She returned to her desk early in hopes of searching Felix's office for his password, but Concetta remained in her office with the door open, so that was out. Berry looked up the number for Wilburn and White, the law firm Cammy Osborne worked for. The more she thought about it, the less she wanted to waste time after work meeting Cammy.

"What name did you say?" the ultra-refined voice of the Wilburn and White receptionist asked.

"Cammy Osborne," Berry repeated.

"I am so sorry," the woman intoned. "There is no one here by that name."

"Maybe she's new," Berry suggested. This was weird. If Cammy claimed to know Daniel, that meant she had to have worked at Wilburn and White for longer than six months.

"I can assure you," the woman said frigidly, "that we do not employ so many people, we have lost one of them. Obviously, you have the wrong number." She hung up in Berry's ear.

Berry replaced the receiver. Something was going on, all right. She just wished she knew what it was and who was involved.

She flicked on her computer screen and accessed the bookkeeping files since she seemed to be alone for the time being. Concetta ran back and forth among the salespeople's offices. Now was as good a time as any to do some snooping.

Enter your name: the screen said, when she sought to enter the bookkeeping program.

Berry typed in Felix Farley's name.

Enter your password: the screen responded.

Berry thought a moment, and inside her mind she heard the word *Topdog*.

That would be about right for Felix. She entered *Topdog*.

The veil metaphorically parted. To her total amazement, the program accepted her login. She had tricked it into thinking she was Felix Farley.

She sat there a moment in blank disbelief. Then she frantically began searching the screen for clues to financial data. This was not a time to pat herself on the back for her brilliant hacker qualities. She printed out page after page of anything she could call up, starting with pages and pages of inventory figures.

Other than the inventory, Berry had no idea what was important data and what wasn't. She printed out twenty pages of journal entries, several financial statements, and a few balance sheets. She just hoped Tyler and Corrigan could get something out of it.

She printed out everything she could get to and slipped the papers, group by group, into the thin, leather briefcase she had prudently been carrying to work in hopes of this opportunity.

She called up Accounts Payable and hit the print key. She was not meeting Cammy Osborne after work. She was taking these papers straight home to Tyler.

"And just what do you think you're doing?" Concetta demanded.

Berry jumped and nearly knocked over Daniel's paperweight. "*Mercy*! You startled me." She reached for Mary MacGregor's personality. "I'm searching for some *facts* Mr. Farley asked me to find. *Unfortunately*, I'm not really sure what I'm searching for, so I'm printing out *everything* for him."

Concetta came closer. Her brown eyes narrowed with suspicion. "Those are journal entries from the bookkeeping files." A distinctly ugly look twisted her face. She reached for the set of papers Berry hadn't yet transferred to her briefcase. "These are Mr. Farley's private files. Who are you really? Did Walter hire you to spy on his brother?"

Berry put her hand at her throat—where her heart had taken up residence—and looked shocked. "*Walter*? Are you saying Mr. Walter *Farley*?"

"Don't play innocent with me. You're up to something. I knew it the day I met you. You're no secretary. You're a spy. Who are you really working for?"

"A *spy*?" Berry let her jaw drop artistically. "*Me*?"

"Yes, *you*," Concetta mimicked her. She sorted through the papers in her hands. "These are the Accounts Payable entries for June. Just what are you up to?"

Berry decided to go for broke. "I'm 'up to' doing my *job* as Mr. *Farley* requested of me." She stood and snatched the papers out of

Concetta's hands. Several tore in half because Concetta refused to let go. "Now look what you've done. Mr. Farley is *not* going to be pleased."

"I'll say he's not," Concetta sneered. "How'd you manage to get into his private bookkeeping files in the first place? Who's your contact?"

"I don't have a *contact*. Mr. Farley gave me his own password. Check with *him* if you don't believe *me*." She put so much vehemence in her voice, Concetta paused and glared at her.

"You'd better believe I will." Concetta marched toward Felix's office.

"He's at the Westheimer number two store," Berry said sweetly. Concetta reappeared. "Mr. *Corrigan* called this morning and said he was going there because someone had discovered why there were big discrepancies in the *inventory* counts."

Concetta's tawny skin whitened. Her brown eyes went wide with shock. "He *what!*"

"Mr. *Farley* said *exactly* the same thing," Berry said with considerable enjoyment. "He left this morning, and I haven't heard a *word* from him since."

"This morning," Concetta said, almost whispering. "Oh, my God!" She rushed away.

Berry gritted her teeth and swiftly ran through the accounts payable screens again, printing new copies of the entire file. When it was done, she put the torn stack on conspicuous display in the center of her desk and slipped the new set into her briefcase.

She was probably going to be fired as soon as Felix and Concetta returned. She needed to get out with every piece of hard data she could. And if Tyler had what he needed, she just might not go back. Things were getting a bit too hot for Miss Mary MacGregor.

She checked her watch against the computer screen. Shortly before five, she would walk out with her briefcase full of data she hoped would help Tyler prove Daniel's death was the result of his uncovering company fraud.

Now that she had Felix's password and was probably about to be fired, she cruised through every program she could get into. The password worked on the company personnel files, much to her delight. Daniel's file was still intact. She printed it out. Maybe the killer had entered something that would turn out to be a clue.

At ten minutes before five, neither Felix nor Concetta had returned. Berry decided to take a chance. Since she couldn't reach Cammy Osborne, whoever she really was, by phone, she'd leave early and avoid the woman.

She picked up her stuffed briefcase and walked to the door. No one was interested in her. In fact, without Concetta at her post on the front desk, most of the salespeople had already left.

Outside the door, Berry sighed and leaned against the wall, then rubbed her aching forehead. Lack of sleep, she supposed, along with taking a tumble down a long flight of concrete steps really took it out of a woman.

But she had succeeded. Now Tyler would use her data to find out what Daniel had discovered that got him killed. She pushed herself upright and tried to conjure up the sense of triumph she'd expected to feel when this moment arrived.

"Miss MacGregor! Wait, please. See there, Kel? I told you she was the type to make it out the door ten minutes early. I'd like a word with you, Miss MacGregor."

Berry turned so swiftly, she almost toppled over on her high red heels. Debra Reid hared down the hall toward her, giving her usual appearance of elegant disarray, and with Kelley Reid, trim in jeans and a sweater, at her heels.

"Sorry," Berry said in her sweetest tones. If she didn't get out fast, Cammy Osborne might show up. "My *lover* is expecting me. Gotta fly."

"If you mean Tyler," Debra said, "you ought to be ashamed of yourself. In spite of what you may think, he isn't rich."

Berry observed the stunned and slightly envious way Debra eyed her red linen suit. It was an eye-catcher, all right, and worth every penny she had paid for it.

"He *isn't?*" Berry mimed surprise and tried to find a way to get past the sisters. "Why, he told me he had an *inheritance*. A *big* one. Do you mean to tell me he was *lying* to me?"

"Give it up, Deb," Kelley muttered. "While you still can." To Berry, she said, "That's the hottest-looking outfit I've ever seen. Where'd you find it, if you don't mind my asking?"

"She isn't getting out of this little talk," Debra said. She sounded like a woman speaking through gritted teeth. "Now, see here, Miss MacGregor—"

"*Do* call me Mary," Berry said sweetly. "I feel so *sisterly* toward you."

Debra, temporarily speechless, looked nauseous.

"Take that," Kelley said, clearly amused.

Berry cast Kelley a suspicious glance.

"Mary! Oh, Mary!" Cammy Osborne trotted down the hall at a rapid pace. Dismayed, Berry noted absently that although Cammy came from the direction of Wilburn and White, she hadn't come from the Wilburn and White office. "Are you ready? You haven't made other plans, have you?"

Saved, Berry thought. She'd leave the building with Cammy then find an excuse to avoid having a drink. "Not at *all*, dear. I'm just coming. Good day, Miss Reid. Sorry to run, but you understand how it is when one is so *popular*."

"Miss MacGregor! Wait, please." Celia Reid approached from the Wilburn and White direction. "I'd like to speak to you, if I may."

"Mom, what are you doing here?" Debra stepped around the corner and into her mother's view.

Celia Reid looked from Berry to her daughters, clearly shocked. "I came to speak to Miss MacGregor. What are the two of you doing here?"

"Looks like we all came to speak to Miss MacGregor. As she said, she's a very popular person," Kelley said.

"Sorry to disappoint all of you," Berry struck in, "but I *promised* to meet my friend for a cocktail after work, and that is what I'm going to do. Now, if you'll *excuse* me—"

"You aren't going anywhere." Debra blocked her. "You're going to listen to us. You don't want Tyler. You just want to use him. Promise us you'll give him up, and we'll leave you alone."

"What makes you think I don't want Tyler?" Berry tossed her head back. "He's a *very* handsome man, in case you haven't noticed. And so *rich*," she added, recalling abruptly that she was still Mary MacGregor as far as the Reids were concerned. "And I think you're lying to me about his fortune. I'm going to ask *him*."

"He is not rich!" Debra snapped.

Cammy Osborne fidgeted. She glanced from Debra to Celia and looked more than ever like a rabbit facing the barrel of a hunter's rifle. "Let's get out of here, Mary. Who are these people?"

"What the hell is going on here?" a new voice demanded.

It needed only this, Berry thought. Tyler approached from the other end of the hall, with his father beside him. She observed with a sinking heart that his frown was absolutely ferocious.

She smothered a groan. Tyler was not going to thank her for wreaking havoc in his immediate family. She had no doubt that Mason Reid had gone to tackle Tyler while his wife saw to her. Of all people, she should have realized the value of family ties.

She searched her mind frantically for something to say that would defuse the situation before Tyler reached them. She came up with nothing.

She should have taken the Reids into her confidence. Now it was too late. Tyler had a full-fledged scene on his hands, and he was not pleased about it at all. From the way he looked at her, he didn't find her sexy red suit much to his taste.

He still wore the cheap clip-on tie and short-sleeved, white cotton shirt he wore that morning. Judging from the expressions on his family's collective faces, they noted his departure from his usual sartorial elegance and were drawing their own horrible conclusions.

"Would someone mind explaining to me exactly what is going on here?" Tyler said upon reaching the small group. "Is this some sort of family meeting I wasn't invited to? Should I go away?"

He knew very well what was up, Berry realized, and he had decided to play it for all it was worth.

"What's wrong with wanting to stop you from making the mistake of your life?" Debra said. "Whether you know it or not, we care too much about you to let you throw yourself away on this—this—"

"Careful, Deb." Tyler sounded amused behind his stern demeanor. "You're about to heap aspersions on my tastes."

"What *is* all this? A family pow-wow?" Cammy Osborne looked both annoyed and nervous as she stood beside Berry and fidgeted with her purse. "Let's get out of here, Mary. It's got nothing to do with us."

"Good idea," Berry said.

"Hold it right there, Mary." Tyler snagged her arm and dragged her against him. "Mary and I are getting married, you'll be happy to know. She's agreed to let the two of you be bridesmaids." He scowled at his sisters. "Although that may change if Deb keeps shooting off at the mouth."

Berry suppressed a gasp. Now Tyler was going too far in teasing his family. She shot him a warning glare and poked him in the ribs with her elbow for good measure.

Cammy Osborne took a cell phone from her purse and looked at it. Sweat had broken out on her upper lip. Berry thought she looked like a rabbit in a fit.

"Look, Mary, I have to be someplace in half an hour," she said in a high, breathless voice. "Let's go, or we won't have time to talk."

Berry tried signaling Tyler with her eyes. "Tyler, I'll meet you later. Okay, honey?"

"Sorry, sweetie," Tyler said. "We're going to straighten this out right now." He studied Cammy, clearly unimpressed with her. "I'm sorry, but my fiancée and I have a few things to settle. She'll have to take a rain check."

"Tyler, maybe it would be better if I left," Berry whispered.

She wished she'd been able to consult Tyler about the fact that Cammy Osborne had lied about working at Wilburn and White.

"Mary promised to meet me here after work," Cammy said on a furious gasp. Her pale eyes glared at Tyler. "You have no right to interfere."

Tyler's suspicious gaze focused on Cammy. Cammy fidgeted with her purse and backed away.

"Is that right?" Tyler asked.

Cammy Osborne's hand suddenly appeared from inside her purse. She pointed a black revolver at Tyler's chest.

"Get back." The gun shook in her hand. She was visibly falling apart. "You. Beryl Challoner. Come with me." Her voice had gone peculiarly flat.

Berry stood rooted where she was. "You know who I am."

"Damned right, I know who you are. Come with me. Now."

"I knew this was a bad idea," Kelley whispered.

"Beryl Challoner?" Celia whispered. "Daniel's sister?"

Debra made a peculiar choking sound. "Daniel's *sister*?"

"She isn't going anywhere with you. Would your name happen to be Mary MacGregor Campbell, by any chance?" Tyler held Berry behind him.

"Looks like you were right, Tyler." Mason Reid stepped forward. "It wasn't about fraud at Farley Brothers at all."

"That's right, Dad. Daniel was killed for the oldest reason in the world. Money, in the form of a big inheritance." He tightened his grip on Berry. "In the meantime, why don't you get Mom and the girls away from here before someone gets hurt."

Berry felt as if the floor had just vanished from beneath her feet. "Mary Campbell? That's my cousin, the one named after—" The briefcase fell from her numb fingers. "*You* killed Daniel?"

She jerked against Tyler's hold, but he snagged an arm around her waist and held her behind him.

"Come with me, Beryl," Cammy rasped. "I can tell you what you want to know. I didn't kill him, but I can tell you who did. Come with me, and I'll tell you all about it."

Cammy's pale blue eyes darted from Tyler to Mason, then back to Berry. The gun shook in her grasp, but the desperation on her thin rabbit's face kept both men at bay. Cammy might shoot accidently, judging from her white-knuckled grip on the revolver.

From the corner of her gaze, Berry saw Kelley edge behind her sister and tap something into her cell phone with one finger.

"Forget it," Tyler snapped. "She's not going anywhere with you, and if you didn't kill Daniel, then you helped in some way. Did your husband put you up to this? It seems pretty clear that he married you because you were supposed to inherit your great-aunt's money, but old Aunt Mary was too clever for him, wasn't she?"

"Shut up!" Cammy screamed. "You don't know anything about it! Beryl, come with me, or I'll kill them all. Now!"

"You have five bullets and there are six of us," Mason said. "Spread out, everyone."

"You succeeded even better than you planned, Berry." Tyler kept a ruthless grip on her, as if he sensed she wanted badly to jump Cammy. "It seems your great-aunt Mary has made a few major changes in her will. She left everything to you, and that's why they had to kill Daniel. If you died, everything would have gone to him, and that would have foiled all their plans. You were next, but you foiled them by leaving Austin and moving in with me. By the time they managed to catch up to you, you were rarely alone."

Cammy snarled. She looked absolutely wild. "Come, Beryl. Or I'll kill you where you stand."

"Why do you have to kill her?" Tyler asked reasonably. "Even if she dies, your great-aunt has specified that you are not to inherit one penny of her holdings. Your best bet is to leave now, while you still have a chance to escape."

Berry had forgotten she had left work about ten minutes early, and that only a few minutes had passed. She thought she'd passed through hours of tension. In another few minutes, the halls would fill with people heading home.

"No!" Cammy clenched her teeth, shaking all over. Berry thought suddenly she looked like a drug addict in desperate need of a fix. "I can't leave without Beryl Challoner. If I have to kill you to get her, I will."

"Go ahead," Tyler invited. "Because that's the only way you're going to get her."

"You bastard." Cammy raised the pistol, gripping it with both hands.

In that instant, Berry realized Cammy was really going to do it. She was going to shoot Tyler, then shoot her.

She couldn't lose Tyler. She'd lost both her parents. She had lost Daniel. Everyone she loved had died. She had only one chance to put a stop to the killing here and now.

She twisted out of Tyler's grip and swung herself in front of him as the gun fired and the sound filled the hall. She saw the gun buck violently in Cammy's hand, then felt a giant fist slam into her shoulder. She staggered against Tyler.

At the same time, both Mason and Debra moved. Debra flung her purse into Cammy's face, and Mason grabbed Cammy's gun hand when the purse distracted her. Up and down both hallways, doors opened and people poured out.

Berry was dimly aware of slamming doors, shouts, and Tyler's voice calling her name. Since she was not a fainter, she refused to give into the rising dark pillow of unconsciousness.

But she did feel faintly surprised to realize she was still alive and sitting on the floor. She was so numb, she couldn't feel her body, or orient herself in space, or tell what was holding her up.

You idiot, a familiar voice said fondly.

"Same to you, Daniel Challoner," she said.

Then she recollected she might well be a jinx. It was all her fault Daniel had died in the first place. Or something like that. She considered it with a mind that slowly sank into blackness.

"Berry? Berry, answer me," Tyler said sharply. "Oh, God, she's going to bleed to death. Someone call an ambulance."

Mason hovered over them, breathing hard. "She got away. Just let go of the gun and ran. Don't touch that gun! Leave it for the police to handle."

Tyler knelt on the floor, cradling Berry in his arms. Her eyes were open, but she took no notice of anything going on around her.

"Berry, wake up. Talk to me." He shook her slightly.

"This is all your fault, Daniel Challoner," she whispered. She saw and heard nothing except the other world she gazed into.

"Don't shake her, Tyler," Celia said. "You'll make the bleeding worse. Here. Let her lie on the floor. Give me that tie. We'll use it to stop the bleeding."

Berry's lashes fluttered as she struggled against unconsciousness. A face, familiar and beloved, but the focus of much current annoyance, formed before her vision.

"Daniel?"

"I never thought you were this eager to join me." Daniel's smile reflected love and peace; unlike anything she had ever seen before, and certainly not from Daniel.

"After all I've been through on your behalf, it's high time you showed some interest," she said.

"As usual, you aren't making any sense." Daniel shook his head. "Since you're here, follow me. I've got a few things to tell you."

CHAPTER 11

"Well, Razz," Daniel said in the superior tones Berry had hated as a child—and still did. "I see you're trying to join me before your time."

"Bug off, Daniel." Daniel looked handsomer than ever, though he looked a little peculiar wearing a white robe that reached to his feet. She decided not to mention it. "I have no intention of joining you. I love you, even if all we ever do is fight. But I don't mind visiting a while, provided I can leave when I'm ready."

Daniel laughed. "Believe it or not, I love you too, Razz. Would a brother who didn't love you go through everything I've gone through these past six months just to keep you alive?"

Berry wondered briefly how it was that she was talking to Daniel when Daniel was supposed to be dead. He wasn't dead at all. Anyone could see that. She puzzled over it a moment, then dismissed the thought. She'd worry about it later.

Daniel grinned as if he'd heard her thoughts. "The only thing I've lost is my physical body—and my ability to communicate with you. One thing you still know how to do is give a fellow hell. How do you think I felt when the creep who shot me started putting the moves on you?"

"Tyler? Don't be disgusting."

"Not Tyler, idiot. Grady Craig. I sent you to Tyler for help. If you'd stayed another day in Austin, Craig would have found a way to stage a 'suicide' on your part. He was working mighty hard at catching you alone."

Berry shrugged. She remembered a peculiar sense of urgency to leave Austin, but she hadn't been aware of Grady Craig. So far as she had known, Grady's urge for revenge had faded. Daniel was probably exaggerating. As usual.

"You have a way of shutting out things you don't want to see, especially when you're concentrating on one of your projects." Daniel smiled again. "You might thank me, you know. Look how things worked out. I've finally gotten you fixed up with the right man."

"My memory of events is a tad different from yours." Berry regarded him irritably.

Daniel's smile spoke for him. Berry thought longingly about punching him.

"I'm sorry I was never there for you after Dad died," Daniel said. "At the time, it never occurred to me how lonely and insecure you were, or how much you needed a family."

"Don't be silly. I'm an adult, after all." Berry hastened to change the subject. "Do you think Tyler will find any clues in those printouts I got today?"

"Boy, are you still hardheaded," Daniel said. "Didn't you hear me?" He studied her a moment. "No, I suppose you didn't. I spent so little time listening to you, you now see no reason to listen to me. Believe me, I've had my punishment. To care so much, and to be so powerless to reach you ... " Daniel shook his handsome head, still smiling. His blue eyes crinkled at the corners. "I've spent the last six months trying to make up for my failings as a big brother. As a nice token of gratitude, you might think about naming your first kid after me."

"I'm not planning on having children any time soon." One thing she didn't need was advice from Daniel about her love life. It was none of his business.

"You will have a baby very soon," Daniel said. "Think about the name, will you?"

"Oh, all right," Berry said. Daniel was like that. He'd harp away on something forever, until she finally gave in. "If it's a girl, I'll name her Danielle."

"Get over yourself, Razz. Tyler wants to marry you," Daniel said. "He's crazy about you. Ever since he saw you in that pink getup at graduation, I think."

Berry ignored this. What did Daniel know?

It struck her suddenly that discussing Daniel's murder with Daniel was a peculiar thing to do. "Look, why don't we go have a bite to eat and talk things over," she suggested. "I've been wanting to ask you about going back to school and majoring in accounting. What do you think? I didn't know accountants knew so much about fraud and skullduggery. I could really get into that."

Daniel chuckled ruefully. "You're the most hard-headed person I've ever met. Your trouble is you're still looking for a family. Now that you've found one, you've got cold feet." He backed away slowly. "It's time for me to go. It's time I got on with my real work."

"On second thought, maybe I'll just go with my original plan and teach earth science." Berry frowned and struggled to think. "What work? I thought you just got this job. Where are you working now?"

"I have a very good job," Daniel said, grinning. "I'm responsible for greeting and helping to orient new arrivals. Goodbye, Razz. And remember, I loved you a lot more than you—or I—ever realized."

Berry grew even more annoyed. "Hold on a minute, Daniel. Where do you think you're going? I'm a new arrival. How about giving me a little orientation?" She stared around and saw only gray fog. "Otherwise, I'm totally lost in this place."

"Actually, you're only making a brief visit." Daniel took another few steps back. His lower body began to fade from view. "See you, Razz. But it won't be anytime soon."

Berry found herself alone in surroundings that had grown so dark, she could no longer see where she was.

She stared frantically in all directions. "Daniel!" she yelled into the thick blackness. "Daniel Challoner, you come back here this minute!"

"Calm down, Tyler," Celia Reid said. "She's waking up at last."

"Where's that nurse?" Mason Reid demanded. "Debra, go get the nurse."

"Quiet, all of you," Celia said. "She mustn't have a lot of noise and confusion. She won't know where she is, or what's happened to her."

That was for sure, Berry thought. What was more, she wasn't sure she wanted to know. Perhaps she'd keep her eyes closed a while longer.

"She's probably going to take one look at Tyler and go unconscious again," Kelley said dryly. "You should have made him go home and do something about himself, Mom. He's still covered with blood."

"Open your eyes, Berry," Tyler commanded softly. "Come on, darling. Wake up."

Berry liked the voice calling her. It was deep and compelling. She wanted to see who owned that voice.

"She's too pale," Tyler said. "Call that doctor back and ask him why she isn't waking up yet."

"Calm down, Tyler," Celia ordered. "She's pale because she's been asleep and she lost a lot of blood. But the doctor says she'll bounce back quickly."

"A few good steak dinners will bring her color back in no time," Mason said. "Celia, we'd better get Tyler's old bedroom ready for her. He won't be able to look after her during the day."

"She's staying where she is." Tyler sounded as if he spoke through his teeth. "Berry, please wake up, darling."

On that, she struggled really hard and managed at last to lift her lashes. At first, she couldn't see anything but bright lights then the hovering blobs of color resolved into people.

"She looks so different without those violet contacts," Debra murmured. "I can't get over it."

Someone leaned over her and Berry stared into Tyler's face. The broad, slashing brows and brilliant, turquoise eyes looked familiar. He looked both coldly angry and desperately anxious. Since he couldn't be anxious about her, he must be mad at her.

Detached, she wondered what she had done.

"Berry," he said tenderly. "How do you feel, darling?"

Berry frowned slightly, unsure how to answer this. She didn't feel anything at all at the moment. She liked it that way.

She sensed movement overhead and looked up. Several unfamiliar faces hovered over her.

"She does look a little like Daniel," Kelley said.

Berry thought this over. She didn't want to look like Daniel. She was thoroughly miffed with Daniel, although she couldn't remember exactly why.

"Berry?" Tyler touched her chin and turned her face toward him. "Talk to me. Tell me how you're feeling."

Her voice felt rusty. "I feel fine. I think."

When she spoke, tension seemed to flow out of him. He relaxed visibly then his brows drew together once more. "Thank God. How could you have done such a thing? I ought to—"

"Leave her alone, Tyler Reid," Debra said. "You're so buried in bottom lines, you can't see the nose on your face."

Tyler ignored Debra. "You almost got yourself killed."

Berry blinked. "Daniel said something about how he felt when the guy who shot him started putting the moves on me ... " Memory returned in a rush that made her squeeze her eyes closed. "I don't think I understand anything anymore. That Cammy person. They said they didn't know her at Wilburn and White. She kept implying that she knew something she needed to tell me."

She suspected this whole mess had something to do with Great-aunt Mary MacGregor. She couldn't think about it now, or she'd burst into tears in front of all these people.

Tyler shifted. He sat on the edge of her bed, and now he moved to take her face between his two palms. "You spoke to Daniel?"

"He said he has a new job—" She broke off, realizing suddenly that she must sound nuts, since Daniel was officially dead. She focused dizzily on Tyler. His white shirt was wrinkled and covered with large, brown stains, and he could have used a shave. "Tyler, where am I? What happened to Cammy Osborne?"

Tyler traced his finger tenderly around her mouth. "She got away in the confusion. But she dropped the gun, and the police have identified her from the prints on it. Her real name, by the way, is Mary MacGregor Campbell."

Berry closed her eyes again. "That's Daddy's cousin's daughter. You were right, Tyler. It goes back to Great-aunt Mary. She must have rewritten her will."

"She did. I had a private detective check into it." Tyler frowned heavily. "Apparently, Cammy was a drug addict and kept trying to borrow money from your great-aunt. When Cammy broke into her house and tried to steal and sell some old coins and antiques, your great-aunt called her lawyer and rewrote her will."

Berry opened her eyes. "She left everything to Daniel?"

"That's right, and if Daniel were to die before your great-aunt, everything would come to you. That's why Daniel was killed, you see, so everything would come to you."

Berry stared up at him, noting his frown. "I don't understand."

"Can't we talk about this later?" Tyler asked. "Nothing is going to make much sense to you until you've had a chance to recover."

He didn't want to tell her the truth. That much Berry divined at once.

"I have to know," she said. "No matter how bad it is I need to know, Tyler."

"Grady Craig," Tyler said gently. "That's why he worked so hard at getting you to marry him. Then when you broke the engagement and set the cops on him, he decided to get revenge and achieve his goal in another way."

This made no sense. Berry pondered this in silence a moment.

"What was his goal?" Berry asked, at last. "What's he got to do with this?"

Actually, the relief almost overwhelmed her. Grady Craig had nothing to do with Great-aunt Mary, so whatever his goal might have been, it had nothing to do with Daniel's death.

"Grady Craig was a junior lawyer in the law firm that handled your great-aunt's affairs," Tyler said. "That is, he was before he was fired for dipping into clients' trust funds to support his gambling habit. His real name, by the way, is Craig Robinson. That's why the police couldn't find a Grady Craig when you filed those assault charges on him."

"Tyler, she isn't in any shape to understand all that," Celia said softly. "Maybe you'd better save it for later, after she's more cognizant."

Berry supposed something was wrong with her. Although she wanted badly to know why Daniel was killed, she found it difficult to think. And if his death had anything to do with her, or with Great-aunt Mary, she wasn't so sure she wanted to know.

But something had happened at Farley Brothers. Something about fraud in the inventory counts at the stores under Felix's management. So maybe Daniel really was killed because of something he'd learned in regard to his job.

"I need to know," she said doggedly. "I came all this way and went through all this to find out why Daniel died." She fixed her gaze on Tyler's nose. "I just need to know one thing, Tyler. Did Daniel die because of Great-aunt Mary's will, or because of whatever was going on at Farley Brothers?"

Tyler scowled ferociously. "As usual, you get right to the heart of the matter, Challoner. The bottom line is Craig killed Daniel so that under the terms of your great-aunt's will, all her money would go to you. Craig intended to marry you and stay married to you until you inherited your great-aunt's fortune. Once the money was yours, he probably intended to kill you, too."

Berry's head whirled in an effort to follow this. "Then he must have believed in the myth of Great-aunt Mary's money."

"As it happens, your great-aunt really is rich, sweetheart. She's got something like five or six million, most of it tied up in real estate and government bonds. The law firm he worked for would have been in a position to know that."

"I see." Berry wondered if she'd been stabbed in the heart. She moved her hand to cover her chest protectively. "Then Daniel died because of me."

"No, darling, Daniel did not die because of you," Tyler said, enunciating clearly. "Daniel died because of Craig Robinson's greed. Don't think for one minute that you had anything to do with Daniel's death. Berry, listen to me. None of this was your fault."

Berry said nothing. Her hand clutched the covers in the vicinity of her heart, and she closed her eyes. Why hadn't she joined Daniel when she had the chance? Then she wouldn't have to worry that someone was going to kill Tyler to get to her, with or without Great-aunt Mary's alleged money.

But Tyler had said Great-aunt Mary really did have money. The very idea blew her mind.

She felt his large, warm hands frame her face.

"Berry, listen to me," he insisted. "It wasn't your fault. Craig Robinson planned this. Do you understand me? He planned to kill Daniel, and he planned to kill you. But you were too smart to fall for his line."

Berry kept her eyes closed. It was her fault. Anyone could see that. Why hadn't she died? She'd much rather that than lose everyone she loved.

"It wasn't your fault," he repeated. "You threw a monkey wrench into his big plans. When he couldn't marry you, he married Cammy Osborne instead, and they both tried to kill you. If you and Daniel are both dead at the time of your great-aunt's death, then Cammy inherits by default as the only remaining relative. He planned this, Berry. You were supposed to die, too. He's been tracking you. That black car that shot at us the other night was the same car I kept seeing around my apartment. You are not responsible for anything."

"It was my fault," she whispered. "I shouldn't have come here."

"How could it possibly be your fault?" Kelley Reid burst out. "It's this Grady Craig or Craig Robinson who's the villain here."

"The man's a killer without conscience," Mason Reid growled. "A cold-blooded murderer. He's a menace to society."

Berry covered her face with her right hand.

"Daniel's death wasn't your fault," Tyler repeated sternly. "This is Grady Craig's fault, and don't you forget it. Do you hear me, Berry Challoner? He wanted your great-aunt's money, and he was willing to kill your entire family to get it."

A loud, melodious beeping began.

Berry ignored it, lost in her own misery. Everything had gone wrong. She'd wasted Daniel's insurance money on an investigation that actually had nothing to do with his death, and she'd alienated Tyler's family. To top everything off, she'd fallen in love with Tyler and had almost gotten him killed. She was a jinx, that was all. Everyone around her either died or got killed.

"Berry, dear, stretch out your arm." Celia gently pried Berry's hand from her face. "You've twisted your IV line."

Berry submitted to having her arm stretched out on the bed beside her. The beeping stopped.

"Now, dear, don't cry," Celia said briskly. She brushed Berry's curls back from her forehead. "As Tyler says, none of this was your fault. Things will be a lot clearer tomorrow, when the anesthesia has worn off and you've had some rest. Say good night, everyone. This young woman has talked all she's going to tonight."

Berry wished the roof would fall on her. She didn't deserve for everyone to be so nice to her when she'd almost gotten Tyler killed.

Tyler bent over her. "I gave all those printouts of yours to Nathaniel Corrigan." He bent close and smiled into her eyes. "He actually drove all the way over here to get them, chortling like a fiend. It seems you managed to crack into Felix's private version of the accounting files—before they're doctored and released to the company accountants."

"Topdog," Berry whispered.

"Exactly." He touched her face tenderly with his fingertips. "Felix wanted to entice the stockholders into voting him in as president. It's giving Corrigan great pleasure to lower the boom on Felix. Walter Farley had hired him especially to investigate the goings-on in the accounts at the Westheimer number two store."

Berry's lips curved into a small smile. "Then there really was something illegal going on?"

"Your instincts were right on target." Tyler stroked his finger carefully over her cheek. "It was a highly specialized fraud designed to make Felix's stores outperform the others. He was fencing stolen auto parts through the Westheimer number two store and putting the profits back into the business. Corrigan suspected something of the sort when the inventory counts didn't jibe. Then I happened to be there when the mag wheels off Daniel's Mustang entered the stock room."

Berry's eyes went wide. "What? Do you mean they're the ones who stole my wheels?"

"Not precisely, but they sure would have been glad to sell them back to you," Tyler said, grinning. "Bernard Warren and Felix Farley were running a fencing operation. They bought stolen parts from professional thieves and resold them through an established business with a good reputation."

Berry took a deep breath. "I knew something bad was going on at that place. Thank you, Tyler. If you hadn't been clever enough to get that job, we might never have known what it was." She tried to reach up and hug him, but a searing pain shot through her shoulder. She fell back, gasping. What was wrong with her? "You're a real hero."

"*He's* a hero," Kelley exclaimed. "What about you?"

"I didn't do much." Berry inched her right hand up carefully to test her left shoulder. "After everything I went through to get into that office, I never did find any real clues, not counting all the personal melodrama. It was all due to Tyler actually getting into Felix's store that we solved the mystery."

"You didn't do a thing," Debra agreed, leaning into Berry's vision. "You just saved Tyler's life, that's all."

Berry winced. Debra thought she was a gold-digger, so why was she being so sweet? "I didn't save Tyler's life."

"Leave her alone, Deb," Tyler commanded. "She probably doesn't remember much about what happened today."

Berry thought back. "I was coming out of the office with my printouts and hoping to avoid Cammy Osborne ... Tyler, did she shoot me?"

"You have a hole in your left shoulder," Tyler said tersely. "You've been in surgery to remove the bullet. You lost a lot of blood, but you're going to be fine. Do you hurt anywhere?"

"They must have given me a lot of painkillers, because I don't feel a thing." That was true. Her body felt numb, unless she moved. It was her heart that ached. She touched the bandage on her left shoulder gingerly.

"We thought you never would wake up," Kelley said. "Poor Tyler was going crazy, what with pacing the floor and talking to the police and all. What a night. But it was worth it to find out Tyler's got himself a real woman at last."

Berry looked blankly at Kelley and wondered what she was talking about.

"When you jumped in front of him, we knew you loved him, so that made everything all right," Debra said. "But you don't seem to realize that it isn't Tyler who's a hero. You are. You saved Tyler's life."

Berry thought dully that no one understood. If Tyler had died, she might as well have been dead, too. She studied Debra curiously. Every hair was in place, but Debra gave the impression she'd been standing in a stiff wind.

"You saved his life," Debra repeated slowly, "and we love you for it."

"I had to," Berry said slowly. "Everyone I loved is dead because of me. I couldn't let Tyler die just because I love him."

"Oh, gosh," Kelley said. "She really believes that."

"That's ridiculous, young lady," Mason Reid said. He stood at the foot of Berry's bed and looked sternly at her. "No one died because of you. And no one's going to. You're going to marry my son and live happily ever after. I refuse to worry any longer that one of those silly women he's been dating is going to trap him into marriage."

Berry regarded him in wondering silence.

Mason stared back. "I don't want to hear another word on the subject."

"Now, Dad, you can't intimidate Berry that way," Tyler said. "You're talking to the woman who dumped a full plate of spaghetti over Daniel Challoner's head and ran him out of the house."

To Berry's dismay, the Reid sisters regarded her with enormous respect.

"You don't deserve her, Tyler Reid," Debra said.

"I know I don't," Tyler said, "but all the same, I'm going to have her."

Berry pondered this with a brain that had trouble taking in the simplest of concepts and decided she had no idea what they were discussing.

"You can't keep her here in Houston right now," Mason said, fixing Tyler with a ferocious frown. "Not with that Robinson psychopath running around."

"You're right, Dad." He leaned over the bed and said gently, "Berry?" When she looked up at him, he said, "How would you like to go to Grand Cayman?"

She thought it over carefully with a brain that grew more sluggish by the moment. "Grand Cayman? Isn't that an island?"

Tyler smiled. "As a matter of fact, it is. It's a Caribbean paradise, or so I'm told. The perfect place to spend a honeymoon. But in order to have a honeymoon, we've got to have a wedding."

"A wedding?" Berry studied his chin.

Tyler stroked his finger over her cheek and carefully traced her lips. "You have a terrible habit of breaking engagements. That's why I've decided not to give you the chance to break another one."

Berry considered this. In her current confused state, it made no sense. "I can't get married unless I get engaged first."

"You're not listening, Challoner." He slipped his hand behind her head and entangled his hand in her curls. "You have a bad habit of reneging on your promises when it comes to marriage. So I'm not asking you. I'm simply showing up tomorrow morning with a preacher and a license."

"Can you do that?" She had no idea what he meant.

"I sure can, considering one of my father's best golfing buddies is a judge," Tyler said. "He'll get us a license fast under these circumstances."

"Sheesh," Debra muttered in the background. "What a romantic. No wonder he's thirty years old and unmarried. If I were her, I'd dump a bowl of lasagna over his head."

"Tyler is very romantic," Berry defended. "He's much more romantic than Daniel ever was."

"It's true love," Kelley said. "Go get that preacher right now, Tyler. You can't take the chance of letting her get away."

"It's four-thirty in the morning," Tyler said. "I don't think he'd be very happy with anyone wanting to be married at this hour. Besides, Dad needs some time to coax Judge Harlow into granting us a license. The judge will be much more amenable if Dad doesn't wake him up."

Berry yawned, still baffled and too tired to work things out. She knew only one thing at the moment. She had caused Tyler nothing but trouble, and had wound up almost getting him killed. That much was clear. Everything else remained hazy.

"Let the judge sleep," she said. "He's probably going to be mad because I almost got Tyler killed." She yawned again. "If he doesn't get any sleep, he'll be twice as mad."

"You didn't almost get Tyler killed," Debra said. "You saved his life when that crazy woman tried to kill him."

Berry said nothing and closed her eyes. That "crazy woman" was her cousin, who wanted her great-aunt's money. That meant she was responsible for this whole mess.

"Open your eyes, Berry," Tyler commanded softly.

She opened her eyes reluctantly and focused on his face.

"We're getting married. No engagements or rings. I don't want you to have a chance to think you made a mistake and call it off. This is a case where once I put the ring on your finger during the ceremony, it stays on. Do you understand?"

She frowned. "Of course I understand. But that doesn't change the fact that it was my cousin who tried to shoot you."

"Second cousin, I believe," Celia said. "She's the daughter of your father's cousin, or so I understand. It's a much more distant relationship."

Berry considered this and decided Celia was just trying to be nice. "A second cousin is still a cousin. That's way too close."

"Too close for what?" Tyler asked. "The fact that a distant relative of yours tried to kill you for money you don't even have has nothing to do with our marriage—I'm not marrying *her*. I'm marrying you."

"You can't marry her," Berry pointed out. "She's already married. I think." She struggled to remember what someone had said about Cammy's marriage.

"I wouldn't marry her anyway," Tyler said. "I'm marrying you. Tomorrow, as soon as possible. Then we're leaving on our honeymoon. You can bring along all those fancy office outfits you bought and give me a proper thrill."

Berry thought this over and suddenly recalled what Tyler had said about having to look at auto parts all day while Felix got to look at her. She smiled.

"That would be perfect, Tyler," she said. "I've got two or three outfits that I haven't even worn yet. Somebody has got to appreciate them."

"If they're anything like that red suit you wore today, old Tyler will probably chase you all over Grand Cayman island," Kelley said, snickering.

"Berry." Tyler leaned over her and brought his face within inches of hers. "I need you. Will you marry me?"

Berry blinked, confused. Tyler was asking her to marry him? After she had almost gotten him killed?

"I've just said the magic words," he said. "Now put out your left hand."

He did want to marry her. In spite of her confusion, she suddenly understood that Tyler really did want to marry her.

"This isn't fair. You're using everything I've told you against me." She lifted her left hand, which was strangely uncooperative, a few inches. "Are you sure you want to marry me?"

"Yes, I am, and I'm not giving you a ring until it's too late for you to give it back." He lifted her hand to his lips and kissed her ring finger. "Besides, I haven't had a chance to get one. It's been a busy day."

"Here, Tyler." Celia tugged her diamond from her finger. "You can borrow mine. Who knows what might happen if you don't do things properly."

"Thanks, Mom." Tyler slid Celia's diamond solitaire on Berry's finger. "You can have it back as soon as she falls asleep."

Berry stared at her left hand through tears that suddenly rose in her eyes. "It's the most beautiful ring I've ever had. Thank you, Tyler."

"Now tell him you love him," Debra said. "In these cases, it's important to be very clear about expectations and emotions."

"I am clear," Berry said. "Tyler is the only man who was ever willing to go out of his way in order to help me. How could I not love him?"

"That's the ticket," Debra said approvingly. "Now you go back to sleep with a good conscience. You love Tyler, and Tyler loves you. Tomorrow you're getting married. Everything is perfect."

"Everything is perfect," Berry repeated, finally believing it.

She drifted back into sleep and dreamed of diamonds and white dresses.

• • •

Tyler stepped off the hospital elevator and headed toward Berry's room. He had the marriage license from Judge Harlow in his pocket, and Pastor Miller was due in half an hour. He also had his car packed with luggage, and a pair of plane tickets in his jacket pocket. He just hoped Berry was up to traveling so soon. Even the Houston police detective agreed with him about getting Berry out of Houston until Craig Robinson was apprehended.

Her doctor had assured him that she was fully able and would have her strength back in a few days. Tyler supposed it would be a while before he believed that. The memory of her injury, the image of the blood pouring from her shoulder and the long period of unconsciousness following would be with him a long time.

She loved him. The thought sent his mind flying into a paradise that had nothing to do with Grand Cayman or anything earthly. He'd never dreamed of all it meant to have a woman love him the way Berry loved him. His determination increased. This was one engagement she wasn't getting out of.

He pushed open the door to her room. Berry was alone, sitting up in a chair beside the bed. Her hair had been brushed into a mass of shining curls, her face delicately made up, and her own gray eyes were clear. Her left arm reposed in a sling, and she wore a loosely fitting white pants outfit one of his sisters had bought for her.

She turned her head and saw him. Joy flooded her face, then confusion. She paled then flushed with color. Tyler was relieved to see the color, considering she'd lost so much blood.

"Good morning, darling," he said and bent to kiss her. "Where's Mom?"

"She went down to the lobby with Mr. Farley." She slipped her right arm around his neck and clung. "Oh, Tyler, Walter Farley came to see me. And look." She nodded at a grapefruit-sized chunk of rock on the bedside table. "He brought me Daniel's paperweight and thanked me for helping Mr. Corrigan uncover Felix's fraud. I hope he never finds out I was really there to prove Felix was a murderer."

Tyler chuckled. "More rocks, Challoner?" He didn't care if she filled his house with rocks, so long as she married him. "You're beginning to make me nervous. I hope you aren't planning on taking that rock with you to Grand Cayman."

"Tyler, what's happening? Why are you doing this?" She clutched his lapel.

"Reneging already?" He smiled at her. "I've got news for you. It's too late. This is one wedding you're going through with."

"Yes, but—"

"You said you loved me," he reminded her. "I have witnesses. My whole family heard you. Are you going to try reneging on that, too?"

She withdrew her arm. "No, I am not. But you might want to think about this, Tyler. Grady Craig is still on the loose, you know."

"I know, darling, but Cammy is now in custody. Without her, he'll never touch a cent of your great-aunt's money." He knelt on the floor before her, clasping her good hand. "If you're worried, maybe we can visit your great-aunt and ask her to leave her money to her church or some charity she likes."

Berry stared at him, clearly struck by this suggestion. "That's a great idea. I'd rather not have her money, and especially not since Daniel got killed because of it." She paused and seemed to swallow hard. "Tyler, are you sure? I mean, we can still go to Grand Cayman, but we don't have to get married."

He laughed and shook his head. "My first—and only— engagement was to a woman who was using me to keep her father from finding out about her real lover because she was afraid he'd disinherit her. It was a humiliating experience all the way around."

"That's horrible," Berry said. "At least, I never got engaged unless I thought I meant to go through with it."

"I know." Tyler laughed up at her. "This time, you aren't going to think about it. You're going to do it."

"Oh, Tyler, do you mean it?"

"As a matter of fact, I am." He produced the license and showed it to her.

"You aren't marrying me just to protect me from Grady Craig, are you?" she asked, struck by horrible suspicion.

"No, Challoner, I'm marrying you because you're an heiress." Tyler saw the expression on her face and rose, lifting her to her feet with him. "Idiot. Can't you see I'm in love with you? I have been ever since you showed up in my office and brought all the color back into my life."

Berry looked into his eyes and saw it was true. "I've never put color into anyone's life before."

"It was those violet eyes of yours," he said roughly. He held her gently, with all due respect for her injured shoulder. "Berry, I love you."

"I—"

"Back away from her slowly." The low, flat voice interrupted from the door. "Otherwise, I'll kill you, too."

CHAPTER 12

"You," Craig Robinson ordered Tyler. "Get back. Now."

Craig Robinson, whom Berry still thought of as Grady Craig, held a short black rifle pointed at them. His formerly handsome face was disfigured with desperate fury, and his blue eyes were coldly empty. He sported a day's growth of beard, and his blond hair was matted. The black trousers and shirt he wore were wrinkled and dirty.

Berry collapsed weakly back onto her chair. She noted with fatalistic horror that the rifle was easily hidden beneath the black windbreaker he had tossed over his arm. She thought of Daniel, how he had opened the door to this man and failed to notice the rifle until it was too late. Terror filled her.

"Come, Beryl." Robinson gestured with the rifle. "You thought you'd get away, didn't you? You really should have known better than to call the police on me."

His crisp, staccato speech told Berry more certainly than anything else how determined he was to kill her. He cared nothing for being caught, so long as he could kill her first. He blamed her for the failure of his brilliant plan.

She had to protect Tyler. She had brought this evil on him. She balanced her right hand on the chair arm and struggled against waves of fright and dizziness to stand.

"Let me by, Tyler," she said. "I'd better go with him."

Now that Berry accepted the fact that she was about to die, she felt strangely calm in spite of her fear. It wouldn't be so bad. Daniel would be there.

"Hold it right there, Robinson." Tyler placed himself in front of Berry. "You're too late. Mary MacGregor died last night. In the eyes of the law, her fortune has already passed to Berry. Killing her now won't do you a lick of good. Your best bet would be to make a deal with her. A couple of million—"

Robinson snarled. "It was all mine! It belongs to me. I worked for it. If I don't get it, neither does she."

"Berry married me two days ago," Tyler said. "Once you've killed my wife, Mary MacGregor's money is all mine."

"You're lying," Robinson said flatly. The muzzle of the short rifle he held never wavered from Tyler's chest. "That money belongs to me."

"Too bad you couldn't hold the pose of an urbane young engineer long enough to marry Berry yourself," Tyler sneered. "You lose, sucker."

"Tyler, stop it," Berry hissed, anguished. She felt sick and dizzy from just sitting up straight. How could she save Tyler if she was too weak to even stand up?

Robinson swore. The muzzle of his rifle vibrated with his fury.

"Go ahead," Tyler invited. "Kill me. I have two brothers, three sisters, and two parents just waiting for their share of that money, and that's not counting all my nieces and nephews." He stuck his hands in his pockets and gave Daniel's killer a friendly smile. "My father is bosom-buddies with the D.A. and the coroner. They'll swear Berry died first, then me. Face it, Robinson. There's no way your wife is going to inherit one cent of Mary MacGregor's fortune. I beat you to it."

Tyler had gone too far, Berry realized. Robinson's face flushed dark red with fury. In Robinson's mind, the MacGregor money was his by right, and Tyler had just bested him in the contest to get it.

Tyler took a couple of casual steps toward him and spread his hands in a placating gesture. "But I'm willing to be reasonable. After everything you've been through—"

Robinson went crazy. He gave an incoherent howl of rage and swung the butt of his rifle at Tyler's head.

Tyler dodged and the rifle butt connected with his shoulder rather than his head. He crashed to the floor and rolled aside as Robinson rushed him, trying to use the rifle as a bludgeon.

Tyler brought his legs up and kicked out. He connected with Robinson's left kneecap. Robinson staggered back, cursing and swinging in blind rage.

Berry groped on the table beside her for something to hold on to so she could stand. Her right hand settled around a familiar object. The chunk of polished Llano granite she had given Daniel as a paperweight fitted her grip as if it had been created for the use she intended to make of it. Summoning every bit of fear and rage, and what little strength she had, she lifted the rock and heaved herself forward out of the chair. With all the force of her body behind it, the jagged edge of the rock connected with the back of Robinson's head.

Robinson staggered sideways, stunned but still standing. He brought the rifle around and aimed it directly at Berry's chest.

Berry's strength was gone. She swayed, lightheaded from exertion. She hadn't been strong enough to deliver a telling blow. Because of her, Tyler was probably going to die.

She faced Robinson fearlessly. All the loud cursing he'd been doing was bound to notify someone of trouble. Perhaps the sound of the rifle as he shot her would bring help before he could turn and shoot Tyler.

Tyler rolled swiftly to his feet. Berry saw his movement from the corner of her vision.

"Tyler, no!" she screamed.

Robinson swung around. His matted blond hair whipped out in an arc, which Berry saw in slow motion. Before he could aim his rifle, Tyler connected with his waist in a flying tackle worthy of Daniel Challoner at his best.

The rifle discharged above Tyler's head with a horrifying roar. Several glass panes of the window shattered and rained to the floor.

Robinson fell with Tyler on top of him. Tyler came up instantly and drew back his fist, but he didn't need to use it. Craig Robinson had finished himself off by throwing his head back as he struck the hard tile of the floor.

Berry collapsed to the floor, faint with a combination of fright and over-exertion. Blackness closed in on her from all directions. Sick and dizzy, she struggled to stay somewhat erect.

Tyler's arms came under her, supporting her. He lifted her to the bed and laid her on it.

"Challoner, we are going to have to have an understanding," he said, panting. "If you don't stop throwing yourself in front of people with guns, I'm going to have a heart attack before I'm thirty-one."

Berry opened her eyes and gazed on his face, full of joy and gratitude. "It was worth everything to be able to bash Grady on the head with a rock one more time."

The hall resounded with screams and pounding feet. No one entered, however, until a security guard, gun in hand, cautiously pushed the door open a moment later.

"Call the police," Tyler said with credible calm. "This guy's a wanted killer." To Berry, he added, "I hope they get him out of here before Pastor Miller arrives. Having that creep in the room would detract from our wedding."

• • •

Berry stood shakily at the wide, picture window of a white stucco cottage and pretended to study the lush, tropical splendor spread before her in the late afternoon sunshine. Tyler had rented a honeymoon cottage at a resort on Grand Cayman with both a garden and an ocean view. It was incredibly exotic and beautiful, but Berry had other things on her mind than the scenery.

She glanced over her shoulder. Tyler had placed their suitcases on the bed—an enormous, king-sized affair with a spread covered with tropical flowers—while he methodically unpacked. He had tossed aside his light blazer, and the thin cotton of his shirt showed the fit, muscular body beneath the material all too clearly.

Although she felt stronger, Tyler had decided she was too weak to even think about getting on with the usual honeymoon activities. Berry bit back the comments she longed to make and glowered out the window. A honeymoon with no lovemaking? What kind of *non sequitur* was that?

"How's your shoulder?" Tyler asked.

"It feels fine." Her shoulder ached, but she wasn't about to say so and swallow one of the painkillers Tyler had sitting ready on the dresser. She walked carefully to a white wicker chair and sat down.

"Good," Tyler said, smiling at her. "I thought we'd have dinner here tonight. You're worn out."

"How can I be worn out? I've done nothing but sleep all the way here," she grumbled.

She regarded the bed with a lackluster gaze. It was the only bed in the small honeymoon cottage. The sofa wasn't long enough for a man of Tyler's height. That meant he intended to share the bed with her, and she was so tired she might not be able to take advantage of the situation. Some honeymoon.

"The doctor said you'll be tired for a few days while your body replaces all the blood you lost," he said. "You'll have to take it easy for a while."

Berry looked down at the sling holding her left arm. "Do I have a whole lot of choice here?"

"No, thank God," he said, laughing. "If the doctor hadn't found a way to immobilize you, I'd have been forced to come up with something."

Berry muttered beneath her breath. She'd been too weak to brush her own hair. If it hadn't been for Celia Reid's tender ministrations, she'd have boarded the plane looking like a wild woman.

"Don't worry," Tyler said, rightly interpreting her mumbles. "You'll be a lot stronger tomorrow." He lifted colorful wisps of nylon from Berry's suitcase. "Well, Challoner, you outdid yourself buying fancy underwear. Did you have some sort of premonition about a wedding trip?"

"Darned right, Reid." Berry flushed, vividly conscious of his hands on her lingerie. He ought to be putting his hands on her. "For your information, I lied all the way around. I didn't come to Houston to investigate Daniel's murder. My real plan was to seduce you and trick you into marrying me."

"So, that's it. I've been seduced and tricked." Tyler tossed the colorful wisps of nylon on the bed and came to stand in front of her. "No wonder I've been wondering how it happened that I'm married and honeymooning in Grand Cayman, all in less than twenty-four hours."

Berry focused her gaze on his chest. Her heart pounded with longing. "You see? I'm so good, you never knew what hit you until I had you wrapped up and bow-tied."

Tyler knelt on the tiled floor in front of her so that she was forced to meet his gaze. "There were a few parts of the scenario I must have missed completely," he said. He cupped her face in both his hands. "For instance, the big seduction. I must have slept through it."

"I'll tell you all the titillating details one of these days." She felt heat sweep across her face.

"Was I good?" he asked, grinning.

"Were you—?" She grasped his meaning and felt a sudden rush of a different kind of heat. "You were fantastic. Why do you think I went through with the wedding?"

"Smart, Challoner. Try out the merchandise before you buy." Tyler stood, bringing her up with him. Before she knew what was happening, he lifted her in his arms. "I'm glad to know I passed your most rigorous test. And it's a relief to know you're a satisfied buyer." He laid her gently on the bed, shoving aside a suitcase.

Berry gazed up at him, bemused. The room whirled overhead so that she couldn't follow what he was saying. He concentrated on not jostling her shoulder as he slipped his arms from beneath her. She found his ability to concentrate fascinating.

He arranged her to his satisfaction and straightened. She tried to reach for him, but he stepped back. Now she found the movements of his broad shoulders intriguing and watched him closely as he sat on the edge of the bed.

"In fact," he said, "I feel so cheated, I'm going to have to ask you to repeat the scene."

"What?" Her heart beat faster with hope.

"The big seduction," he amplified. "I want you to repeat it, down to the last titillating detail. Before you start, kindly make sure I'm awake and aware. I don't want to miss a thing the second time around."

"In that case, there's no time like the present," she said, and held up her good arm.

Tyler bent slowly to her. He brushed his lips over hers and smoothed her hair back from her forehead. Berry's arm closed around his neck, holding him close. He smelled of green-forest aftershave and the male scent that was his alone. Berry nuzzled his neck, breathing deeply of him.

Tyler made no move to take their lovemaking to the next level. He simply stretched out beside her, holding her gently, and let her snuggle against him to her heart's content.

Too late, Berry realized she'd been tricked. Her body grew too heavy to move, and her brain could no longer hold a thought. Whatever she'd been dosed with was potent. Even without the painkillers, she could barely stay awake.

"You tricked me," she whispered.

He sat up and leaned over her, smiling. "Just get well fast, Challoner. I'm not sure I can wait much longer."

As badly as Berry wanted to wake up, she found it impossible to so much as pry her eyes open. This was, she reflected, one heck of a time to find herself incapacitated.

She drifted into wakefulness the next morning at the sound of Tyler's voice.

"Maybe I should call a doctor." Tyler sounded almost frantic. "She hasn't had a bite to eat since yesterday at the hospital. How's she going to regain her strength if she doesn't eat? Is she supposed to sleep this much?"

Berry stirred, opened her eyes, and turned automatically toward the voice. Tyler stood at the window with his cell phone in his hands. He had his back to her.

She pushed herself up on her right elbow, ignoring a complaint from her left shoulder. He wore only a pair of khaki trousers. His hair was rumpled, as if he'd run his fingers through it, and his feet were bare.

Judging from the sun coming through the window, it was late in the morning. After staring appreciatively at Tyler's bare back a moment, she struggled up from the bed. She still wore the loosely fitting pants outfit she had worn on the plane. He hadn't undressed her. She must have passed out cold yesterday afternoon.

She felt so dizzy, she had to prop herself against the wall a moment before she could make it to the bathroom. When she emerged, Tyler awaited her, looking both eager and relieved.

"It's about time you showed signs of life, Challoner. I was about to call in a doctor."

Berry yawned. "It's been a heck of a week, if you want to know. Life as a high-class-bimbo executive secretary isn't all it's cracked up to be."

"Neither is life as an auto parts counter salesman. I'll never look under the hood of a car again." He took her arm gently. "Your breakfast is waiting."

"Who were you talking to?" She let him seat her in a chair before a small table, where a covered dish waited.

"My mother, of course. She called to see how you were. It's a good thing she did, because I was inches away from total panic."

Berry discovered she had worked up quite an appetite. In fact, she was starving. She set about delicately devouring eggs, toast, fruit, and a small breakfast steak while Tyler entertained her with a description of his final day as an employee of Farley Brothers Westheimer number two store.

"I'm so glad you found out what was going on," Berry said. "Otherwise, I'd probably still be convinced Farley Brothers was behind Daniel's death." She sighed deeply. "And Walter Farley was so kind when he brought Daniel's paperweight up to me. I felt like such a sneak."

"Mom said he offered you a full-time job with the company. He was impressed with your initiative and your computer skills."

Berry made a rude sound. "What skills? It was sheer luck, guessing Felix's password." She paused and added, "And maybe I did have a little help from Daniel."

"Definitely, you probably had a hint from Daniel." Tyler smiled across the table. "Lord knows, I've been getting them all week, and ignoring them until yesterday afternoon. Dad and I were having a great time playing private investigator, but the more I learned about how the fraud was run, the less I could see either Felix or Warren as a murderer. Then I got an email from the private detective, with the particulars of Mary MacGregor's will and realized you were probably the killer's next target, so Dad and I went running to your office."

Berry's fork halted midway to her mouth. "What? Are you telling me that little fiasco yesterday afternoon was Daniel's fault? I was never so embarrassed in my life."

"I don't think Daniel had anything to do with my mother or my sisters showing up to have it out with 'Mary MacGregor,'" Tyler said, rightly interpreting this. "That was strictly their own idea, I'm sorry to say. In fact, Dad had followed me to the Westheimer number two store in order to have it out with me, and about two seconds later I spotted Daniel's wheels."

"I warned you they loved you very much," Berry muttered. "Naturally, they don't want any gold-digging bimbo latching onto you."

"That's funny," Tyler said. "Dad almost shoved you into my arms this morning and prompted me at the proper time to say 'I do.'"

The wedding had taken place soon after Craig Robinson, sullen and silent, had been hauled out of the room in handcuffs and on a stretcher. Pastor Miller had been understanding enough to delay the ceremony while Tyler and Berry gave statements to the police. But the moment the door had closed behind the officers, Mason Reid had positioned the participants and beckoned the pastor to begin.

"This is really all about Daniel making sure he passes his name on," Berry grumbled. "That's about like him."

"Did you really see him while you were unconscious?"

Berry thought this over and replied cautiously, "Well, I do remember having this weird dream ... "

"Confess, Challoner. If you'll tell the truth, I'll tell you about waking up and finding Daniel sitting on my bed."

Berry's gray eyes went wide. "I hope you're kidding."

Tyler added, "By the way, I like your own eyes a lot better than those purple contact lenses."

"They're *violet*. I keep on telling you." She laid down her fork again. "You saw him, too?" She gazed down at her plate in silence a moment then looked up. "Do you know, I've thought and thought about that day I was rushing to answer the door and fell so hard, I lost a contact? There was nothing there to trip over, but it felt as if I'd run into a wire stretched across my path."

"Remember the drive-by shooting, when we fell down the stairs just in time to keep from being shot? Someone put a hand in the middle of my back and shoved, but there was no one directly behind us."

"I can't believe this." Berry covered her face with her hands. "Not content to ruin my entire childhood by demanding all Daddy's attention, Daniel is now resorting to physical mayhem to get attention."

"I think he was trying to keep you alive, darling. He kept interjecting thoughts into my head," Tyler said. "I'd dismiss them as aberrant creations of my own subconscious and try to find alternate explanations. But whatever tripped you saved your life by keeping you from answering the door. Craig Robinson would have killed you the same way he killed Daniel."

Berry shivered. "Do we have to talk about him? This is supposed to be our honeymoon."

"All the more reason to get this out of our way now."

She looked up and met his tender gaze. "Do we have to?"

"Daniel loved you, and he did his best to keep you alive. That's the important thing for you to remember from all this, Berry."

Her eyes filled with tears as she looked away. Blinking them back, she lifted her gaze to Tyler's so she could enjoy that brief moment of pleasure that squeezed her heart every time she looked at him.

"He said he'd gotten me fixed up with the right man at last." She laughed through her tears. "That's Daniel for you. Always taking credit for anything good that happens."

Tyler laughed with her. "How well I remember that."

Berry dried her eyes and ate in silence a moment. "Walter Farley told me that Daniel's special assignment was to investigate the Westheimer number two store. He thought something peculiar must have been happening that made it so much more profitable than all the other stores. But Daniel died before he could get started on the project."

"So now we know." Tyler smiled at her. "Daniel's death had nothing to do with the fraud, but because of when it occurred, the two things seemed connected."

"Tyler?"

"Yes, darling?"

"You don't have some silly idea about waiting until I'm completely healed before you touch me, do you?"

Obviously caught by surprise, Tyler stammered something incoherent.

Berry fixed him with a stern gaze. "Daniel wants a baby named after him. How am I supposed to have a baby if you keep behaving as if I'm made out of fragile china?"

"They said you'd be tired for several days," Tyler said. "When I make love to you again, I want you full of all the passion and enthusiasm I remember."

"How am I supposed to have any passion and enthusiasm if I have nothing to look forward to?"

Tyler opened his mouth then closed it again. "This is the sort of argument a man has no hope of winning, isn't it?"

"Glad you realize that, Reid."

"Actually, I'm nervous. I had no idea I was marrying a rich woman."

"You'll have to think of something better than that. I'm not a rich woman until my great-aunt dies, and she's so mean, she's liable to live to be over one hundred. Besides, as soon as Daniel's namesake is safely underway, I intend to do as you suggested and pay Great-aunt Mary a visit."

"Glad I could help." Tyler watched her quizzically.

"Maybe if I'm rude and sassy enough, she'll take pity on Cammy Osborne and change her will again." Berry took up her knife and fork again and vanquished the remainder of the breakfast steak. "At any rate, you can't use the rich woman argument. Aunt Mary is just too mean to count on."

"I'm beginning to see why Daniel held you in respect. You must have wiped out his best arguments constantly."

"That was because Daniel persisted in thinking the male brain was better than the female brain, in spite of every piece of evidence I gave him to the contrary." Berry fixed Tyler with a challenging stare. "What I want to know is, are we going to be real partners here, or am I going to have to let you take Daniel's place in training?"

"I've already been trained," Tyler said meekly. "Mom and my sisters consider me a promising work-in-progress."

"Good." Berry sat up straighter. It was amazing how much better she felt after eating a good meal. In another hour, she should be full of energy. "In that case, you may now help me take a shower."

Tyler's eyes widened and he visibly drew in a breath. "No deal, Challoner. The doctor said you couldn't get that shoulder wet for another week."

"In that case, you'll have to help me take a tub bath."

"Berry ... " He started to speak then looked at her face and laughed. "All right. I can see you're just waiting for me to say something stupid. Would you like me to help you hobble into the bathroom? Maybe I should carry you. Help conserve your strength."

"We're partners, remember? You're supposed to help me when I ask, and I'm going to need help getting this blouse off over my head."

Tyler raised his brows suggestively. "Maybe you'll need help removing some of that sexy lingerie. What an opportunity."

"I knew you'd think so," Berry said, satisfied. "It's too bad I'm not wearing a bra. It's really unfair to rob you of taking it off me."

"Why do I get the feeling that you've got more than a simple bath in mind here?" Tyler watched her stand and steady herself with a hand on the table. "Are you sure you're feeling okay?"

"Tyler, I feel fine. Just fine. And I'll feel a whole lot better as soon as you quit acting like you expect me to faint every time I stand up."

"You'll be a lot stronger in another day or two." He rose reluctantly and followed her to the bathroom.

"I'm a lot stronger now."

"Do you like hot water or warm?"

"Very warm."

She watched the play of muscles in his bare back as he reached for the faucets and adjusted the water flow and temperature. It was asking too much of her to look and not touch, so she laid her palm on his back.

"Challoner, that is not a good idea if you want to have a bath."

"I thought you might like to have a bath with me," she said innocently. "That way, you'll be right here to help me."

Tyler straightened. "You're really devious, aren't you?" He took her in his arms, careful not to hurt her shoulder. Behind him, the water flowed into the tub and released tremendous quantities of steam. "There's no need to rush anything. We're going to be here for two weeks."

"I don't want to waste a single day." Berry's arm went around his neck. "You make me feel so good, Tyler. I love you so much. Since the day I met you, I've felt more secure and more cared about than I've ever felt in my life. I want to show you how much it means to me."

Tyler touched her mouth gently with his fingertips. "Berry, I love you. I'd never forgive myself if I hurt you. Can't we wait another day or two?"

"You won't hurt me. If you do, I promise to tell you. How's that?"

"I suppose it'll have to do," he said, letting his breath out in a long sigh.

For a moment, Berry stood in the security of Tyler's hold, savoring his warm strength and the feeling that she'd finally found the one man in the world who could make her feel loved and cherished the rest of her life. She just hoped she could make him feel half as good as he made her feel.

And she would never be alone again. Tyler's family had more or less adopted her. Having both Tyler and a family made her feel … she didn't know how she felt, but it translated roughly into *fantastic.*

•••

Tyler breathed in Berry's flowery scent mixed with steam and wondered if he'd ever get used to being with a woman who made him feel like one of those heroes in male adventure novels. It was a heady feeling, one he found himself enjoying more than he'd have thought possible.

He didn't dare kiss her. If he kissed her, he'd be a goner for sure.

When she turned and held up her arms, clearly expecting him to help her undress, he faltered. He wasn't ready for this. He wanted to savor every inch of her body. He wanted to throw her down on the bed and make savage love to her for the rest of the day and night.

Instead, he managed to gently remove her sling and lift the loose, blue blouse over her head, exposing her beautiful breasts and the ugly bandage that covered the front and back of her left shoulder.

He caught his breath. He wanted her so much, but not if it would make the wound in her shoulder bleed again.

"If bashing Grady Craig over the head didn't make it bleed again," Berry said, rightly interpreting his expression, "why should making love make it bleed?"

"You have a point," he admitted.

Berry placed both hands on his shoulders, enjoying the feel of his skin and muscle beneath her palms. "Of course, I've got a point. We're going to be very careful. There's nothing to worry about, Tyler. Nothing at all."

That was what she thought, Tyler thought grimly. He helped slide her slacks down over her hips, then the pair of blue lace bikini panties she wore. It was a miracle his sanity remained intact.

He helped her step into the tub of steaming water then had trouble unfastening and stepping out of his own trousers. Berry's interested gaze on him made him twice as clumsy. If he made it through this day, it would be a miracle.

He settled into the water facing her. "I thought the object of this was to provide Daniel with a namesake."

She gave him a siren-like smile. "It is."

"Wasn't it the Roman Empire that collapsed because of hot baths?"

"I don't think it was one hot bath." She used her hand to push water toward him. "Those ancient Romans spent hours and hours in hot baths every day. I don't know about you, but I don't care to stay in here until my toes wrinkle. We've got a nice bed in there just waiting for us."

Tyler looked his fill of her. Even with the bandage covering her shoulder, she was the most beautiful creature thing he'd ever seen.

He found her lack of shyness enchanting. She expected him to look at her. She wanted him to. She even encouraged him to touch her all over under the pretense of washing everything she couldn't reach, and then she tried to do the same to him. By the time Tyler got her out of the tub, he was breathing as if he'd just run a marathon.

"If you keep this up," he said hoarsely, "I won't last much longer."

Berry rubbed him with a towel using her good hand. "Good. I was getting worried."

He finished drying her and tossed the towel aside. "You're not going to be satisfied with anything less than making love to me, are you?"

"I'm glad you've finally begun to realize that, Reid. We're partners, remember. Partners do not leave each other in the lurch on their honeymoon."

Tyler chuckled faintly, even as his entire being reached for her. "We have our entire lives together, darling. Are you sure you don't want to give yourself a day to heal?"

"You don't understand, Tyler," she said.

Her gray eyes were filled with love. All for him, he realized, amazed.

"You're the only one who can heal what's really wrong with me," she said. "I'm ready to get well, starting now."

Tyler saw the truth in her eyes and lifted her in his arms. As he healed her loneliness and gave her a sense of security and belonging, she healed his restlessness and put a sense of color and adventure in his life.

"In that case, partner," he said, "let's be healed together."

Kathryn Brocato

ABOUT THE AUTHOR

Kathryn Brocato is a lifelong reader and writer of romance who lives with her husband, dogs, and chickens in Southeast Texas. Learn more about her at
www.kathrynbrocato.com, and visit her Facebook page at
http://www.facebook.com/pages/Kathryn-Brocato
-Author/130436237088005.

MORE FROM THIS AUTHOR
Bride by the Book
Kathryn Brocato

Angie Brownwood looked around her office in search of items to toss into the cardboard box she was using to pack her personal belongings prior to leaving her job at BrownWare Business Software Company. She found almost nothing to pack, other than her personal coffee cup and her personal coffee maker, which were already lovingly settled in the box.

After spending a grand total of five years working at BrownWare, you'd have thought she would have at least two cardboard boxes full of miscellaneous personal items. Angie looked around regretfully and shook her head. She had no life, and that was the whole problem. Apparently, if you had a life, you collected personal items as something to show for all the time you spent in a location.

"He's on his way here, Ang." One of her colleagues from the software development lab stuck his head in her door. "He's really gone ballistic this time."

Angie shrugged. She was so tired, she literally no longer cared. "It doesn't matter. I'm on the way out the door. In case he hasn't heard, I quit."

Her friend glanced over his shoulder. "He's heard. See you."

Angie watched the young man dart off. A fraction of a second later, her father appeared in the doorway.

"You can't quit," he snapped. "For your information, I've already fired you."

Angie looked at him in wondering silence. Five years of striving to excel, striving to win his approval, and what did she have to show for it?

Not much, if she counted the contents of her cardboard box. She had been such a disappointment to him, he even used her one spectacular success to fuel his anger at her.

"You think that stupid game has made you somebody," he raged, as if he read her thoughts. "Everything you know, you learned here, and now you think you can take over my company. The company *I* founded."

There was more, but Angie tuned out and cast her gaze around her office. Nothing else caught her eye, so she folded in the cardboard tabs and picked up the box.

"Since I no longer work here, you should have nothing further to complain about," she said. "Maybe you can get back to business instead of fighting with me and Peter."

"You're darned right you don't work here anymore. You're fired!" her father yelled.

Angie rolled her eyes and headed out the door for the last time. "Bye, Daddy."

He didn't follow her as she had feared. Angie exited the building that housed BrownWare and another software company and headed for the parking lot. To her own surprise, every step away from BrownWare caused a corresponding surge of energy and a lift in her spirits. She had been so tired, she figured she'd need a nap before she could begin implementing her plans.

She intended to get a new life, and she had laid careful plans as to how to go about it. The first step involved updating her wardrobe. The second step involved moving halfway across the country to the house she had just inherited. The third step involved readying herself to step into a whole new career.

The further she got from BrownWare, the more Angie could hardly wait to get started.

•••

Garner Holt stared, temporarily stunned, at the sheet of paper he had just extracted from an envelope and unfolded. In spite of his recent trials and tribulations, hope sprung eternal within his breast.

"Oh, Lord," he breathed prayerfully. He pressed the paper flat and pushed it across the diner booth toward his brother-in-law, Clifford Jones. "What do you think, Cliff?"

The two men shared office space in a house across the street from the New South Diner and had formed the habit of meeting for breakfast every morning. Cliff, a short man with curly, blond hair and a tendency to gain weight easily, cast a swift glance over the elegantly typed résumé.

"Sounds like your salvation, buddy." He grinned. "It also sounds too good to be true. A Stanford grad who wants to be a legal secretary?"

Garner frowned and studied the résumé once more, then shrugged. "As long as she can type, file, and is willing to clean up some of the mess in my office, I don't care if she went to clown college."

"Hire a maid," Cliff recommended. "It's a lot safer. How much would you like to bet this is Mindy Adams using some phony name to get to you? I heard she took some computer course once upon a time." Cliff regarded the résumé suspiciously. "I've been wondering why Mindy hasn't pretended she was a legal secretary and applied for a job in your office before this."

Garner tried in vain to imagine the spoiled daughter of the town judge at a computer for longer than five minutes at a time. "Mindy would fall apart the minute she was expected to do more than type her name. According to this, the woman is new to the area. Look at these skills." Garner grew almost reverent when he reread the sheet. "I'll bet she's middle-aged and tough. Just what I need to chase off husband-hunters like Mindy."

In spite of having lived in Smackover most of his life, Garner still wasn't accustomed to the attention he received from the single women in town. He definitely wasn't rich, he didn't consider himself particularly handsome, and he wasn't a man who enjoyed much of a social life. In fact, he'd have said he was a poor risk for marriage, considering his past romantic experience and his tendency toward suffering every stress-related illness in the medical texts. But he was single, and apparently that was all that counted these days.

Yes, a tough, efficient, battle-axe of a woman who could keep his business in order was just what the doctor ordered.

"Yeah," Cliff said, chuckling. "Just what you need. A secretary who'll organize you like you were a kid in grade school."

"Who cares? I could use a little organizing, and I need a secretary. *This* secretary."

"You could use some organizing, all right," Cliff agreed, with sinister emphasis.

Garner flushed but said nothing. During the two years he'd been practicing law in his hometown of Smackover, Arkansas, he'd let more than a few things slide. Although he never neglected his clients, his entire attitude about life had undergone a major readjustment.

For instance, he was no longer a fanatic about anything except his physical well-being, and that had become second nature. Garner had learned first-hand what stress could do to a man. For that reason, he avoided many situations and cases that might raise his stress levels, and in spite of that, he still found himself overwhelmed with work.

"I don't know what happened to you in Dallas, and I'm not sure I want to," Cliff muttered. He glared at his plate. "But I'll tell you this much. Chicken breast was never meant to be a breakfast food."

Since Cliff had put on a few pounds recently, he was allowing Garner to dictate his choice of food.

"Shut up and eat. Your stomach doesn't know it's getting chicken," Garner said without taking his gaze off the thick sheet of paper in his hand.

"My nose and my mouth sure know they're getting chicken instead of bacon with buttered toast and two eggs over easy." Cliff studied his plate with a definite lack of interest then lifted his guileless, brown gaze to focus on something behind Garner. "Wow. Get a look at that. There's someone new in town."

Smackover was small enough that any stranger was instantly noticed. Garner twisted in the narrow booth to look at the woman entering the diner. This particular stranger was more visible than most. Every male in the small diner took careful note of her.

She was a leggy, young girl of average height with a mass of pale blond hair floating around her shoulders. She could have done with a judicious application of makeup, thanks to the excessive paleness of her skin and the big, dark circles beneath the most beautiful, innocent blue eyes Garner had ever seen. She wore a pair of white Bermuda shorts and a shocking-pink blouse that attracted any eye not already focused on her. She created a welcome splash of exotic color in the small cafe.

But the most striking thing about her was the fascinated way she gazed at everything and everybody. She seemed enthralled by each item her gaze fell upon, including the waitress, crusty old Dolly Sims.

Garner, who had forgotten what it was like to greet each day with eager expectation, paid special attention to the girl's enthusiastic expression. It made him feel extra-old on this particular morning.

Too bad she was still in her teens, he thought cynically, watching the girl approach. He knew from experience that once a woman got older, she lost her enthusiasm for life and centered on one thing—herself. Garner let himself enjoy the gentle sway of her hips and the tiny waist above them. Some lucky male would probably snap this one up the minute she turned twenty.

The girl walked to the booth behind Garner with the springy, elastic step of youth. When she passed their booth, she cast a happy smile in their direction. A fresh, lemony scent that reminded Garner of a spring meadow followed her.

"Now there's a darned good-looking woman for you," Cliff said, lowering his voice. "She reminds me of Laura. It's that look of happy expectation."

"That'll change," Garner predicted with disgust. "What do you expect from a sixteen-year-old?" He studied the résumé again— the résumé that promised salvation. "I'd better call this number first thing. She's bound to be in huge demand."

"Your sister hasn't changed." Cliff peered over Garner's shoulder. "She's still got that joy in life that first attracted my attention, and we've been married three years now. Three *great* years, by the way." He watched the girl a moment. "What makes you think she's sixteen?"

"She looks sixteen, therefore, she must be sixteen." Garner studied the résumé again, conscious of his brother-in-law's steady gaze. He knew Cliff was curious about his time in Dallas and his failed marriage. Even after two years, Garner still didn't care to tell anyone, including his relatives, what a fool he'd been. "If you're through torturing that chicken, let's get back to the office so I can hire my new secretary."

"But I haven't had anything to eat," Cliff said plaintively He picked up his knife and fork and bravely attacked the chicken breast. "Calm down, Garner. She's probably sitting by her phone, waiting for calls.

"Her phone has probably been ringing since six this morning if she sent résumés to every lawyer in town." Garner plucked a pen from his shirt pocket and circled the phone number. "Let's hope I'm the only one who needs a secretary."

Dolly Sims, the crotchety waitress who had been at the small diner since it was the Old South Cafe, stalked past them with a glass of water and a menu in her hands. She glared at the girl. Garner bit back a smile and wondered if the girl's expression of enthusiasm would dim in the face of that glare.

"Don't mind Dolly." Cliff smiled past Garner's shoulder. "She always looks like she just finished eating a sour pickle."

Dolly sniffed and ignored Cliff. Garner bit back a laugh, knowing that Dolly disapproved of Cliff's diet and would likely retaliate by setting a dish piled high with butter before him.

Garner turned. He might have known his kind-hearted brother-in-law would be unable to resist soothing the stranger in their midst. In spite of knowing she was too young to rate serious interest on his part, Garner couldn't resist basking in such youthful vivacity. The girl smiled. Garner almost flinched in the face of that beaming smile directed at Cliff.

"Thank you." The girl smiled up at Dolly when the glass of water plunked down on the table. "If it isn't too much trouble, may I please have some fried eggs and hash browns?"

"Ain't no hash browns in this place," Dolly said, with enormous contempt for the very concept of hash browns. "You'll eat grits with breakfast like everyone else, or you'll eat nothin'. That's the menu. Take 'em or leave 'em."

"Grits," the girl repeated. Another beaming smile spread over her face. "I'll take them. Thank you so much for mentioning them."

Dolly glowered. "Shouldn't have to mention grits on a breakfast order."

"Come on, Dolly," Garner coaxed. "Can't you see she's a Yankee? How's she supposed to know every breakfast down here comes with grits and only grits?"

Dolly scowled, but her voice lost some of its bite.

"She could look at the menu for starters," she said and stalked back to the counter.

To Garner's surprise, the girl's dancing blue eyes followed Dolly. Her mouth twitched with enjoyment. The realization that this girl had the most kissable lips he'd ever seen was like a kick in the gut to him. Since when had he gone around ogling teenyboppers?

The girl's laughing gaze met his, then Cliff's, and the two broke into outright laughter. Garner wondered what it would feel like to be able to laugh like that. He was surprised to note he felt mildly jealous of Cliff, because Cliff could laugh so easily with this young girl.

"Is she always like that?" the girl asked.

"I've lived here five years," Cliff said solemnly, "and she hasn't changed a bit during that time."

"I've lived here most of my life, and she hasn't changed since I was a kid," Garner agreed, studying the girl closely.

She smiled back at him. Her eyes widened, but to give her credit, she employed no coy come-ons. Garner frowned, remembering how he'd caught a glimpse of himself in the bathroom mirror that morning and had decided he was beginning to look saturnine. In his opinion, there was nothing about him worthy of feminine admiration. A wise female would leave him alone.

"She must own the place," the girl said. "By the way, how does one eat grits?"

"It depends on how thick they are," Garner said. "The proper consistency of grits is a philosophical matter of great seriousness to connoisseurs of Southern cooking."

She gave him a beaming smile. "I can't wait to try them. This is so exciting."

Exciting? Eating grits? Garner studied her again. There was such a thing as an excess of enthusiasm. Especially when it made a man in his early thirties feel like a dour sixty-year-old.

Still, she appeared to be enjoying the exchange for what it was worth, and to have no feminine designs on him. Or was she just being exceptionally clever?

"Not getting any grits at all is a matter of even greater seriousness," Cliff said, looking regretfully at his plate.

"Shut up, Cliff," Garner said. "When you've taken off those ten pounds, you can have grits again. But I'd advise you to leave off the butter—"

"Not now," Cliff said, groaning. "This is my brother-in-law, Garner Holt, the resident health nut. If he mentions butter one more time in my hearing, I'm going to go berserk."

The girl smiled sympathetically. "I know exactly what you mean. I'm from California, and everyone there is counting fat or carb grams except me. You can't even buy a hamburger without being made to feel guilty by all the vegans." She rolled her eyes. "And don't get me started on the no-gluten freaks."

"No wonder I'm always on a guilt trip." Cliff fixed a meaningful stare on Garner. "Hamburgers are my favorite food, and my brother-in-law here acts like I'll die tomorrow if I eat one."

Garner ignored him and focused on the girl's delicious gurgle of laughter. Her unbridled joy in life made him long for something he had lost years ago. He stared at her full, smiling lips and wished she was old enough to date. He hadn't been interested in a woman in the past two years, but he'd love to spend some time in this girl's company, getting his battery recharged, so to speak.

The girl looked at Garner reproachfully. "I used to leave pizza boxes and French-fry cartons lying around my office in hopes that they'd keep the resident health freaks on the other side of my door."

"Did it work?" Cliff asked.

"Does it work with him?" she asked, nodding at Garner.

"It gets me a nice lecture on the fat and salt content of French fries and pizza slices," Cliff said mournfully. "What kind of work did you do in California?"

"I was a ... an office worker." Her smile bloomed forth once more. "I do hope they have lots of offices around here. I'm looking for a job."

That did it. Garner slid out of the booth, clutching the envelope with its precious contents. "See you later, Cliff. I've got to get busy on some telephone calls."

"I'm coming. I'm coming." Cliff cast one more glance of dislike at the remains of the chicken breast on his plate. "It was nice meeting you. You've just moved here? We hope you enjoy living in Smackover."

"Oh, I love it already," the girl said, beaming at them. "I adore the flowers and the big shade trees. Now, if I can just find a good job ... "

"Try one of the employment agencies in El Dorado," Garner recommended. "We'll be seeing you around, I'm sure."

He paid his bill, feeling vaguely guilty about his curt behavior. He had to squelch the desire to go back and say something friendly by reminding himself she was far too young for a man who felt as ancient as he did this morning.

"You're in another weird mood," Cliff complained. "That was the nicest-looking woman to come along in years, and you hardly gave her the time of day. What the hell happened to you in Dallas that made you hate women so much?"

Garner felt vaguely ashamed of himself. "I don't hate women." He glanced at the ad in his hand. "Although I'll have to rethink that statement if this résumé turns out to be from Mindy Adams."

Cliff shrugged good-naturedly. "Why not hire Mindy and be the boss from hell?"

"Because I'd have to spend a few minutes with her before I could fire her." Garner headed out the diner's glass door.

"Why not give our little friend a try?" Cliff nodded toward the wide, picture window. "She does office work."

Garner glanced back as they waited on the curb for a car to pass before they could cross the street. The young blond was sipping her water. Garner noted she wasn't watching them and felt vaguely surprised, both because she wasn't watching them, and because she was enjoying Smackover water. Garner had thought he was the only person who liked the strong sulfur taste.

"She probably answered the phone for her daddy during Spring Break," he said.

"Well?" Cliff grinned at him, brown eyes twinkling. "Wouldn't getting your phone answered help you out some?"

Garner laughed and slapped his brother-in-law's back. "You have a point there. If this ad doesn't pan out and your young friend shows up looking for a job, I'll let her take Mindy's calls. That'll get Mindy off my back, at least."

"You ought to take Mindy out a couple of times." Cliff pretended to have a great interest in Garner's battered green Blazer as they approached the driveway of the house that contained their offices. "You could stand a little social life, and Mindy would probably never bother you again once she finds out what a bear you really are."

"Come on, Cliff." Garner paused at the sidewalk leading to the front door. "Mindy's convinced she can make me over into a society lawyer, but I didn't know you and Laura thought I needed making over, too."

"We don't." Cliff headed down the driveway to the front door of his own office and said over his shoulder, "We just think it's time you quit mourning over whatever happened in Dallas and start living again."

Garner remained on the sidewalk with his mouth half-open and no retort available while Cliff opened a door at the side of the house and disappeared from sight.

Garner shoved his hands in his pockets. So. Everyone thought he was mourning his dead marriage and his dead corporate law career. Maybe it was time he did something about that misconception.

But not with Mindy Adams.

The young blond in the diner across the street passed fleetingly through his mind. Garner took wistful note of the faint desire to get to know her better. It was too bad she was so young. By the time she was old enough for Garner to ask out, she'd have lost that attractive zest for life.

Garner entered the small front room that served as a reception area, refusing to glance toward the unoccupied secretary's desk that held central position. He went into his own office, tossed the résumé down on the desk in the single bare spot he maintained for actual work, and studied it once more.

He dialed the number, conscious of a curious feeling of impending ... something. He couldn't call it disaster. It was more like fate, or destiny, or some other approaching event that would change his life forever.

He ignored the craven impulse to hang up the phone. He had to have a secretary, at least for long enough to clean up some of the paperwork inundating him.

While he waited, he surveyed his surroundings. If he wanted impending disaster, he need look no further than his own office. Papers, legal tomes, and thick file folders representing current and settled cases were stacked everywhere. The wastebasket brimmed over with his aborted attempts at typing his own documents.

Also, the floor could use a good sweeping, and every surface needed dusting. Garner shrugged. If he managed to get a secretary, he'd be able to rehire his old cleaning service. The service had quit a month ago because of the impossibility of cleaning around the stacks of books lining the floor of his office.

Garner had only been practicing law in his hometown of Smackover, Arkansas, for two years, but a visitor to the office would have thought it far longer. Never a neatness fanatic, Garner preferred to stack things where he could lay his hands on them. The problem was, many of the surrounding stacks contained folders and papers he no longer needed to lay his hands on.

Garner studied the résumé once more as he counted the third ring. It was amazing how three months without a secretary could back things up, even in a small office like his.

And now he'd received this résumé with its promise of succor. Garner held his breath while the other phone shrilled a fourth time.

You'd have thought secretaries were available for hire, even in a small place like Smackover, Garner thought resentfully. But that wasn't the way things were. People who claimed to be secretaries these days couldn't type, couldn't spell if they could type, and as for asking them to file a folder away in alphabetical order, forget it. In the past weeks, he'd given up on finding someone with computer skills or the ability to use a dictating machine. He was now willing to settle for a person who could use the old typewriter he kept for addressing envelopes.

The phone rang another ten times before Garner gave up at last and picked up the file of a case he needed to work on. After twenty futile minutes spent on that, when he realized the amount of typing that was going to be required before he could file the necessary motions, he tried the number once more.

On the third ring, a woman answered the phone in crisp, businesslike tones. "Miss Angelina Brownwood speaking."

In spite of himself, Garner's hopes rose. At least the woman knew how to answer the telephone, and she didn't mind having everyone know she was a "Miss" rather than a "Ms."

"I'm calling about the résumé you sent out," he said. "I'm a lawyer in need of a legal secretary who knows how to use a computer."

He sounded too eager. He should have beat around the bush a little and tried to feel out her skills and experience.

Miss Angelina Brownwood was silent a moment. Just as he was about to ask if she was the person who had sent out the résumé, she spoke.

"I'm a secretary who knows how to use a computer, although I've never done legal work before," she said, in cool, even tones. "May I know to whom I'm speaking, please?"

Garner concentrated hard on her voice but found himself unable to identify her accent. She was definitely what Southerners called a "Yankee," but that term was liberally applied to accents hailing from New England and the Midwest, all the way to California.

"I'm Garner Holt. My office is located on West Hickory Street, across the street from the New South Diner."

"I've seen the diner," she said, still cool and precise. "Very well, Mr. Holt. I'd better come in and discuss the job requirements with you. When would you like to see me?"

Just like that, Garner thought, amazed. No nonsense. No equivocating. His heart beat fast with hope. But she was bound to be in enormous demand with some of the local business offices.

Unless she was an ax murderer. Garner looked around his dusty, cluttered office once more. But if she could clear up some of this mess …

"How long have you been a secretary, Miss Brownwood?"

"Five years," she said. "How long have you been a lawyer?"

Garner blinked at the wall, which held his framed diplomas and certifications. "About seven years," he said drily.

Having her as his secretary was probably going to be like having a tough maiden aunt who saw through you to the bone, Garner decided. No matter how much you loved her, you were always terrified she was going to take you over, body and soul.

In the corner, a tottering pile of old newspapers and legal briefs suddenly gave up the good fight and spilled onto the floor.

Maybe someone needed to take him over. Or, at least, take his office over.

She was perfect. He was tempted to offer her the job right now, but supposed he should at least ask about her skills to try to preserve some dignity. "Do you know how to use VP-Base and Microsoft Word?"

"Of course," she said. She recited an entire list of other programs she used, including two he had never heard of before.

"Oh." Garner wondered what they were for and decided not to ask.

He glanced at the résumé more carefully. To his surprise, it stated that she'd graduated college—Stanford University, at that—six years ago. Younger than he'd expected. At twenty-seven she was old enough to have some sense, and young enough to have some stamina. But why would an Ivy League grad be looking for a secretarial position?

"I didn't realize they taught secretarial courses at Stanford," he commented. "No wonder you have so many computer-related skills."

She coughed delicately. "Exactly." Was that relief he heard? "Stanford is rather … computer-oriented. Don't worry, Mr. Holt. I'm quite skilled at what I do."

He blinked at her silky-voiced assurance and wondered briefly what Miss Brownwood looked like. Not that it mattered. He had three cases coming to trial in the next few weeks, and needed help. He didn't care what the woman—or man—he hired looked like if they could type at least 50 words per minute.

"I'm sure you are, Miss Brownwood," he said. "That's all I need to know for right now. I'll see you at two o'clock sharp on Wednesday. Bring another copy of your résumé along, please."

It wasn't until he'd hung up that Garner realized she had sounded a bit eager to bypass any further discussion of her academic career.

Perhaps she had flunked. Perhaps she had never received a degree. Surely a place like Stanford didn't have the associate degree programs popular at many community colleges.

What did he care? Garner asked himself and decided against calling Stanford. Lots of good secretaries had never gone to college at all. Either she could do the work, or she couldn't. In the meantime, he needed a secretary, and Miss Angelina Brownwood was a secretary.

Garner opened a desk drawer and dropped the résumé into the overflowing desk drawer. God bless the United States Postal Service, he thought, grinning at his own silliness. Just when he'd given up hope, the solution to his problem appeared in an ordinary envelope in the day's stack of mail.

He peered over the tall stack of folders on his desk at the crumpled paper lying on the floor beside the trash can. A man who'd been without a secretary for three months had a right to act a little silly, but in the meantime, maybe he'd better do a little picking up and straightening. He didn't want to make a bad impression the minute she walked in.

He opened the drawer and gazed at the résumé once more. If Miss Angelina Brownwood worked out, he was having that sucker framed, by God.

For more from this author, check out:

Old Christmas

Sutherland's Pride

Georgie's Heart

The Counterfeit Cowgirl

The Look-Alike Bride

"... a sweet and fun romance about second chances and forgiveness that will keep you hooked till the last page." —Harlequin Junkie

"The setup was hilarious, the heroine sympathetic, and the hero was a doctor-to-die-for, so what more can a romance lover ask for? This book is filled with love and laughter. I can guarantee you it will brighten your day." —5 stars, Rae's Romance Reviews

In the mood for more Crimson Romance?
Check out *Building Mr. Darcy by Ashlinn Craven* at
CrimsonRomance.com.